Murder in the Devil's Half Acre

Penrose & Pyke Mysteries, Book 1

Rose Pascoe

Published by Flax Bay Books, 2022

Copyright

MURDER IN THE DEVIL'S HALF ACRE

ISBN: 978-0473627881
Publisher: Flax Bay Books, New Zealand

Cover design: Rose Pascoe
Cover images from Adobe Stock Images by mimadeo, dervish15 and Irina Korsakova

Contents

Acknowledgements

A huge thank you, as always, to my fabulous beta readers and friends.

This novel is dedicated to all the women and men who worked tirelessly to achieve worker's rights and women's suffrage in New Zealand, putting our small country at the forefront of a peaceful social revolution.

Lest we forget how it used to be … and sometimes still is.

Miss Bones

An unholy yowl pierced the grey clag of misty drizzle and coal smoke, chased by a clatter of metal and a woman's scream.

Grace Penrose dashed in front of an approaching tram, gripping her medical bag as she dodged a pile of horse droppings and leaped over a pothole filled with vile sludge. A fluffy ball of soot streaked past her in the opposite direction, fleeing under the tram wheels without a care for any of its nine lives.

A woman stood, ghostly pale, outside the tobacconist's shop. Soapy water spilled into the gutter from the overturned bucket at her feet.

Grace ran a practiced eye over the woman as she approached, but she appeared unscathed. "Mrs Kelly, whatever is the matter? Has your husband had another one of his turns?"

The tobacconist's wife pointed across the street with a quivering finger. "Did you not see that black cat crossing right in front of us, Miss Penrose? I swear it stared at me with the eyes of Lucifer himself."

"Wasn't that just the baker's mouser, Mrs Kelly? I can see it gave you a terrible shock, but I suspect it was just as frightened as you were." Grace nodded towards a brawny ginger tom, sitting with feigned nonchalance outside the seed-merchant's warehouse, washing a much-torn ear with a battle-scarred paw.

"Fair made me jump out of my skin, seeing that black demon hissing and arching its back right in front of me, so soon after hearing of a ghastly death. 'Tis a bad omen, indeed it is."

"Has someone died? I hope it wasn't anyone dear to you."

Mrs Kelly clutched her hands to her bosom. "They found a body in the Devil's Half Acre last night, brutally beaten, so I heard. I pray no one we know will be next. Death always comes in threes, you know. You mark my words, there will be two more by week's end. I feel it in my bones."

7

Mr Kelly stepped out of the shop. "Now, now, my dear, don't you fret. Everyone we know is as healthy as a horse out to grass."

"What about Mrs Campbell? And old Mr Jones?"

Mr Kelly patted his wife's arm. "No need to upset yourself over Mrs Campbell, my love. She is only having a baby."

"And Mr Jones has the heart of an ox, " Grace added, "even though he must be close to eighty years old."

Despite their reassurances, Mrs Kelly's fear was so palpable, Grace couldn't help but feel a touch of anxiety. She wasn't superstitious, but death was an all too frequent presence around here, whether it came in omen-heralded threes or not. Contagious diseases, malnutrition, accidents, the scandalously high rate of mortality in childbirth … but it was best not to get started on that vexing line of thought, with a busy day ahead.

A pair of painted ladies joined the fray, their paint rather the worse for wear as they trudged home after a hard night's work. "We heard screaming. Has someone else been murdered?"

"There is no cause for alarm. Nobody has been murdered." Mr Kelly turned his back on the two prostitutes and addressed his remarks to Grace. "The mortuary assistant came in this morning to buy his usual Ruby Twist tobacco and a spare pipe. He told us that a drunken vagrant fell and died in an alley near here last night. Nothing to worry yourself about, Miss Penrose, although you ought not to be out on your own in this part of town. The police should clear the rabble out, so decent people can go about their business unmolested."

"Thank you for your concern, Mr Kelly. I promise I will be careful."

"Then I'll wish you a good day, Miss Penrose." Mr Kelly picked up the bucket and held the door open for his wife. "Come inside for a nice cup of tea, my dear."

The woman in the bilious green dress tutted at the closed door. "Shows how much he knows, silly old coot. Word on the street is murder, but not one of us, thank the Lord."

"Do you know who died, Connie?" Grace asked.

"Ain't heard nothing yet, Miss Bones, which probably means the victim was slashed beyond all recognition."

Across the street, a pair of lurching drunks stopped to see what the fuss was about. When one of them made a lewd gesture, Connie rolled her eyes. "No point you dangling your eyeballs at me, Harry me lad," she yelled at him, "not unless you're the long-lost son of Her Bleedin' Majesty, with a pocket full o' gold."

"We'd best be leaving you to your work, Miss Bones," the woman in scarlet added, with a weary smile. "Off to sever a limb or two, are ye?"

"Not so much as a fingertip, if I can help it," Grace replied.

Miss Bones was the nickname Grace had picked up on her first day of work at the women's refuge, two months ago, after facing an urgent case requiring a minor amputation. The name had stuck like surgical tape, while the incident had escalated into major surgery in the retelling.

"You watch yourself, Miss Bones. Ain't nobody safe with a vicious killer on the loose."

Grace shrugged. "If the mortuary assistant said it was an accident, I expect we're in no danger. Pleasant dreams, ladies."

As if her reassurance would stop the rumours from escalating into the macabre. Not much more than a year ago, the newspapers had been feasting on the gory details of a string of killings in London. It would be many months yet before the public could hear of a death in an alley, even half a world away in New Zealand, without recalling Jack the Ripper.

The women sauntered off, chortling like a pair of magpies, seemingly untroubled by such dark thoughts. They turned in unison at the corner to give her a friendly wave. Grace waved back and turned in the opposite direction, along Princes Street.

To Grace's surprise, her presence and limited medical expertise had been welcomed by the residents of the Devil's Half Acre – from the destitute, the prostitutes, the beaten wives, and the immigrants shunned for the slant of their eyes or colour of their skin, to the ordinary working

9

folk of Dunedin. The last few years of depression had hit this community hard. With 1890 just three weeks in, they eked out a living in whatever way they could, praying for better days ahead.

Grace counted herself blessed to have a full belly and a warm bed. The only vexation in her life was being thwarted in her goal of becoming a doctor. Her letter of application to the Otago Medical School, then a follow-up letter, had disappeared into the gaping maw of enrolments. No doubt the Admissions Clerk had had a jolly good laugh with his fellows, before consigning her future into a wastepaper basket, without the courtesy of a reply.

As she strode along, acknowledging the occasional greeting with a distracted nod, Grace allowed herself the luxury of a moment to fume at the ridiculous reluctance of the male establishment to admit that women could be more than brood mares and human scrubbing brushes.

Turning on to Walker Street, as the bells of the clock-tower chimed eight times, Grace steeled her thigh muscles for the steep climb, distracting herself by recalling the names of the muscles of the leg. She hadn't got beyond the four muscles that made up the quadriceps when a man staggered out of the mizzle, carrying a large bundle wrapped in cloth. He barged past her with nary a word, let alone an apology.

Grace watched him disappear into the murk, his unsteady gait suggesting either a man in distress or a mug of grog too many. Before she could resume her journey, a second wraith appeared from the mist, heading straight for her, extending a bony hand to grasp her arm.

The girl was painfully thin, with the inflamed eyes of an old woman, and skin of a deathly pallor. Anaemia. Grace hadn't been here long, but the diagnosis was not difficult to determine. Nearly every factory girl she saw had it, from long hours inside and a starvation diet. She reached for her purse, secured underneath the folds of her skirt.

But the girl shook her head at the coin, instead pointing to the black leather bag Grace was carrying. "You're Miss Bones, ain't you?"

"That's me. What's your name?"

"Bess Todd. But never mind that. You gotta come quick." Bess tugged Grace's arm, pulling her down a narrow lane beside the looming brick wall of a factory and into a small courtyard. "Please. I don't want her to die too."

The urgency of the girl's words knocked all other thoughts from Grace's mind. She hurried after her, towards a pile of discarded refuse. When Grace got closer, she saw a body slumped against the wall, beside the rubbish. A woman of Chinese ancestry, propped up like a china doll, with a dribble of blood running down her alarmingly motionless face.

Ignoring a stab of foreboding, Grace kneeled by her body, letting out a grunt of relief on detecting a strong pulse. A quick examination of her patient revealed a minor head wound and lacerations to one arm. As she pressed a dressing to the woman's forehead, she noted the web of fine lines around her eyes, suggesting her two score or more years had known both laughter and hardship.

The girl was staring at her with enormous eyes. "Mrs Wu tried to save a boy. He got caught in the old loom."

Grace laid a comforting hand on her trembling arm. "Well, Bess, thanks to your quick thinking, this lady will be fine. Knocked out for now, but with a steady pulse and only minor bleeding. Is the boy injured too?"

Bess shook her head and crossed herself. "Alfie were underneath the loom, trying to clear a tangle, when the foreman must have forgot he was there and started it up again. I hope to God I never have to hear a scream like that ever again, when Alfie's arm got pulled into the rollers. Reckon it must have snapped his neck, cos he went quiet as a tomb, all sudden-like. I didn't see no more, on account of fainting at the gore."

Grace forced the gruesome image from her mind. "What happened to his body?"

"They done take him away, Miss, like a sack o' rubbish. Alfie Watts was his name. A sweet lad, always cheering us girls up with a kind word and a laugh."

Grace pushed aside her mounting anger. The living came first, although the dead boy would not be forgotten, if she had anything to do with it. "Do you think you might be strong enough to help me carry Mrs Wu to Lavender House? It's less than a quarter-mile."

Bess Todd's eyes flicked between the body and the door into the factory. "Mrs Wu has been good to me. Helped me learn the trade. But I been gone too long. Can't lose my job or none of us'll eat."

As Grace followed her line of sight, a door slammed open. A disembodied arm flung the contents of a bucket into the courtyard, with a spray of watery red, before the door closed again.

Panic crossed the girl's pinched face. "They be done cleaning up the blood. I gotta go. Me brother Johnny will help. Down on Princes Street. Ask for Johnny Sticks."

Grace watched the girl race to the door, her matchstick arms pumping, unable to decide if Bess was so slight because she was malnourished or if she was underaged to be working long hours in a factory. Both probably. The girl looked no more than twelve, with not an ounce of fat on her.

She sighed the brief, heartfelt sigh of a woman who sees too much that troubled her, every hour of her working day, and retraced her steps to Walker Street, then down to the main thoroughfare.

Sure enough, a ragged lad stood next to a small barrow with a scattering of sticks poking out at odd angles. The barrow was cobbled together with odds and ends of wood, making it hard to tell the barrow from the sticks.

"Kindlin' fer yer fire, goin' cheap," he yelled to the heedless scurry of passers-by. He turned a grimy face to her, his eyes lighting up with hope. "Kindlin' milady? Best quality."

"Are you Johnny Todd?"

His eyes darted in alarm as his muscles tensed, ready to sprint off like a hare at the sight of a fox. Grace guessed he was about ten years old and fearful of being dragged away from his trade to attend school.

She crouched down beside him, blocking his escape route. "It's all right, Johnny, your sister Bess sent me to find you. I wish to hire you and your barrow. Perhaps a shilling for half an hour's work? And maybe a bite to eat?"

His eyes boggled at the outrageous generosity of her offer, but he was quick to rein in his eagerness. "I might be willing, Miss, but I don't want no trouble."

"No trouble, I promise."

Johnny "Sticks" Todd glanced around, but the pedestrians seemed more intent on getting to their work than stopping for a few twigs of kindling. With a nod, he picked up the handles of the barrow and followed her across the street and up the hill, his short legs scampering to keep up with her longer stride.

The midsummer morning clag had turned to a half-hearted mist, which would soon be dispersed by the light breeze trickling around the edge of hills, carrying with it the acrid reek of the Hillside railway workshops and a hint of the sea. Sunbeams slanted through the haze, promising a warm day ahead. People would be out and about, no doubt spreading the news of a second death so close on the heels of the first, albeit entirely unrelated.

Ten minutes later, they pushed the wobbly barrow and its dainty cargo up to the steps of a rundown boarding house. A discreet sign welcomed them to "Lavender House, no vacancy, women only, except by appointment". The peeling paintwork and rusted roof sang a ballad of hard times, but the neatly tended row of medicinal herbs, flanked by lavender bushes, played out a softer descant of welcome to women seeking refuge and free medical care.

Grace and Johnny lifted Mrs Wu out of the barrow with little effort, thanks to her tiny frame, and up the steps. She was awake, but groggy and unable to stand unaided.

Inside, a middle-aged woman looked up from a desk, casting Grace a stern look. "Miss Penrose, we were expecting you earlier. There are several women waiting."

"My apologies, Miss Newland. I have an emergency case." She turned to the waiting women. "Could someone please help this lady into the pink room while I get Mrs Macmillan?"

A bleary-eyed woman lifted a grizzling baby from her shoulder, leaving a trail of regurgitated milk down her shawl. She looked at the woman beside her, who was holding a blood-stained cloth to one cheek, underneath a black eye the exact shape and size of a man's fist, complete with knuckle-marks. The beaten woman was swaying unsteadily, so the mother looked across at a girl in a patched dress. The girl cooed at the baby and was rewarded with a slobbery grin, sporting two new teeth. With a shrug, the mother handed her the baby and went to relieve Grace of her patient.

Grace flipped a coin to the barrow boy and turned back to Miss Newland. "Perhaps we could find a crust of bread for Johnny?"

Miss Newland inspected the scruffy runt of a lad with an imperious gaze and nodded. No doubt the boy would soon be devouring a thick slice of bread spread with homemade blackcurrant jam. Despite her stern exterior, Miss Newland was as soft as duckling down on the inside.

Anne Macmillan was in her office, poring over a leather-bound ledger with an expression bordering on despair. She wore, as always, her unofficial uniform of black, relieved only by a ruffle of white shirt at the neck and the tartan trim she always wore in memory of her husband. Dunedin might be half a world away from Scotland, but the many immigrants with Highland single malt running through their veins still wore their heritage with pride.

Grace hesitated in the doorway. Her great-aunt was now well into her seventies, yet still running this refuge for local women with far less help than she needed. The stream of desperate women needing succour was never-ending. As were the bills, whether or not there was any money to pay them.

Anne looked up from the ledger. "Gathering wool, Grace? If you have nothing better to do that stare at an old woman, I can find you a thousand more worthy tasks."

"Only a thousand, Aunt? It must be a slow day. As it happens, I have brought you another patient. Blow to the head, minimal bleeding externally, but significant concussion and minor lacerations to one arm. She tried to rescue a boy who was probably too young to be working, and certainly too young to have died a horrible death."

Anne snapped to attention. "A boy died?"

14

"Alfie Watts. Caught in a mechanical loom, according to a factory girl, who was likely no more than twelve herself. It seems Alfie's body has been spirited away – one hopes to the proper authorities, or at least to a church."

Anne was on her feet now, reaching for her walking stick. "Better see to this woman."

Grace watched her great-aunt's slow progress across the room, knowing her assistance would not be welcome. Anne didn't like to admit to any infirmity, especially within these walls, although she accepted help readily enough when it was necessary.

Indeed, the only way Anne could get to Lavender House these days was by taking the cable-car up High Street and shuffling her way down Maitland Street, as tackling the steep uphill ascents was beyond her. Anne had a bevy of willing helpers to assist her onto the slow-moving, open-sided car – the conductor, the coalman, the grocer's boy, the footman from the house across the road, practically any passer-by – as everyone knew Anne and her routine. More often than not, another of the regular passengers would help her off again and see her safely down the precipitous slope to the refuge.

"The patient is called Mrs Wu," Grace said. "She works at Kendall's factory on Walker Street."

The walking stick stopped its rhythmic thumping on the wooden floor for a beat. "Does she indeed. Well, that explains the 'accident'. I'll have to have another word with the Tailoresses' Union to see if they can rouse the Inspector of Factories to do his job."

"Better to close the factory down entirely. From what I've heard, the pay scarcely covers the girl's board, and the place is a death-trap."

Anne stopped at the door to the pink room, as the surgery was known. "Most of the workers are young girls living at home. Many a family would starve without the paltry wage their daughters bring in." She tipped her head at the woman with the black eye. "Especially with their fathers drinking away their wages every night."

Mrs Wu was lying on the bed, her eyes flicking woozily between them. Johnny Sticks had disappeared, but the mother who had helped

15

was still there, holding the patient's hand. Her own eyes were half closed, as she enjoyed a moment's respite from caring for her children.

"What happened? Why am I in hospital?" Mrs Wu's voice may have been weak and quavering, but her vowels were as crisp and rounded as a lady from the genteel salons of London.

Grace couldn't help but wonder at her unexpected accent. Chinese people had been living in the Otago region for quarter of a century – more than many of the Scottish and English immigrants who made up the bulk of the New Zealand's population – but many also kept to themselves. Not surprising, given the harassment and prejudice they suffered. Even the government could not resist lumping them with unfair laws and extra taxes.

"Good morning, Mrs Wu. You are in Lavender House. We provide refuge and medical care for women in need, not far from the factory where you were injured. My name is Grace Penrose. I brought you here."

Their patient closed her eyes and breathed in and out with slow, deep breaths. When she spoke again, her voice was stronger. "I remember you. You're the one they call Miss Bones. I was there the day you cut those fingers off. You seemed no older than a schoolgirl to me, but you didn't hesitate."

"I was petrified," Grace admitted, "but very grateful it was only the tips of a few fingers, not a hand or arm. How is the man?"

"Mr Duncan is as careless as ever." Mrs Wu shook her head, wincing at the pain this caused her. "You would think he might learn from his mistake, but sadly, he hasn't, and now a boy is dead."

Grace gestured at Anne, who was busy taking her patient's pulse, inspecting her injuries and waving her fingers across Mrs Wu's line of sight. "This is Mrs Anne Macmillan, the resident medical expert."

"The resident everything," Anne grumbled. "You appear to be in fair condition, considering. Your name is Mrs Wu?"

"Lily Wu."

"Did you see the accident?"

16

"I was concentrating on my work, until I heard that awful scream, so loud I could hear it over the clamour of machinery. I remember seeing Alfie Watts caught up the rollers at the front of the loom, but nothing else."

"You tried to rescue him and got knocked out." Grace gave her hand a reassuring pat. "A girl called Bess Todd risked her position in the factory to get help for you. Luckily, I was passing by."

A tear slid down Lily's cheek. "Bess is a good girl. Too young to work, of course, but she does what she must, same as the wee lad. I hope she didn't get into trouble for helping me."

Grace and Anne looked at each other and refrained from stating the obvious – it wasn't the girl who should be in trouble, but the factory owner.

"I don't think anyone saw Bess," Grace replied. "We'll report the boy's death to the authorities, don't you worry."

"I will have a word with Harriet Morison at the Tailoresses' Union," Anne said. "You and the girl may be required to give a witness statement to the police, Mrs Wu. I will see that no harm comes to you if you lose your job because of it."

"There is little doubt my employer will not want me back, especially if I make a fuss about the boy, which I intend to do. But do not concern yourself about me. I am very experienced. If it were not for being half Chinese, I could earn decent wages in one of the better factories."

"Do you have family I should inform?" Grace asked.

After a fractional hesitation, Lily replied, "I am a widow, living alone in a boarding house."

The momentary wrinkle of her nose at her mention of the boarding house told Grace all she needed to know about their patient's accommodation. She glanced at Anne and saw the same awareness.

"It would be best if you stayed here at Lavender House today," Anne said, "so we can keep an eye on you. Tonight, you will come home with me and stay until you have recovered. I have a spare room and could do with the company."

"You overwhelm me with your generosity, Mrs Macmillan, but I will be fine after a little rest."

Anne was not swayed by Lily's assurance. "I insist. I don't suppose you play cribbage, Mrs Wu? A favourite of my dear departed husband."

"As a matter of fact, I do. My English mother taught me as a child when we lived in Australia. When we followed the gold rush to New Zealand, my sister and I would play to while away the long, cold Central Otago nights. But, honestly, Mrs Macmillan, I feel well enough to go to my usual lodgings."

"Nonsense. One ought never to take a concussion lightly. I'm afraid I must insist that you stay for at least a night or two. And please call me Anne. We do not stand on ceremony around here."

"You are most kind, Anne." Lily's eyes glistened. "And you, Grace. Am I correct in thinking you are Anne's granddaughter?"

"Anne is my great-aunt." Grace took it as a great compliment that she was often mistaken for Anne's granddaughter. In fact, although they were similar in build, temperament and interests, they were not related by blood, as Anne Godwin Macmillan was her grandmother's sister-in-law from her first marriage. Grace had seen little of her during her childhood in Wellington, but she was an inspiration, brought to life through the tales spun by her beloved grandparents. Like Grace, Anne had wanted to become a doctor as far back as she could recall.

Lily nodded and attempted to sit up. Before she could say another word, her eyes rolled back, and she collapsed onto the pillow.

Anne bent down and eased her patient's eyelids up to examine the pupils. "Concussions are fickle, Grace. Never underestimate them when you become a doctor. Always observe for a day or two in case internal bleeding is causing swelling around the brain, even when the patient appears fully recovered." Anne stood upright again, with a barely audible groan and a painfully audible click of her back. "I suppose we will have to track down a dogcart or gig to take Lily home. Life would be so much easier if we had access to a reliable means of transportation."

Grace got up from the bedside chair. "I'll see if Johnny Todd is still here, being fussed over by Miss Newland. We brought Mrs Wu here on his kindling barrow. I expect another coin will be enough to secure his services to push her up and over the hill to High Street later today. Not very dignified, but perfectly serviceable for a woman of Mrs Wu's tiny build. After that, I'm off to have a stern word with the factory owner."

Anne dropped Lily's wrist and clamped a hand on Grace's shoulder. "You will do no such thing. Mr Kendall may be lauded as a man of wealth and position, but I assure he is more ruthless than a stray cat in a nest of rats."

Grace evaluated the expression on Anne's face and deduced that her warning was not given lightly. "But I must inform the police that a boy has died, because nobody else will care to or dare to. If the policeman shows any shred of diligence, I will need to accompany him to the factory and back here to take witness statements."

"You might simply give the policeman directions, Grace, and leave him to his job." Anne shook her head. "But I know you, always determined to be in the thick of it, even as a child."

"I expect the police force will show little interest, regardless of my protestations."

Anne's fingers tightened on her shoulder. "Promise me you will not venture into Kendall's factory unless accompanied by a policeman, and only then if he appears a trustworthy sort. Everyone around here knows that certain officers can be bought for the right price. I mean it, Grace, take care and place your trust wisely. Your parents would have me hung, drawn, and quartered if anything happened to you."

When Grace walked into the police station fifteen minutes later, the sergeant was busy berating a hapless constable. Faced with the blatant hostility of the ruddy-faced, bewhiskered sergeant and the stony silence of the constable, her natural optimism drained away.

Nevertheless, she stepped forward to bring herself to their notice. Both men turned to her, with expressions that leached her confidence still further. The sergeant looked her up and down with hard eyes, no doubt assessing her station in life, and thus whether she was worthy of his time.

Ordinary male arrogance she could deal with. It was the constable who gave her the heebie-jeebies. His mandibular muscles were so taut, it was a wonder his jaw didn't explode. When he turned his gaze on her, her knees turned to India rubber. Never before had she seen eyes like his. Unusually shaped and an arresting colour, like emeralds streaked with gold.

She shivered but held her ground. This was how a big-game hunter must feel when he has stalked his quarry all day, only to turn and find the tiger behind him, ready to pounce.

Tarnished Coppers

Constable Charlie Pyke stood to attention in front of his sergeant, his spine rigid, his uniform immaculate. Above all, he allowed no inkling of his foul mood to show on his face. Up half the night, when all hands had been roused to raid a gambling den, then back up again a scant few hours later, to turn out for his assigned shift from five to nine o'clock this morning. It was a wonder he hadn't forgotten to put his trousers on, let alone shine his badge and straighten his collar.

He wouldn't have minded so much if he hadn't spotted a wad of money being transferred from the owner of the gambling den to Sergeant Lynch, right before he deemed the raid "no longer necessary, there being no evidence of wrongdoing".

Lynch had looked up as he took the cash, and seen Charlie watching him. Charlie held his gaze long enough to convey his disapproval, before stomping past the illegal gambling tables to the door with his teeth clenched. To think he had given up his much-needed sleep for this parody of policing. His father, a man of strong principles, would be disgusted.

And now Charlie was supposed to be off duty for four short hours, with nothing to do but force down a late breakfast of cold, lumpy porridge and fall into his cold, lumpy bunk for a quick nap, before turning out for the one o'clock to five o'clock afternoon shift. Instead of which, he was being ordered to attend to another matter during his precious down-time, by an arrogant sod of a sergeant with illicit cash burning a hole in his pocket.

"Are you listening, Constable Pyke? Almighty Lord, save me from the dim-witted oafs that headquarters have the gall to call recruits these days. I've few enough men with these retrenchments, especially with all the thieves and charlatans in the country making the most of the crowds at the Exhibition. I haven't the time to repeat myself."

21

"Yes, Sergeant Lynch. Visit the mortuary, sir, to track down a deceased body which appears to have vanished."

The sergeant rolled his eyes. "Nothing so fanciful. Merely mislaid, no doubt. The sawbones needs to sign off the death and can't find the body. Couldn't be bothered to look past his nose, more like."

"A murder victim, Sergeant Lynch?" Charlie tried not to look hopeful. Months of trudging a beat were all very well, earning his way by breaking up bar fights and liberating the ill-gotten gains from the grubby hands of pick-pockets, but he yearned for a case to test his hankering for proper detective work.

"I'd not be sending you if it was, Pyke." Sergeant Lynch turned back to his pile of paperwork and rosters. "Just a drunken degenerate who kicked off his clogs in a seedy alley in the Devil's Half Acre. Fell and hit his head according to Constable Nolan's report. Not that anyone will give a damn, but still poor form to lose a body if there are relatives who want to claim it. No mystery about it. Just find out where the damn corpse is and get it back to the mortuary, so the police surgeon can write it off as an accident."

Charlie stifled a sigh and placed his cap squarely on his head, adjusting it so the badge sat precisely in the centre. Lynch was a stickler for the rules, at least as far as they applied to other men and, especially, to third-class constables. Rabid dogs came higher up the pecking order than third-class constables. Damn it, the fleas sucking on the hides of rabid dogs could scarcely be treated with more contempt.

"And, Pyke, make sure you track the body down before your next beat. I've no men to spare, as you well know."

When Charlie turned to leave, an elegant young lady was blocking his way, wearing an expression that would curdle milk. She was as slim and delicate as a whippet, with the same sense of wound-up energy waiting to burst forth. A victim of an assault, he guessed, judging from the flecks of blood on her tailored white shirtwaist and the filth up to knee level on her fine wool skirt.

No lady – no woman of any stripe – was safe out on the streets alone, even in daylight hours. Another cause for shame amongst the so-called upholders of the law.

He went around her in a wide arc, sensing trouble out of all proportion to her size. She ignored him and stalked straight towards the desk, brushing dark strands of loose hair out of her face, back towards the coil of hair pinned under her plumed hat.

Unfortunately, another member of the public now blocked his escape. A distinguished gentleman of middle age, with a precisely trimmed moustache and the posture of a military man, dressed in a neatly pressed worsted suit of excellent quality. He had his bowler hat tipped forward, shading the upper third of his face, but Charlie glimpsed of a pair of intelligent grey eyes, which flicked in his direction for an instant, then slid away.

Usually, gentlemen of his type would send a message requesting that the police call on them. Charlie was half-tempted to linger to see what matter of urgency had brought the gentleman here, but time was short if he was to have any hope of getting breakfast before supper-time.

The young lady, who looked to be not yet twenty, strode up to the desk with all the assurance of a well-bred woman of middle age. "I wish to report the death of a young boy and an injury to a woman at a local clothing factory."

The sergeant waved his hand at the desk clerk and continued browsing through his paperwork.

The clerk picked up a pen and plonked an incident form on the counter. "Name and details, Miss?"

"The dead boy's name is Alfie Watts. The injured woman is–"

"I meant *your* name and details, Miss," the desk clerk continued, as if she were merely reporting a lost handkerchief.

Colour flared in her cheeks, but she soldiered on, undaunted by the clerk's attitude. "I am Miss Grace Penrose, residing at the Macmillan house on High Street. More to the point, the incident took place at Kendall's clothing factory on Walker Street."

Sergeant Lynch stopped shuffling papers. He and the desk clerk exchanged the merest hint of a nod.

The desk clerk turned back to Miss Penrose, laying down the pen with deliberate care. "Mr Kendall being a pillar of Dunedin society, it would be wise not to make hasty allegations without proof. Miss Penrose, a young lady such as yourself may not be aware that the police force does not investigate accidents in the workplace. I assure you I shall pass your concerns to the Inspector of Factories. You mark my words, he'll find the woman has made a mistake or fallen asleep on the job, causing her own injury. If women did as God intended and stayed at home looking after their husband's children, such foolish accidents would not happen."

Constable Pyke watched the young woman with growing interest to see how she would react to the clerk's inflammatory words. If he was a betting man, which he wasn't, he'd be laying better than even odds that she would not back down, and two to one that they were about to be treated to fireworks. Sergeant Lynch was pretending to read, but watching the scene being played out with as much interest as he was.

Miss Penrose calmly took the pen and form from the clerk and began filling in the details of her evidence, the pen dashing across the page with remarkable speed. When she finished, she signed with a flourish that all but ripped the paper. Then she set the pen down again, with the same deliberate care as the clerk had used, and said, "What is your name, Sergeant?"

Lynch gave a start at this unexpected question. "Sergeant Lynch, Miss."

"Well then, Sergeant Lynch, I suggest you provide immediate and thorough training to your men regarding the requirement to report all deaths occurring under suspicious circumstances to the police, who, as employees of the people, are obliged to act in the interests of all citizens."

"Miss, I don't–".

"*All* citizens, Sergeant Lynch. Need I also mention the provisions of the *Employment of Females and Others Act*, in relation to offences pertaining to unsafe work-places? Must I note that the dead boy was probably not yet twelve years old, and therefore illegally employed, as it appears are several of the girls working in the factory? Or that his death was likely due to serious negligence?"

She paused for breath, ensuring everyone's full attention. "If you wish, I can produce a list of all the other violations in that death-trap they call a factory." She turned to the desk clerk, who was standing with his mouth agape. "I will need several additional forms, if you please. Perhaps you could also manage a cup of tea? I may be here for some time."

Charlie sincerely hoped that the astonishment bubbling up inside him was not being betrayed by even the smallest twitch of a grin, as he watched his sergeant turn beet red. He knew he should scarper as quickly as possible, before Lynch redirected his anger and humiliation onto his lowly constable. But he couldn't help himself – the scene playing out was far too riveting.

"Your concerns are duly noted, Miss Penrose," Sergeant Lynch said. "I assume that you witnessed the alleged death?"

"I did not, Sergeant, but I have a witness who was there."

"And who would that be, Miss Penrose?"

"The injured woman, Mrs Lily Wu."

Charlie could not control the jerk of his head as the name registered. His heart hammered so hard, he felt as if the polished buttons of his uniform would start quivering and give his distress away.

The sergeant raised one bushy eyebrow as he stepped up to the desk. "You wish me to take the word of a *Chinese* woman over that of Mr Kendall and his foreman, both good *Christian* men?"

Miss Penrose squared her dainty shoulders and thrust her chin out. "Yes, that is exactly what I expect."

Charlie could not keep still a moment longer. "Perhaps I could look in on my way to the mortuary, Sergeant Lynch? The boy's body will have to be transferred there anyway, for the post-mortem."

"A post-mortem is not required for an accident, Constable Pyke."

"Of course, sir, if a doctor has certified the death as accidental." Charlie saw the narrowing of his sergeant's eyes and the pinching of

25

his nostrils, an all too familiar sight. Damn it, when would he learn to keep his big mouth shut?

Miss Penrose rounded on him, with a jaw clenched so tightly, her voice came out as a hiss. "They dumped boy's body, Constable, as if he was no more than a stray mongrel."

Sergeant Lynch leaned across the counter towards the young woman. "You are reporting a death, which you did not see, for which there is no body?" Sarcasm was all but dripping down his chin.

Miss Penrose arched backwards, away from the sergeant's bushy whiskers and rancid breath, without moving her feet. "The workers at the factory witnessed the lad's death and no doubt an experienced officer will find evidence, despite their cleaning efforts."

"Sir, I–".

"You have your assignment, Constable Pyke," Lynch snapped. "Constable Nolan has that beat this morning and can attend to the *alleged* incident." He turned to the desk clerk. "See if Nolan is still here."

"Yes, sir." The desk clerk hurried out.

Charlie was about to make his escape when Constable Nolan sauntered in, flaunting six feet of muscular arrogance. The boyish scatter of freckles and blond hair might charm the ladies, but his broken nose and calculating squint gave away the true character of the man.

Nolan blocked his path by standing right in front of him. His elbow jerked back, catching Charlie square in the gut. "Darn it, Pyke, didn't see you loitering there. You wanted to see me, Sergeant Lynch?"

Lynch looked up from the sheaf of papers he had buried his nose in, conveniently missing the wayward elbow. "This young lady is reporting the possibility of a death at Mr Kendall's factory this morning. Drop by on your rounds and see that all's well, Nolan."

"And Pyke," Sergeant Lynch continued, "if I hear you've been within a mile of Mr Kendall's factory, I'll have you assigned to D&V for a year. Is that clear? And if you dare question my orders ever again, I'll have you out of the police force so fast, your backside will leave skid marks on the pavement."

"Yes, Sergeant Lynch." D&V, the night shift devoted to dealing with belligerent drunks and fetid vagrants, could grind a man down. Charlie knew it better than most, as Sergeant Lynch took delight in assigning him the shift.

Charlie turned towards the door, but the young woman blocked his way again. Miss Penrose turned her penetrating gaze on him, leaving him with the uncomfortable sensation of being dissected alive. Pity the poor man who is brave enough to marry that one, he thought, but he tipped his cap and gave her the courtesy of a bow of his head.

"At least Constable Pyke has an ounce of manners," she muttered, as the gentleman still standing in the doorway hurried to stand aside for her.

The man raised an eyebrow at Charlie. Fine lines crinkled around his eyes, suggesting that he too was trying to conceal his glee that the flit of a girl had bested the sergeant.

The gentleman turned to follow her, hurrying to catch up, despite the obvious discomfort it caused his left leg. Charlie hurried out after them, eager to get away before he landed himself in more trouble. He stopped for a moment to watch the man hand the young lady a calling card and exchange a few whispered words.

Without warning, a shove to his back flung Charlie forward, stumbling over the gutter. He turned to find Nolan standing with his feet apart and fists curled.

"You need to learn to mind your manners in front of your betters, Pyke."

Charlie edged one foot back for stability and allowed his eyes to linger on Nolan. With slow precision, he adjusted his uniform cuffs and brushed a speck of dust off his sleeve. "Whatever you say, Constable Nolan," he replied, with as much casual disdain as he could summon.

Red splotches flashed across Nolan's face, highlighting his freckles. He took a step forward and drew back his fist as Charlie stood side on, ready to parry the blow.

The gentleman stepped between them. "I think that is quite enough, Constable Nolan."

"Who asked you, old man?" Nolan sneered.

The gentleman, who was several inches shorter and probably forty pounds lighter than Nolan, stood firm, exuding a quiet confidence. Nolan turned and swaggered away without another word.

"My apologies, sir," Charlie said.

"No need for you to apologise, Constable Pyke. The police force would be a better off without the likes of Nolan."

"Still, there was no need for you to step in and risk his wrath."

"The only risk I saw was in you losing your temper and laying him out flat. Indeed, it is most commendable that you did not do so. No wonder the lad has a broken nose, if he approaches a fight with flat feet and square-on to a better man." The gentleman raised his hat. "Good day to you, Constable Pyke, and to you, Miss Penrose."

Charlie watched him limp away, as if he hadn't a care in the world. "A relation of yours, Miss Penrose? You two appear to share a certain unexpected … fortitude."

"I've never seen him before in my life." Her lips twitched in amusement. "Shall we go, Constable Pyke?"

"*We*, Miss Penrose?"

"Yes, we. Am I wrong in assuming you will wish to discuss the incident and the condition of Mrs Wu, out of earshot of the delightful Sergeant Lynch? You recognised her name, if I am not mistaken."

Charlie stared at her for a long moment, willing his face to shut down to an unreadable mask. "You are an astute observer, Miss Penrose. Are you perchance one of these private detectives one reads about in the penny dreadfuls?"

"Oh, I think you'll find that undercover detectives exist outside the realms of literature, Constable, although I assure you, I am not one of them."

She smiled angelically, giving him the distinct impression that she was holding back on him. Given her feisty determination on behalf of factory workers, he guessed she must be part of the Dunedin

Tailoresses' Union. No wonder they were so effective at making gains for their workers.

"You may walk with me towards the mortuary." Charlie spun around and set off at a brisk pace.

Between indomitable young women and pugnacious fellow officers, his day was not getting any better. But Miss Penrose was right. He was desperately keen to have done with the missing corpse, so he could see to Mrs Wu before his afternoon shift began. Preferably without this woman hounding his footsteps and most definitely when Nolan had long gone from the factory.

She jogged along behind him, breathing as steadily as if she was on an afternoon stroll in the park. "I should very much like to see inside the mortuary too."

Charlie stopped so suddenly she bumped into him. "Miss Penrose, you shock me. I applaud your sense of adventure, but the inside of a mortuary is a sight no lady should see."

The lady in question let out a raucous snort of laughter, which wouldn't have disgraced a drunken bullock-driver. "How sweet of you, Constable Pyke. However, I fear you have a great deal to learn about what some young ladies can confront without swooning."

"You're a very determined young woman, Miss Penrose."

She flicked a stray fragment of fluff from her shirt. "It has been said I am as tenacious as a limpet, with the social graces of a mule."

Now that they were well out of sight of the police station, Charlie didn't bother to suppress a bark of laughter. "I trust by someone who did not know you well?"

"My own mother, actually. I consider it high praise. Charm and delicacy are terribly over-rated as character traits."

"Nevertheless, this is police business now. Viewing corpses is not a public spectacle."

She didn't give an inch. "Constable Pyke, I doubt you will find Mrs Wu without me."

"Is she not being cared for at the factory?"

"Have you ever visited the Kendall factory, Constable? They don't even have a place for the workers to eat their meal and only one closet for them all, which smells worse than any sewer, never mind such luxuries as ventilation and light. Why would they bother to care for an injured worker when they expend so little effort on the productive ones?"

"Then what happened to Mrs Wu?" The pitch of Charlie's voice rose with his growing unease. "I hope she isn't so badly injured that they had to take her to the hospital."

"She was knocked unconscious. They left her outside in a courtyard amongst the discarded refuse, to recover from her concussion, or not. One of the girls from the factory saved her by coming to find me." She must have seen his horror, because her voice softened. "Please do not worry unduly, Constable Pyke, Mrs Wu is in safe hands now."

"They put her outside, alone and unconscious?" Charlie could feel his face burning, but he no longer cared if she saw his fury at full blast. "Come along then, but don't expect me to slow down for you. And turn your back if you happen to see me in the vicinity of the factory later, in case I lose my temper entirely."

"Duly noted, Constable Pyke. I will not only turn a blind eye, I will cheer you on, as it seems unlikely that justice will be done any other way." She set off beside him, matching his long legs with a rapid stride-and-a-half of her own.

As Charlie glanced back at her, he wondered if it was not too late to take up an easier vocation, such as breaking wild horses or highway robbery.

A Missing Corpse

Grace dashed along behind the constable, determined to keep up. Cursed man had legs like a piston. But there was no doubting the anger he felt at Mrs Wu's treatment. For whatever reason, she was sure that he would be on the side of right, no matter how unscrupulous his fellow officers were. If only she could get the sergeant to assign Pyke to the investigation instead of the repellent Nolan … which seemed about as likely as the entire criminal population of Dunedin giving up their dark deeds in favour of growing daffodils.

She glanced up at Constable Pyke, trying to make out his character. She had taken him for a dull oaf at first – a big man with a bland expression, standing to attention and taking orders. But, out of sight of his sergeant, he showed signs of both intelligence and a sense of humour.

And, when she had told him about Mrs Wu, he had transformed into a completely different man again. He was already so tall that she scarcely reached beyond his chin, but suddenly he had towered over her, as if he had gained ten pounds of solid muscle and menace by magic. A handy skill to have, although not one she had any hope of emulating. No wonder Nolan and Lynch felt the need to dominate him.

Constable Pyke slowed his pace so she could catch up. "Will you accept my apologies for taking my vile temper out on you? I would be grateful for news of Mrs Wu, if you would be so kind. Is she badly injured?"

The softly spoken apology caught her by surprise. He had a pleasant, melodious voice when he wasn't furious.

"Mrs Wu appears to be out of danger, although concussions can be unpredictable. Aside from a knock on her head, she has some minor cuts on her arm, now clean and bandaged. I took her to a place called

Lavender House, where she is receiving the best of care. I will take you there after the mystery of the missing cadaver is solved."

"Thank you, Miss Penrose. I am very grateful that you took care of her. I know of Lavender House."

"You do?" Grace's words came out more sharply than she intended. Lavender House aimed for discretion, to avoid unwelcome attention.

"I have heard nothing but words of praise for Doctor Macmillan and her medical care."

"You have been misinformed, Constable Pyke," Grace replied. "Lavender House is a refuge for women, providing hot soup and compassion. Although it is true that the care extends to simple medical treatment if required, such as tending to minor wounds and infections, there is no trained doctor on the premises. At least, not since Mrs Macmillan's husband passed away."

His watchful eyes crinkled. "Of course, to practice medicine without a licence would be illegal. Strange that the new assistant is called Miss Bones. Rather an appropriate name for a doctor, don't you think? I understand surgeons are often known as Bones, short for sawbones."

Grace tried to read his expression for signs of a trap. "In this case, the name is used in jest. Amputating thoroughly mangled finger-tips in an emergency hardly counts as surgery. The man would have bled to death, as nobody else in the vicinity was willing to do what was required."

"You know this Miss Bones then?"

"I see her in the mirror every morning, Constable. If you encounter Mr Duncan, the foreman at Kendall's factory, and he assures you of their impeccable safety record, ask him how he came to get his hand stuck in the same rickety, rusted, grossly unsafe loom the boy died under. It's so old, it's a wonder it hasn't shaken itself apart entirely. The term death-trap is tragically appropriate."

"*You* are the new doctor at Lavender House? But ... but surely, you cannot be."

Grace smiled at his confusion. "And why is that, Constable Pyke? Because I am a woman?"

He ran a hand over the lower half of his face, which was devoid of the whiskers and moustaches that most men cultivated, while he composed an appropriate answer to her razor-sharp question. "Because you are so young. You cannot be more than twenty, surely."

"That's true. I am not a qualified doctor, but I am from a family of doctors who had the decency to acknowledge their daughter's interests, as well as those of their sons. Most of what I do at Lavender House involves little more than the cleaning, bandaging, soothing and distributing soup."

"And severing the occasional finger," he added, with a grin. "I must admit that courage, intelligence and medical expertise are not a combination I have previously encountered amongst the well-to-do young ladies of this city."

Grace found herself grinning too. "Do you have much experience with well-to-do young ladies, Constable Pyke?"

"None at all, Miss Penrose," he admitted cheerfully. "I do their bidding on command, but otherwise, I am as invisible to them as the air they breathe. You are the exception. I take it you wish to add the examination of a corpse to your medical repertoire?"

"I certainly do," Grace said, before realising he must think her a madwoman. "Because one must take every opportunity to gain experience, Constable, when one wishes to become a fully trained doctor."

"Does the medical school allow young women to train as doctors, Miss Penrose?"

To Grace's surprise, he appeared genuinely interested. Incredulous disbelief was the more usual response whenever she told a stranger about wanting to become a doctor. Outright laughter was not unknown.

"The medical school has no specific regulations against it, but the unwritten rules have precluded any actual enrolments so far. It is time for that to change. Women have been practicing medicine for centuries. It is only the formal training and official registration that is lacking."

"Such as the much-lauded Mrs Macmillan at Lavender House perhaps," Pyke suggested.

"Quite so. As it happens, Mrs Macmillan is my great-aunt."

"That comes as no surprise. I'm sure that if anyone can do it, you can. Your handling of Sergeant Lynch was a joy to witness. I am in awe."

They turned a corner, so deep in conversation that neither of them noticed the pretty, buxom lass standing in their path, with arms crossed and lips pouting, until the last second before colliding.

"Constable Pyke," the woman said, "aren't you going to say hello and introduce me to your lady friend? It's the least you can do after you failed to come to the New Year dance, leaving me like a wilted wallflower."

The constable halted abruptly a few inches away from her, looking puzzled.

"You don't even remember me, do you? Miss Maggie Fraser?" She paused, waiting for a sign of recognition. With a huff, she added, "You bought a cap from the shop I work in. I was talking about the dance and you said that sounded nice."

"My sincere apologies, Miss Fraser," Constable Pyke stammered. "I remember purchasing the cap, but nothing about the dance."

Miss Fraser took a step closer and looked up into his eyes, fluttering her lashes. "I will accept your apology, but only if you take me to the New Zealand and South Seas Exhibition. Shall we say Thursday evening? You may pick me up from the shop at seven o'clock. Bye!"

Grace watched her walk away, hips swinging, half-turning at the corner to give a pert little wave over her shoulder. "Pretty lass, your girl."

"She's not my girl," he grumbled. "I hardly recall her and certainly did not ask her to a dance. Now I suppose I am obliged to step out with her on Thursday, my first night off in a week."

"Can't be worse than D&V, Constable, surely?"

He grunted and changed the subject. "The entrance to the mortuary is down those steps. Shall we attend to the case of the vanished corpse?"

Grace smiled to herself as she walked towards the steps. The young constable clearly had a lot to learn about the wiles of determined young women. She'd pack in her scalpel if he wasn't engaged to the girl within three months. Miss Fraser had the makings of a perfect policeman's wife – assertive enough to keep the home fires burning and sweet enough to warm both the shepherd's pie and the bed after a long shift.

Constable Pyke held the door open for her. "You will have to remain in the waiting room, Miss Penrose. Only authorised persons may enter the mortuary."

"And relatives of the deceased," Grace said.

"I will not lie to get you in."

"And I would not ask you to, Constable Pyke. I will merely say I am looking for a missing relative who happens to match the general description of our corpse."

He closed his eyes for a moment, but let her comment pass. They followed a maze of corridors and found the mortuary without difficulty, down in the bowels of the building.

The clerk looked up from his meat pie, standing a little straighter at the sight of a police uniform. "How may I help you, Constable?"

Grace tried not to think of Sweeney Todd, as the pie spilled its unidentifiable innards onto the plate, adding to the unpleasant smell of the basement room. She gladly left the talking to Constable Pyke.

"A corpse was brought in late last night. A drunken vagrant found in an alleyway. The body should have gone for a post-mortem, but the police surgeon could not find the body this morning. He informed the police station."

"Most irregular. I've only just come on duty, so please wait while I examine the register." The clerk wiped pastry flakes onto his trousers and opened a thick ledger, which looked big enough to have recorded every death in Dunedin back to the first colonists. "Ah yes, this appears to be the cadaver in question." The clerk ran a greasy finger over the words. "Hmm. Regrettably, there appears to have been a slight mix-up. That body was transferred to the medical school for dissection."

Constable Pyke closed his eyes again and suppressed a sigh. "The police surgeon will not be happy if he receives a dissected victim."

"Not our fault," the clerk said. "Constable Nolan, who filled in the ledger, noted that there were no suspicious circumstances and the man had no family." He spun the ledger around so that the constable could see for himself. "See here? Accidental death due to a fall on iron stairs while drunk. He's put 'no post-mortem required'. That would be why the body was released to Professor Scott at the medical school."

A question formed on the constable's lips, but he left it unasked. Grace wondered if it was the same question that had occurred to her.

The clerk relented a little at their calm acceptance of the mistake. "I will send an orderly over directly to retrieve the deceased."

The constable glanced at Grace and she shot him a pleading look in return. With another sigh, he said, "No need, I will see to it personally."

When they were out of earshot of the clerk, Grace said, "Were you wondering how Constable Nolan could know that the man had no family when the victim hadn't been identified?"

Pyke nodded. "And how he had the gall to record 'no suspicious circumstances' before the police surgeon examined the corpse."

"Stupidity, laziness or outright deception, do you think?" Grace asked.

"Short of wringing Nolan's neck to find out," Pyke replied, "I am open to believing any or all three of those motives, although laziness seems the most likely. We're all overworked and tired, so the temptation to cut corners is strong." He held the door for her again on the way out. "Come along then, Miss Penrose. Your destiny awaits you and time is wasting."

She looked up at him with surprise. "You're not going to argue and tell me a dissecting room is no place for a woman?"

"Of course not. However would I manage without you?" With an air of amusement, he strode off towards the university, looking remarkably cheerful for a man who was clearly having a terrible day. "Somehow, I have the feeling you will be as interested in the science of detection as in the anatomy of the human body. Am I correct?"

"I feel as if I am an open book before you, Constable Pyke. The process used to determine the cause of death is a fascinating subject, in the rare cases where the cause is not immediately obvious. The smallest details can be the most telling, according to the doctors of my family. I have little experience myself, but I am eager to learn more. Not a fact I divulge to many people, I assure you."

"I am honoured to be taken into your confidence, Miss Penrose."

When they reached the bridge over the Water of Leith, Grace stopped for a moment, gazing at the university buildings before her, as another might gaze in awe at a magnificent cathedral. Truly, the grand façade of black rock, trimmed in pale stone, was both commanding and beautiful. As elegant in structure as the science and art of medicine.

A few students hurried by, laden with books and satchels. By the start of term, this place would be heaving with lucky students and dons in black gowns. She slowed again as she mounted the short row of steps to the arched entrance, closing her eyes for just a moment before she entered the Otago Medical School, whispering a silent prayer to the God of Enrolment.

A Hand Up

Inside the hallowed corridors of the Otago Medical School, the porter directed them to the body man, Mr Jefferson.

Constable Pyke explained the situation. "You will see, Mr Jefferson, that we must retrieve the deceased at once. The police surgeon will need to establish the cause of death and formally identify the victim. The body must be returned intact in case there is a family wishing to claim their loved one."

"Ah, there may be a slight problem there," Jefferson replied. "Professor Scott requested a fresh body to assist with preparing his drawings for anatomy lectures for the upcoming term. I believe he was intending to make a detailed drawing of the tendons of the hand. With luck, the rest of the corpse might still be intact. Follow me, Constable. The lady may wait here."

"The lady is a medical expert, Mr Jefferson. She will accompany me."

Jefferson raised a disbelieving eyebrow. "Indeed? Most irregular. I will have to ask Professor Scott's permission."

They ascended the stairs to the dissection room, which was empty of the living, although a sheet-covered corpse was laid out on a central table. Anatomical drawings of astonishing quality lined the walls.

"You will wait here, please, and not touch the deceased, while I fetch the professor."

As soon as Mr Jefferson left, Constable Pyke went over to study the drawings more closely, while Grace took the opportunity to study the body. Or rather, the hand, which was the only visible portion of the anatomy, laid out on top of the sheet.

The constable glanced around from his perusal of a cross-section of a torso. "Do you never do as you are told, Miss Bones?"

"On the contrary, Constable Pyke, I am doing precisely as told, by not touching the body."

A deep Scottish lilt boomed from the doorway. "Miss Bones is it, lassie? Is that really your name or is there a lady surgeon in town who has escaped my notice?" He ended the question with a good-natured chuckle.

Grace turned to the man in the doorway, a distinguished-looking Scotsman with curving sideburns, a thick moustache, receding hair and piercingly intelligent eyes. He was younger than Grace had expected for the head of a medical school. His attire and manner were as impeccable as his drawings. Altogether an impressive figure.

The constable stepped forward to shake his hand. "Professor Scott, I presume. I am Constable Pyke of the Dunedin Police Force. Allow me to introduce Miss Grace Penrose, who saved a man's life by amputating fingers caught in machinery, hence the surgical moniker. The local community values her medical skills, despite her youth."

Grace wanted to throw her arms around the constable and embrace him for giving her this glowing introduction to Professor Scott, but she was so overwhelmed she was rendered incapable of action.

Scott gave her a penetrating look, as if he felt he should know her name, but couldn't quite place why. "And what do ye make of this poor laddie, Miss Penrose?"

Grace snapped out of her daze and picked up the hand, inspecting it in detail as seconds ticked by. "The hand is not without interest, as we were told it belongs to a drunken vagrant, found dead in a disreputable alley." She turned the hand over, leaning down to study it. "I would say the hand belongs to a short, educated, left-handed man of middle-class occupation. Certainly, neither a vagrant nor a habitual drunk."

Scott inspected her as closely as she had the hand, no doubt looking for signs that she was indulging in wild speculation. "You have my attention, Miss Penrose. Please explain your deductions."

Grace felt like curling into a protective ball at his steely gaze, but she knew this was her one chance to impress. She cleared her throat and took a moment to consider her words. "His nails are precisely trimmed, and his hands show only superficial dirt, not ingrained in the creases, so not a vagrant. The hand is largely devoid of thick callouses, so not the hand of a labourer, but by no means as smooth as that of a gentleman. His pale skin suggests an inside occupation, but not an entirely safe one, given the scattering of scars and burn marks. This is his left hand, yet it shows distinct traces of ink. I understand it is almost impossible not to smudge ink when writing with the left hand."

"You might consider a career in the police force, Miss Penrose. You have an excellent eye for detail." Constable Pyke took up the man's hand, examining the nails and knuckles. "No sign of a fight, but there appear to be fragments of skin under the middle three nails, suggesting the possibility that he was attempting to defend himself."

"An impressive set of observations." The professor clicked his fingers. "Aye, I recall your name now. I believe I received a letter from a Miss Penrose?"

"Two letters, in fact, sir," Grace said.

Scott raised his hands in surrender. "I've got a medical school to run single-handed. Non-urgent correspondence tends to slip through the cracks o' my twelve-hour workday."

Grace took a deep breath and persevered. "The letters concerned my application to enter medical school, sir."

"I have a pile of them to consider after I have sorted out a mountain of more pressing issues – funding, staffing, equipment, finding adequate premises, reports to the faculty. Nevertheless, I assure you, your application will be duly considered."

"I am relieved to hear that being a woman does not disbar me entirely."

"Don't raise your hopes too far, Miss Penrose. Even if I support it, the application will have to be approved by the faculty, medical staff and hospital trustees. There is a general feeling that women are too delicate to cope with the unpleasant sights that medical training inflicts upon the student."

"With respect, Professor Scott, women have been attending births, caring for the sick, and laying out the corpses of their own loved ones since the dawn of time. May I see the rest of the body?" Grace whipped away the sheet, with rather more of a dramatic flourish than was strictly necessary.

All three of them stared at the long gash on the side of the victim's head.

"The constable who found him reported he had fallen in an alley, hitting his head on an iron step as he fell." Pyke sniffed. "Reeks of whisky." He stooped and sniffed again. "His clothes smell as if they have been doused in it."

Grace studied the rest of the corpse. "Again, no signs of habitual drunkenness. Indeed, he seems like a young man who took good care of himself. No broken veins in the nose, trim figure, neatly coiffed hair, carefully shaved."

The constable shrugged. "Even a teetotaller can be led astray on occasion. However, the man's clothes are remarkably neat and clean for someone found in a grimy alley. No rips or stains, just fresh grease marks. The suit, waistcoat, shirt and cap look relatively new and a more expensive material than a labourer would wear, even as Sunday best. But as you noted, Miss Penrose, still a well-to-do working man rather than a gentleman."

"Decidedly odd that he has a head wound, yet no broken bones or even contusions, aside from the slight bruising around the lower face. I suppose he might have fallen at the bottom step and cracked his head. Although, as you pointed out, Constable, the skin under his fingernails suggests the possibility of an attack." Grace leaned down to inspect the face, almost pulling back at the stench of whisky and another slight odour, which she could not place. "Odd. There are a few fibres in his nasal cavity."

Scott stopped her hand as she reached for a pair of forceps. "Best leave that to the experts, Miss Penrose. If his death resulted from foul play, we should not touch the body before the official post-mortem." He stepped back, watching her with interest, as if conducting a viva voce exam. "Tell me, what do you make of the head wound? Without touching."

41

Grace came close to crashing heads with the constable as they both bent over.

He grinned at her. "Ladies first."

"How kind of you." Grace bent down again. "The wound is flecked with rust and dirt, but it is not nearly as deep as one might expect from a fall from stairs. At least, not from the top. But it makes little sense as a fall."

"You're right. Not with so little blood," Pyke said. "His hair should be soaked in it, given how much a head wound will bleed. Has he been cleaned up, do you think?"

"I think it is more likely that the wound was inflicted after death," Grace replied. "He must have died from other causes, then been hit on the head or dropped onto the stairs. I wonder why?"

Pyke tapped his fingers on the edge of the dissecting table. "Perhaps to make the death appear accidental? Which would have worked had Constable Nolan's report been accepted without further investigation."

"Cause of death, Miss Penrose?"

Grace jumped at the professor's sharp question. May as well get used to being interrogated, she thought, if I'm going to be one of Scott's students. Her heart drummed against her ribs as she examined the body again. "I would be speculating, sir, without a proper examination and autopsy. The fibres in the nose and slight bruising around the nose and mouth might indicate suffocation. And there is a faint trace of a smell around his mouth, aside from alcohol."

Professor Scott leaned over the body, sniffing carefully. "Aye, a hint of something more aromatic than alcohol alone. A pity the body wasn't examined sooner. Perhaps the autopsy will determine what it is." He used a probe to ease one eyelid open. "Bloodshot eyes, consistent with your theory of suffocation."

Pyke harrumphed. "It doesn't feel right to me. A respectable-looking man drunk in the seediest alley in town, possibly suffocated, yet he puts up only token resistance?"

"His assailant might have been much stronger," Grace suggested. "Our victim has a slight build."

Pyke shook his head. "Even if the victim was drunk, he would have resisted with all his strength if his life was being threatened. At the very least, there would be significant bruising on the arms or body where he was held down. I wonder, could this aromatic smell indicate some type of disabling drug? Chloroform, perhaps?"

"Miss Penrose?" Scott said.

"I think Constable Pyke's hypothesis has merit, sir. As for the substance, I couldn't say. Chloroform would be difficult to administer to an unwilling victim. It's hard to get right even when used as an anaesthetic on a willing patient. But a sedative might work, administered in the alcohol he drank."

"An interesting suggestion, Miss Penrose," Scott said. "Chloral hydrate comes to mind as a possibility."

"Chloral hydrate?" Pyke queried.

"Prescribed as a sleeping tonic or for nervous complaints, commonly administered in alcohol."

The constable met her gaze, his gold-flecked irises incandescent with excitement. "How long would it take for the victim to lose consciousness?"

Grace looked to Professor Scott, as she had reached the limits of her knowledge.

"Twenty minutes or longer to reach the full sedative effect. Rarely fatal, but it is possible to overdose. Seems you have quite the mystery on your hands, Constable Pyke."

"Indeed, Professor Scott. If we are on the right track, I doubt the sedative was administered in the alley. The victim could hardly be expected to loiter for twenty minutes in such a place on a miserable night. So, where exactly did this poor fellow meet his killer?"

"A grog shop or gambling den?" Grace suggested. "Plenty of them around. There are five hotels and three houses with liquor licences in Walker Street alone, and who knows how many sly-grog shops."

"I recall the *Otago Daily Times* calling the area a 'rare hotbed of vice and infamy'. The description does rather stay in the mind." Scott said. "Although, as you pointed out, the victim does not appear to fit the type of man given over to vice."

"A right mystery, indeed." Pyke considered the body again for a long moment, before stepping back. "Much as I'd like to continue this investigation, I am satisfied that the circumstances point to a suspicious death. I must hand the case over to a trained detective and send the body for an official autopsy."

"I wonder who the victim is," Grace murmured. "There was talk of a murder on the streets this morning, so perhaps the local populace can shed some light on his death."

The constable rocked back on his heels, then stepped forward again. "Perhaps I ought to look for any identifying documents, as Nolan's dereliction of duty has already wasted a great deal of time."

Grace watched as the constable searched the man's pockets with nimble fingers. "Anything of interest?"

"Nothing at all. No pocketbook, no diary or letters, no keys, no pipe, no identification. Not so much as a handkerchief. He might have been robbed." Pyke checked the narrow slot in the waistcoat where a man usually carries his watch. "Hmm, what's this?"

He drew out a fragment of paper with part of a drawing, and "8 o'c–" above "Te–". The top corner of a page, the rest long gone. "A meeting time and place, I suppose, but not much to go on." He slipped the fragment into his notebook.

"Excellent work, both of you," Scott said. "It has been most stimulating to make your acquaintance. I assume you wish to arrange an autopsy as soon as possible, Constable Pyke?"

"I will report to the police station first and they will make the arrangements. If I might take a moment, I will make a quick sketch of the deceased, so that we have a likeness for identification purposes."

Scott turned to Grace while the constable made his sketch. "And how is it you know so much about forensic medicine, Miss Penrose?"

"My father and grandfather, who are both doctors, discussed many an autopsy over dinner, sir, until I was old enough to be taken along to see for myself, at about the age of fourteen, as I recall."

44

"An unusual dinner time topic of conversation. I wonder that your mother and grandmother allowed such talk."

"Everyone found it fascinating, except the maids, who were wont to faint if the descriptions became too graphic. My grandmother gave me a copy of *Gray's Anatomy* when I turned twelve, just as she gave a medical text to my great-aunt at the same age. She believed in encouraging a person's passion."

"Is your great-aunt medically trained as well?" Professor Scott asked.

"Unofficially. But she worked alongside her brother-in-law, Doctor George Penrose, and later her husband, Doctor Gordon MacMillan, both sadly now deceased. Now she cares for women at Lavender House, where I am assisting her, until I am accepted for medical school."

Scott let out a snort of laughter. "I can see that I will have to consider your application favourably, if I am not to be hounded by your remarkable family for years to come." Scott turned back to the constable. "You appear to have an aptitude for drawing, Constable Pyke."

"That's high praise from you, Professor Scott. I've seen your own work in the art gallery. I assume the excellent anatomy sketches in the dissection room are yours as well, sir?"

"Aye. Drawing helps a man both to look and to see, I find. A distinction most people seem unable to comprehend. I must say, my estimation of the local constabulary has improved on your acquaintance, lad. I always said the combination of art and science makes for a potent mix."

"Thank you, sir." Pyke pulled his watch out of his pocket, viewing its dial with alarm. "I'm afraid I must be away. I thank you for your time and assistance, Professor Scott."

Grace added a hurried farewell and ran to catch up. "I'm truly grateful that you allowed me to accompany you, Constable Pyke. It was decent of you to allow me the opportunity to demonstrate my skills to Professor Scott. I suspect this morning's adventure will do more to secure my place at medical school than any number of letters."

"The pleasure was all mine, Miss Penrose. I can't tell you how wonderful it is to be involved in proper detective work, after months of walking the beat."

"Are you not appalled by my indecorous interest in morbid pursuits, Constable Pyke?"

"Much as it was unexpected, I have to admit it is an interest we have in common. I have never seen anyone work out so much from such small shreds of evidence. Most instructive."

"I could say the same of you, Constable. I'm sure your sergeant will be impressed by your conclusions."

Pyke grunted. "Then you do not know him as well as I do. I expect to get a stern reprimand for overstepping my orders. The Four Horsemen of the Apocalypse will descend upon me if he finds out I let you come with me. And now I really must dash, or I will be late for my afternoon shift."

"He won't find out from me," Grace called after his rapidly retreating back.

Down and Out

Charlie leapt up the steps into the police station, aware that he was running late – an offence that would stay on his record forever, if not lead to his dismissal. Lynch would be looking for any excuse to get rid of him after he witnessed the bribe taken last night.

The clerk looked up at him and then at the clock. "Sergeant's office, Pyke, *now*."

Three minutes late for his afternoon shift. But only because he'd uncovered a suspicious death, if not an actual murder. A reasonable excuse, surely?

"Murder?" Sergeant Lynch thundered. "And how would you know that, Third-Class Constable Pyke, after nowt but a handful of months of walking the beat? Constable Nolan, who found the body, said he reeked of alcohol and had obviously fallen and hit his head."

"With due respect, sir–"

"I don't want to hear it, Pyke." Lynch picked up a letter opener shaped like a thin dagger and brandished it at the stack of files on his desk. "I'm up to my armpits in unsolved crimes and I don't need an inept constable creating more work."

"Yes, sir."

"All I asked you to do was return the body to the mortuary. Are you too stupid to follow even the simplest order?" Lynch punctuated each sentence with a stab of the dagger into the air between them. "I would dismiss you on the spot for being late reporting for your shift, if there weren't procedures to go through. Can't spare the time to do the damned paperwork."

"But, sir, when we examined the body, there was evidence of foul play."

The dagger slammed into the wooden top of the desk as Lynch's face exploded into a fiery red ball of anger. "On whose authority did you make an examination of the body, Pyke?"

Charlie hung his head and stayed silent, realising that no words could save him from the depths of his stupidity. Not that he was in the wrong, but that he was foolish enough to argue the point.

Lynch poked a whiskery chin closer to his face and said, with ominous calm, "And what do you mean, *we* examined?"

Damnation, why couldn't he have clamped his jaw shut at "Yes, sir"? "The mortuary staff delivered the body by mistake to Professor Scott at the Otago Medical School for dissection, sir. He and ... another medical expert ... made some useful comments."

Lynch hesitated, but the temptation to reprimand his constable proved too much. "Were Scott and this other man qualified to do autopsy work for the police, Pyke? Did you investigate their credentials?"

Charlie knew he was in trouble either way. "It won't happen again, Sergeant Lynch." He edged toward the door. "I will begin my shift immediately and stay late."

"You will do no such thing. I am standing you down with immediate effect while I have your deplorable conduct investigated. If I find out you allowed a civilian to view a corpse, I will have you strung up by your bollocks."

"Yes, sir. How long is my stand-down, sir?" Forever, without a doubt, if the investigation turned up Miss Penrose's involvement, which it surely would.

"Until I get time to investigate. You can clear out your swag from the barracks and take the week's leave that's owing. Or save me the bother and resign forthwith."

The temptation to resign and have done with it was almost overwhelming in the heat of the moment, but Charlie was not about to give Lynch the satisfaction of ruining his career without a fight. He pulled the door behind him with enough vigour to convey his disgust, but not enough to be accused of insubordination.

To his horror, he saw Miss Penrose standing at the desk in the lobby, talking to the clerk in a low voice. Fortunately, she ignored him as he exited out the back door, heading for the barracks.

He reemerged a few minutes later, having switched his smart uniform for worn workingmen's clothes. With a sigh, he pulled the cloth cap low on his head, slung his canvas bag over a slouched shoulder and headed off into an uncertain future, wondering how it had all gone so wrong in such a short time.

Miss Penrose was waiting for him around the corner, observing him with tears in her eyes. Great, just what he needed right now, a weeping woman.

"You overheard?" It came out more harshly than Charlie intended. If there was one thing he hated, it was being pitied. He kept walking. To the devil with good manners.

"I'm sorry." Miss Penrose scurried to keep up with him, cursing her long skirt under her breath. "I wanted to see what Constable Nolan had found out at the factory, but you were gone so fast I couldn't catch up." She caught hold of his arm. "Constable Pyke, can we please stop and talk for a moment? I am mortified that I am responsible for what happened to you–"

He interrupted with an abruptness that crossed the border between curt and rude. "It is not your fault, Miss Penrose. I'm not much of a policeman if I can't even stop a slip of a girl from diverting me from my orders."

"A decent one, who is too much of a gentleman to tell a riled up, pig-headed, mule-brained limpet to clear off and leave him to go about his business in peace."

The ridiculousness of her words diffused his anger and brought an unexpected smile to his lips. "A cross between a pig, a mule and a limpet. Now that I'd pay to see."

"Constable Pyke–"

"I'm not a constable now." He sighed. "You may as well call me Charlie, since it appears you take your limpet duties seriously. My apologies for taking my frustrations out on you once again. It has been an extremely trying day, but not because of anything you have done."

"I'm on my way to Lavender House, Charlie. Perhaps you would like to come and see Mrs Wu?"

"As I said, I am no longer a policeman, Miss Penrose. Someone else will have to take her statement." He took in her raised eyebrows and realised he had nothing more to lose. "But I've nothing else to do."

"Do call me Grace. And don't look so despondent, Charlie. I have a feeling your situation will improve. Mrs Wu's too. I intend to take the matter of the boy's death up with the Tailoresses' Union. Change will come, justice will be done, eventually."

"You're an idealist, Grace. One of the great hazards of youth."

Grace glanced up, no doubt judging him to be no more than a year or two older than herself. And probably no more of an idealist than him. Working in the Devil's Half Acre was a quick way to banish romantic notions, such as freedom and justice.

They walked in silence, each deep in their own thoughts.

Charlie paused on the threshold of Lavender House, reading the sign. "Women only."

"Men by permission, which I hereby grant. Before we go in, I ought to warn you that Mrs Macmillan, my great-aunt, is considered something of an eccentric."

"Does she run around with a meat cleaver threatening male visitors?"

Grace allowed a grin to tweak her lips. "Nothing so dramatic – usually – unless you behave like one of the insufferable specimens of your gender. She is more likely to embrace you, before launching into an interrogation of your views about everything from women's franchise to workers' rights. If she is running true to form, and not too busy tending to her patients, she will finish by peppering you with questions about the intimate details of your digestive habits and intake of fresh air."

"Mrs Macmillan sounds perfectly charming," Charlie said, "much like you."

"I should warn you that the usual rules of etiquette do not apply in her domain, other than common decency and equal care for women from all walks of life."

He opened the door and held it for Grace. "I trust I will not be burnt at the stake for holding the door open for a lady."

"Courtesy is something we value too, Constable."

She gave him a dazzling smile and entered, setting up a clamour of calls of "hello, Miss Bones" from the waiting area. A trio of ladies of questionable virtue, dressed in gaudy colours, put down their cups of tea with a clatter at Charlie's entrance.

The nearest of the trio, a woman in a ruby red dress, brushed back a wisp of auburn hair and gave him a thorough inspection from head to toe, with a disconcerting pause half way down.

"Well, ain't you a sight for sore eyes? I see ye've met our Miss Bones. You want to watch yourself with her. She'll whip off a limb with a carving knife before you can blink."

"Ladies, please stop terrifying poor Constable Pyke," Grace said. "I amputate only when absolutely necessary."

"Shame you didn't cut off his spindle, Miss Bones. Fingerless Fergus having nine brats already and Mrs Duncan fed up to the back teeth with it."

All the ladies laughed uproariously.

"Still don't stop old Fergus coming to visit me when he's in his cups," the woman in the red dress chortled.

Grace rolled her eyes. "Really ladies, spare the constable your sordid tales."

"I'd be happy to share a tale with Constable Pyke anytime. If I have to give myself to you coppers to keep you sweet, I'd rather it was him than that disgusting sergeant and his wonky winkie." More gales of laughter and emphatic head nodding greeted her sally.

Grace hastened to push Charlie down the corridor. "Ignore them. They have little to laugh about. This is probably the only place in Dunedin where they don't get harassed for their bodies or harangued for their souls."

51

"I grew up on the goldfields of Central Otago," Charlie said. "There isn't much that I haven't seen before." Although today was proving him wrong at every turn.

She paused outside a pink door, looking up at him with interest. "Your father was a goldminer?"

"Armed Constabulary. He didn't win any popularity contests, but he always acted fairly. He is rather different from the usual type, being a cultured man and a great believer in education."

"Ah, I did wonder at your signs of education. Not a trait I have noted in my few contacts with the local constabulary. Your father sounds like a man to look up to and emulate."

"Indeed. I had hoped to make him proud." Slim chance of that happening now. Charlie dreaded to think what his father would say when he heard of his son's dismissal.

Grace pushed open the door, revealing a tiny figure swathed in bandages, flat on her back in a narrow bed. Charlie tried to keep the shock from his face, not that he expected he could keep anything from Grace Penrose's all-seeing eyes.

Lily's eyelids opened, revealing her bright almond eyes. "Charlie!" Her joy evaporated in an instant. "You shouldn't have come."

To the devil with being discreet, he thought, stepping to her bedside and taking up her tiny hand. "I should have come sooner."

"Good to see you looking so much perkier, Mrs Wu," Grace said. "Would you like to sit, or are you still feeling dizzy?" At Lily's nod, Grace helped her patient to sit up, before observing her for a few seconds. "I'll fetch some tea." She closed the door behind her.

"Don't look so worried, Charlie. My injuries look worse than they feel. We are amongst good people here. People who care for others, no matter their station in life. Mrs Macmillan has insisted that I stay with her tonight."

"She has? How extraordinary." Charlie felt a wash of relief at seeing her so cheerful underneath the bandages, although her grimace of pain every time she moved her head rather undermined her assurances. "You were lucky that Grace happened by, or you might still be in that

52

rubbish pile. When I find the man who gave that order, I'll make sure he regrets it for the rest of his miserable life."

Lily squeezed his hand. "Don't you do anything stupid, Charlie Pyke. I'd never hear the last of it from your mother."

Too late for that, Charlie thought.

"And how do you know Miss Bones well enough to call her Grace?"

Charlie was about to explain the complicated tale of the day's events, when Grace saved him, by appearing with a tray loaded with a teapot, cups, a bowl of soup and a plate of buttered bread. Hunger welled up inside him after missing breakfast, leaving him unable to take his eyes off the food. He really, really hoped Lily would not want it.

"For you, Charlie. You must be starving." Grace placed the bowl and plate on the bedside table. "There's always a pot of soup bubbling away here for those in need. Would you like some too, Lily?"

"Not for me." Lily leaned forward, sniffing. "Is that green tea I smell?"

Grace poured a cup for her, then waved the teapot at Charlie. "Would you care for green tea too, Charlie, or shall I make you English tea?"

The question was a simple one, but fraught with cultural complications. Finally, he replied. "Green tea will do very well, Grace. It is a pleasure I have not enjoyed for some time."

Grace poured another cup as Charlie continued tucking into the delicious soup with ravenous concentration. Better than cold, lumpy porridge any day.

"I would have liked you to meet my great-aunt, Charlie, but she had to go home to meet with our benefactors. Without the generosity of the Chelmsford family, this place would be falling down around our ears."

Charlie paused mid-slurp. "Mr Sterling Chelmsford? Enormous mansion on Royal Terrace? You're lucky to have him on your side. I hear he intends to run for parliament, if he can drag himself away from making bushels of money."

"That's the man." Grace tucked the blanket snugly around Lily. "I will leave you two to talk."

"Grace, please stay." Charlie put the soup bowl aside and gestured for her to sit down. "You have a right to know the facts, most especially as I understand that your great-aunt has been good enough to invite Mrs Wu to stay at her home tonight."

Grace sat, her hands crossed in her lap, waiting expectantly.

Lily took up Charlie's hand and gave him a nod.

"Mrs Wu is my aunt on my mother's side. My grandfather was a Chinese goldminer. I hope you are not too shocked."

"Why would I be?" Grace said. "I guessed as much. Although you obviously take after your father in size and appearance, you share the gestures and expressions of your mother's side of the family."

Lily smiled and ran a hand softly down her nephew's face. "My clever little Chinese pearl, concealed within a sturdy English shell."

"If it became known that I had Chinese ancestry," Charlie continued, "it might jeopardise my career prospects in the police force. What small hope I have left of a career, that is. It pains me to be deceitful about my origins, but it is my only option for following in my father's footsteps."

"I assure you nobody will hear your secret from me," Grace said. "I have no time for a system that deems the likes of that rotten egg, Constable Nolan, to be a better candidate as a policeman than you. Now, to more important matters. Where will you stay, Charlie?"

"My aunt's room in the boarding house, I suppose. I need to collect her possessions anyway."

"Absolutely not. I insist you stay with us. We have a room in the attic that isn't used. It is the very least I can do, considering I caused your temporary downfall."

"You are too kind, Grace, but that would not be appropriate."

"Nonsense. Besides, your aunt will need you to tend to her while she is recovering."

Charlie hesitated. "But what would Mrs Macmillan say about such an idea?"

"She'll be delighted. Aunt Anne loves lively company. A good dash of crime will make a pleasant change from medical discussions at the dinner table."

Their household must indeed be eccentric if they considered crime as an appropriate topic of dinner conversation. The thought of staying there was becoming more appealing by the second. "Your great-aunt sounds as if she is very like you."

"If you mean stubborn, unconventional, and maddening, you are correct. I suggest you collect your aunt's possessions from her boarding house, while I arrange transport for Lily." Grace handed over a calling card with Anne's address on it and left them to it.

Twenty minutes later, Charlie walked out of Lavender House in a daze. The entire day seemed to be a hallucination, swinging wildly between ups and downs. After the unexpected generosity of Mrs Macmillan and Miss Penrose, he felt the next turn of events could only be markedly for the worse.

Sure enough, the oozing hunk of slime who owned the boarding house was soon prodding a filthy paw towards Charlie's chest from the safety of the far side of the counter. Charlie could have picked him up with one hand and booted his skinny rump into the street, but the last thing he needed in his life was more trouble.

"Mrs Wu can take her swag and get the hell outta here. Bad enough having a Chinese woman living here on her tod, but I don't allow no lodgers without a paying job. I've already had a copper around here asking questions about her. I don't like coppers, I don't like trouble, and I don't like the look of you neither."

Charlie didn't care enough to ask how the landlord knew Lily had lost her job at Kendall's. Presumably it was Constable Nolan trying to track her down and suppress her version of events. He stomped up the squalid stairs, down the squalid corridor, and into the narrow room his Aunt Lily called home. She had tried, with limited success, to raise it from its squalid roots with a few pictures and arrangements of dried wildflowers.

Charlie set about gathering together her meagre possessions – a single bag of clothes and bits and bobs, plus a box of cooking equipment and glass bottles filled with dried herbs. He was furious at himself for failing to realise the depths his beloved auntie had fallen to. How easily she had fooled him into believing all was well, by always meeting him in the park rather than at her so-called home.

He slung the bag over his shoulder and balanced the box on one arm, taking a last look around, before slamming the door behind him and staggering down the narrow stairs. He flipped his aunt's key onto the counter under the watchful gaze of the landlord.

"Good riddance," the landlord shouted after him. "Don't expect no refund on her rent."

Home Sweet Home

Grace showed Lily into the empty bedroom previously used by the cook. Being bumped up and down hills in a barrow hadn't done their patient an ounce of good, so Grace left Lily to rest.

She headed up the stairs to Anne's study, eager to share her simmering stew of thoughts on the day's events. Her great-aunt could always be counted on for forthright advice, undiluted by the usual genteel flatteries and obfuscations beloved of polite society. Although sometimes Grace wondered if a dollop of honey might help her plain-spoken words go down a little easier.

The study door thumped back against the doorstop as Grace flung it open. She stomped in, only to be faced with two strikingly handsome men, dripping with class from their barbered chins to their silk cravats and finely stitched leather shoes. Their age gap and similarity of countenance declared them to be father and son.

Grace had forgotten about her great-aunt's meeting with the benefactors of Lavender House. Anne certainly wouldn't thank her for barging in like a rambunctious child, still dressed in the clothes that had seen her from a blood-spattered living body in a filthy courtyard to a corpse in a room reeking of formalin, via hours of traipsing across town.

"Please excuse my abrupt intrusion, gentlemen. I am terribly sorry to have interrupted your meeting."

Both men rose from their chairs. The father took the lead. "Not at all, young lady. Your need appears to be more urgent than ours."

"Allow me to introduce my great-niece, Miss Grace Penrose, recently arrived from Wellington," Anne said. "You must forgive her vigorous entrance. She lives life at a gallop."

"Like a fine racehorse." The father allowed his gaze to flicker over her body, resting a little longer than was polite in the area between her clavicle and the bottom of her ribcage. Grace had the unsettling impression that he wanted to lift her foot to check that her hooves were sound, before examining her teeth to ensure he was about to purchase a filly of the correct age.

The younger man inclined his head politely. "Miss Penrose, what a delight to meet you. Your great-aunt has told us about you, but I must say she has understated your charms."

The son spoke in a bored monotone, as if reading from a script. Quite the opposite of the hearty bluster of his father. Nor did the son's eyes descend below the level of her chin, although his dull expression suggested that might be because of disinterest rather than politeness.

Grace opened her mouth to get a word in, but Anne silenced her with a glare. "Grace, allow me to introduce Mr Sterling Chelmsford and his son, Mr Edmund Chelmsford." Her eyes bored into Grace's, etching a message into the lenses. "Without their generosity, Lavender House would still be a broken-down boarding house."

Grace recognised the call to duty and took a seat with as much ladylike composure as she could muster, allowing the two men to resume their seats. "The working women of Dunedin are truly grateful for your generous support, Mr Chelmsford."

"I consider it my Christian duty to support all decent people, no matter their status in society, Miss Penrose. Indeed, I am so impressed with what your great-aunt has achieved in transforming the old boarding house, I am minded to offer her a position in my new venture."

Grace kept her face politely blank, but smiled internally to think of the prostitutes who frequented the safety and comfort of Lavender House, feeling sure that they were not the good Christian working women their unsuspecting benefactor had in mind.

"You are too kind, Mr Chelmsford," Anne cut in, "but, as you well know, my work lies in charitable endeavours, not business."

Sterling Chelmsford bowed his head an inch or two. "It is my loss, but society's gain, Mrs MacMillan. I do not wish to keep you from the delights of your charming great-niece any longer than necessary.

Perhaps Miss Penrose would care to show my son your lovely rose garden while we complete our discussion?"

The son's mouth compressed for an instant, presumably at being dismissed from the discussion rather than at having been put in her care, but he turned it into a weak smile as he held out his hand to Grace. "How delightful. Please, allow me, Miss Penrose."

Grace allowed him to guide her down the stairs and out into the garden, as if she was incapable of achieving locomotion on her own.

"The roses are exquisite, Miss Penrose." Edmund said the words as if he meant them. His stiff formality had drained away in direct proportion to the distance from his father.

"I'm afraid they are no longer at their best, Mr Chelmsford. But still delightful, as you say. My great-aunt has given over most of her garden to growing vegetables, so that we can serve a hearty soup to the needy at Lavender House."

"Perhaps you are like your great-aunt, putting your heart into caring for others, rather than sipping tea amongst the flowers with the other young ladies?"

She glanced up at his face, but he showed no signs of disapproval at her unusual choice. "You are quite right, Mr Chelmsford. The need for medical assistance is never ending amongst the poor working women and destitute in this fine city of ours. Why, only this morning, I was called to a terrible accident at a clothing factory. A fatal incident, I'm sorry to say."

He nodded sagely. "Many factories are not what they should be. My father is a great believer in creating a healthful and safe workplace, in the interests of the worker and for the more efficient production of goods."

"I am pleased to hear it." Grace found, to her immense surprise, that she was warming to him. Perhaps she might allow herself to accept that, just because a man was rich and handsome, it did not immediately follow that he was unscrupulous or conceited. Indeed, if anything, Edmund Chelmsford was a little insipid, or perhaps merely rather shy.

"My view is that it is no bad thing for women to show an intelligent interest in their husband's business affairs, to better support their mutual success."

"I applaud the sentiment, Mr Chelmsford, although I think you'll find that women would take a great deal more interest in such affairs if they were allowed to participate more fully. Without the right to vote, and with few meaningful occupations to pursue, the constraints are many."

"Well said, Miss Penrose." His expression finally gained a little animation. "My father and I are of the same mind. He intends to stand for parliament, to pursue his goals more widely. Although, at present, his attention is directed towards his latest venture – an innovative new design for a woollen mill that will exceed the expectations of even the harshest critics at the Tailoresses' Union."

This young man was full of surprises. Indeed, he was the first gentleman she had met since arriving in Dunedin who seemed sympathetic to her views. "I should very much like to see so laudable an enterprise."

"Unfortunately, the mill itself is situated some way out of town. However, it would be my pleasure to show you our local factory, where we fashion the fine worsted from the mill into garments of the highest quality. We are proud of the standards there too."

"Thank you, Mr Chelmsford. If it is not too much to ask to take time out of your busy life, I should be most interested in visiting."

"I am honoured by your enthusiasm, Miss Penrose, which is not shared by other young ladies of my acquaintance. At the risk of being forward, might I inquire if you are free on Thursday morning? Not the usual time for social engagements, I concede, but I regret that I have business to attend to in the afternoon."

Grace consulted her mental diary. With an early start to her medical rounds, she could make time. "That would be splendid. I keep much earlier hours than is common amongst society ladies."

"Shall I call for you at half past ten?" Edmund said. "We could take tea at Chelmsford House before visiting the finishing factory."

"How kind of you, Mr Chelmsford." Grace would have preferred to decline the tea invitation, but she did not wish to be ungracious. "I have heard others commend the beauty of your house. Being recently arrived in this city, I have not yet had occasion to visit any of the homes on Royal Terrace. I must consult with my great-aunt to see if she is free to accompany me."

"Of course, Miss Penrose, we must observe the proprieties. Here is my card. I await your confirmation with eager anticipation." He plucked a perfect white rose, taking care to remove the thorns before handing it to her with the card, with a graceful bow of his head.

She accepted the rose and card, feeling unaccountably pleased to be on the receiving end of one of the delicate little flatteries a gentleman was supposed to show to a lady. Not that she met the definition of a lady, either by birth or inclination, but occasionally it was nice to pretend. How serene and charming Edmund Chelmsford was, after the robust vitality of Constable Pyke.

Grace looked up to see Charlie Pyke staring at the house from the other side of the fence. Speak of the devil. She followed his line of sight, to where the rampant garden was threatening to wrench off the filigree railings and swamp the windows. Another decade and the vines would be wrestling with the gable ends.

Charlie suddenly noticed her with Chelmsford and instantly turned away, swinging the large box he was carrying so that his face was no longer visible.

"Please, will you excuse me for a moment, Mr Chelmsford?"

Chelmsford frowned in Charlie's direction. "Do you not have a butler to deal with the tradesmen, Miss Penrose?"

"Our modest household has no need for a butler. My sincere apologies, but could I ask you to see yourself back up to the study, while I attend to our visitor?"

Edmund hesitated, no doubt unused to being dismissed in favour of a tradesman. Then he left with another polite dip of his head.

Grace hurried down to unlatch the gate. "Charlie, good to see you found us. Do excuse the state of the garden. Our gardener is older than

61

Methuselah and beset by arthritis, but he stoutly refuses to let my great-aunt pension him off. He swears the day he stops working is the day he'll keel over and die."

"Perhaps I might lend a hand while I am here, since I have no gainful employment." Charlie looked up at the graceful lines of the house, which rose above the steep road. "What an elegant home. It must be a daily pleasure to wake up to a panoramic view of the hills and harbour."

"Especially on Sundays, when the beauty of the view is not veiled by the belching smoke of the chimneys on the flats. Please, come in, Charlie. I'm afraid I will have to put you into a rather poky room in the attic until we can clear out a better room."

"After the barracks, I assure you that even a dank cellar would be an improvement. You and your great-aunt have been exceedingly generous, Grace."

"Nonsense. I expect you would like to see Lily and drop off her possessions, while I must rejoin our visitors."

The Chelmsford men were on their way down as she reached the stairs. After seeing them out, Grace herded her great-aunt back upstairs to the study and pulled the door closed.

Anne raised an amused eyebrow. "Grace, dearest, don't glare at me with that ferocious expression. What if the wind were to change, leaving you looking like a cornered ferret forever?"

"Is this better, Aunt?" Grace gave her best impression of a simpering debutante, complete with fluttering eyelashes. "But honestly, what were you thinking, encouraging Edmund Chelmsford like that?"

"Tish, Edmund's a little wet behind the ears, but surely you must concede that he is handsome and wealthy enough to tempt any young lady. Indeed, I have heard him referred to as Dunedin's most eligible bachelor."

"If you dare say 'a single man in possession of a good fortune, must be in want of a wife', I swear I shall scream. Although, I concede he seems quite agreeable, when away from his father's dominant personality."

"Grace, dear, I am endeavouring to extract an enormously large donation from that gentleman's father. Could you not find it within your heart to charm the son just a little, so that we might tend the poor women of Dunedin under a roof that does not resemble a waterfall every time it rains?"

"You would sell my body and soul for a new roof?"

Anne waved a dismissive hand. "Nonsense, child. All I ask is that you be civil to a charming young man until the donation is in our account, then you may reveal the full force of your character. If he is not worthy of you, he will be running for the hills before the ink is dry on the ledger."

"Enough of your flattery, Aunt," Grace said. "Besides, I was on my best behaviour. Come and meet Constable Charlie Pyke. I should warn you, an arrogant sergeant has stood him down from the police force over his determination to see justice done. In fact, Constable Pyke's dismissal is largely my fault, which is why I have invited him to stay until he gets on his feet again. I do hope that meets with your approval."

"Excellent, a man of character. I like him already. I'm looking forward to having some lively company about the place. It has been far too quiet since Gordon died, notwithstanding the stimulating conversation and endless amusement provided by you, my dear Grace."

Grace tapped on the door to Lily's room. They entered to find Charlie setting out bottles of dried herbs and other unidentifiable substances on the top of the upturned box, alongside a high-sided skillet. He had already arranged Lily's few clothes neatly in the armoire.

Lily sat upright on the narrow bed, propped with pillows, her features crinkled into a smile. "Mrs Macmillan, allow me to introduce Charlie Pyke, my sister's son."

Anne looked from the petite Chinese lady to the man filling the room with his shoulders. "Delighted to meet you, Charlie. Do call me Anne, unless you feel uncomfortable doing so. We do not bother with formality amongst the residents of this house. Lily, how are you feeling? No more dizziness?"

Anne moved to her patient's side to check her eyes and pulse, no matter that Lily was looking as chirpy as the tiny silvereyes flitting around the grapevine outside the window.

Charlie moved out of the way, coming to stand next to Grace. "I apologise for interrupting you and your young man in the garden."

"Edmund Chelmsford is not my young man. His family owns a clothing factory empire, which claims to be at the forefront of enlightened design. I have accepted an invitation to view the local factory. Which reminds me – Aunt Anne, are you free on Thursday morning to accompany me to the Chelmsford factory, or would you have me ruin my already tattered reputation by going alone?"

Anne thought for a moment. "Unfortunately, I have to attend a meeting of the Ladies' Society for the Advancement of Prison Reform. Or is it the Ladies' Benevolent Fund for the Welfare and Education of Children? Whichever it is, I cannot accompany you. But I do not wish you to miss your assignation with Edmund Chelmsford. Perhaps you could take Mrs Patterson?"

"Auntie, you are determined to torture me. You know full well I would never hear the end of it if that gossip-monger escorted me. Indeed, the whole town would be abuzz with my impending nuptials by nightfall. Mrs Patterson would be knitting baby booties before the week is out."

Anne chuckled. "Scared of a little gossip, Grace? Perhaps Charlie might like to go. Edmund Chelmsford wouldn't dare take any liberties with a burly policeman guarding your virtue."

"I'm sure Charlie has better things to do with his time, such as catching up on sleep."

Charlie was working hard to hold back a grin. "On the contrary, Miss Penrose, I would be happy to escort you, although I don't doubt you are more than capable of looking after yourself. It is the least I can do after being invited to stay here tonight."

"The pleasure is all mine, I assure you," Anne said.

The grin disappeared from Charlie's lips. "Could I ask you to keep my aunt's location a secret? Constable Nolan was looking for my aunt at her boarding house."

"Isn't it good that the police are investigating the boy's death and Lily's injury?"

"It would be, Mrs Macmillan, if it wasn't Nolan. I don't have any proof, but I know he is rotten to the core. If so, he was not after my aunt to help her, but to ensure her silence. He gave the landlord reason to believe that she has lost her job at Kendall's factory."

"What does he look like?" Lily asked.

"My height and build, but pale-skinned and blond," Charlie said. "Rather boyish in appearance, aside from his broken nose, but a demon on the inside. He may be Kendall's lapdog, but he's as vicious as a cornered pit bull."

"I've seen a constable of that description at the factory on several occasions over the last few months," Lily said. "One time, I caught him coming out of Kendall's office with a handful of money. He realised I had seen him, but he dismissed me with an unpleasant smirk."

Charlie was at her side in a flash. "In that case, you are not safe even here, Aunt Lily. You must go to stay with my parents, well away from Dunedin."

Lily crossed her arms and glared at her nephew with all the force of her five-foot-nothing of outrage. "I am not leaving until I see justice done for a poor boy whose life has been cut short by Kendall's negligence." Her shoulders sagged as she turned back to Anne. "But Charlie is right. I cannot put you and Grace at risk by staying here."

Anne thumped her walking stick on the floor. "Enough! All the more reason Lily must stay in our care, where she has people to look out for her welfare." She thumped again as Charlie opened his mouth to protest. "You will both stay here. I will brook no further argument on the matter. We have no cook at present, so Lily is welcome to stay in this room, and we never use the attic rooms these days."

Charlie looked to Grace for support, but she was doing her impersonation of a mule again. "I see this is an argument I cannot win." He hesitated a moment, then added. "Aunt Lily is an excellent cook."

Lily sent an adoring smile to Charlie. "My nephew is too kind, although I did work in a hotel kitchen when my husband was alive. He was an exceptional chef."

"It seems you have brought your own herbs and spices too," Grace said.

"They are mostly medicinal," Lily replied. "I was training in the art of Chinese healing, before my father took it into his head to move the whole family to New Zealand to make his fortune on the goldfields."

Anne picked up a pair of jars and sniffed. "Chamomile? And ginger? It seems fate has brought us together. We desperately need another healer at Lavender House, and our housekeeper here, Mrs Brown, would be glad of a night off cooking occasionally. Only if that suits you, Lily, and not until you have recovered. The wages would not be much, but you would have no cost for board."

Lily was clearly at a loss for words. Charlie wiped a tear from his aunt's cheek and answered for her. "I cannot thank you enough, Mrs MacMillan. You are an angel of mercy."

"Hardly that, young man. Once you know me better, you will no doubt come to think of me as a stubborn, irritating old lady who terrifies the faint-hearted by speaking my mind. A demon of mercy, if you will. One of the few privileges of advanced age."

Grace rolled her eyes. "Don't believe a word of it, Charlie. My great-aunt has spoken her mind all her life. I recall my grandmother telling me she scared half the tutors in London away with her frank opinions and enthusiasm for anatomy."

"Let's hope Lily and Charlie are made of sterner stuff," Anne grumbled.

"I deal with the criminal classes daily, Mrs Macmillan," Charlie said. "There is little left to shock me, although today has brought more than the usual quota of surprises."

"Then you must have a cup of chamomile tea to calm your nerves, Constable," Anne said. "Grace, perhaps you could ask Mrs Brown to make a batch of her delicious scones. Then I expect you'd like to retire to the drawing room to tackle some needlepoint or something."

Grace let out an unladylike snort. "I shall retreat to the delights of needlepoint just as soon as you retire gracefully and accept that society is perfect as it is, dearest Aunt. Unfortunately, I have an urgent errand in town."

"Do try not to enrage any prominent citizens, my dear. Or lowlifes, for that matter."

"I will endeavour to avoid it, but only if they do not provoke me first."

"Which they always do."

Grace closed the door on a trio of chuckling misfits, reflecting, not for the first time that day, that fate had a wicked sense of humour.

Charlie followed her out. "Might as well make a start on the garden."

"I can imagine that it might be cathartic, hacking through the undergrowth and imagining that every vine is your sergeant's neck." Grace went up the stairs to her room to change, followed by the deep rumble of his laughter.

She switched her blood-stained shirtwaist and muddy skirt for a similar, but clean, outfit. Thank goodness tightly boned corsets and elaborate bustles were no longer de rigueur. The newspapers had been featuring skirts designed to accommodate the current enthusiasm for bicycling. She had already ordered one, thinking how excellent it would be for walking freely.

As Grace detoured via the drawing room, in search of her reticule, she found the maid at the window, staring out with rapt attention. Sadie jumped like a startled rabbit as Grace cleared her throat. A blush of magnificent red burned her cheeks as the maid raced for the door.

What was that all about, Grace wondered, until she looked out the window. Charlie was in the garden, in shirt-sleeves rolled to the biceps, swinging a slasher like a mighty Samurai sword against the undergrowth, which had besieged the path to the vegetable patch. She pulled her gaze away and hurried out of the house, heading for town.

"Cooee, Miss Penrose!"

Grace hovered between impatience and politeness before coming down on the side of the latter. She stopped and turned to their neighbour, a woman of indefinable age, who looked after her husband with the same bustling efficiency she used to elicit donations for the good works of her church group. "Mrs Patterson, good day to you."

"What a grand carriage that was in front of your house, Miss Penrose. Mr Sterling Chelmsford and his handsome son, if I'm not mistaken. Fine Christian gentlemen and wealthy too. I trust the younger Mr Chelmsford enjoyed his visit?" Mrs Patterson covered her ladylike titter with a lace handkerchief, but her eyes twinkled with the thrill.

"You would do well to flutter your fan in his direction, Miss Penrose. I've always said it, my dear. If only you made an effort to dress nicely – perhaps some lace and ruffles or a dash of colour to bring out your blue eyes – you might be pretty enough to turn the right heads."

"Thank you, Mrs Patterson, but Mr Chelmsford was visiting my great-aunt on a business matter. If you'll excuse me, I am late for an appointment."

"About time you were married, my dear," her neighbour continued. "A girl like yourself should not linger on the shelf. Eligible men might begin to wonder why."

Grace fixed a smile on her lips. "I am not yet twenty years old, Mrs Patterson. Hardly beyond redemption just yet."

"The choicest fruits are quickly plucked, my dear. I married my dear husband when I was eighteen."

"I thank you for your wisdom, Mrs Patterson, but I really must leave you to tend those lovely roses, as I have a pressing engagement. Goodbye for now." Grace hurried down the hill at an unseemly pace. Now she really was late for a meeting she did not want to miss. She had a debt to repay.

Two hours later, Grace returned home to find a patch of the jungle tamed. The two aunties were sitting with their heads together at the kitchen table, having an animated conversation over the jars of herbs. Were they actually giggling like a couple of schoolgirls? Anne had never come close to giggling in her presence before. The sight was enough to bring a smile to anyone's lips.

Grace met Charlie on the stairs, his pitch-black hair still damp, and smelling of soap. "Charlie, can you spare a moment?"

When they were seated in the drawing room, with those gold-flecked eyes examining her, she didn't know where to start. The beginning seemed as good a place as any.

"Do you remember the gentleman who was at the police station this morning?"

"It seems like a lifetime ago, but yes, I do. He gave you his card and whispered in your ear, as I recall."

"He would like to talk to you. About what, I am not at liberty to say. But I assure you it will be in your best interests to meet with him in Wains Hotel at nine o'clock tomorrow morning."

"This is most mysterious. Wains Hotel? I doubt they'd let the likes of me through the door."

"Poppycock," Anne said from the doorway. "Fitted out in a decent suit, they'd be bowing and scraping in a trice. Stand up, lad."

Charlie stood while Anne looked him up and down. "My husband was about your size. Come upstairs and we'll see what we can find."

Grace choked back an exclamation of astonishment. Anne treated Uncle Gordon's possessions like sacred relics. Almost two years after her husband's death, she hadn't let a single item out of the house. Anne didn't go to the excesses of Queen Victoria, who had Prince Albert's clothes laid out each morning, but Grace had caught Anne more than once with a wistful expression on her face and her nose buried in her husband's favourite coat.

And now she was handing them out to a man she had known for less time than it would take to brush and press one of Uncle Gordon's suits.

Charlie meekly followed Anne upstairs. Apparently, he had been quick to learn the cardinal rule of the household – that it was easier to sail with the wind than against when faced with Anne's determination.

A Second Chance

On Wednesday morning, Charlie was ready in good time, with a hearty breakfast warming his belly and a full night's sleep in a comfortable bed.

For the first time in his life, he lingered in front of a looking-glass, studying the imposter in the dark tweed sack suit and matching waistcoat. Astounding the difference a quality suit of clothes could make to an ordinary man. Even one that had to be cinched in around the waist and let out in the arms, thanks to the nimble fingers of his aunt.

Anne intercepted Charlie in the hall, swapping his cloth cap for a black bowler hat and straightening his tie. With a final adjustment here and there, she said, "Perfect," and hustled him out the door.

He turned back to look up at the house, pinching himself to see if he was still dreaming.

Standing so high on the hill gave him a new perspective on the city. Dunedin spread out on all sides, around an amphitheatre of steep slopes. Social position could be determined by altitude as easily as by the quality of the bricks and mortar. Wharves, warehouses, and workers on the flats, stretching to the south. Commerce, churches, and enterprise on the lower slopes, with sturdy middle-class homes above them. Mansions on the upper slopes, above the stench and smoke and strife, mantled by the green of the Town Belt, with magnificent views over the harbour and the distant hook of the Otago Peninsula.

The Macmillan house was mid-way up the slope, set amidst a cluster of doctor's residences. Harbouring hands tainted by blood and disease, halfway between the grime-incrusted hands of the flats and the upper-level white gloves, which were rarely sullied by anything more indelicate than champagne.

Charlie was a man with his boots on the flats and his sights on the lower slopes. As his father said, at least a man has the freedom to make his own way here. Not like England, where Debrett's Peerage ruled the waves.

Fortunes here were as likely built off the backs of sheep and the glitter of gold. Many a family on the upper slopes were said to have distinguished portraits on their walls, which bore no relationship to their never-mentioned humble roots. The Chelmsford family was a prime example. He shuddered to think that a portrait of Grace Penrose might grace their walls one day.

A rustle behind the neighbour's hedge roused Charlie back to reality with a jerk. He turned to find a middle-aged woman staring at him, open-mouthed, so he tipped his unfamiliar bowler hat to her and set off down the hill for the short walk to the hotel, humming a jaunty tune.

Not that his present situation warranted such good cheer. Grace and her great-aunt may have provided him with shelter and kindness for a night, but he knew his career and future were hanging by the thinnest of threads. He ought not to take advantage of their generosity for more than another night at most. They might choose to skirt the usual etiquette of society, but he owed it to Grace Penrose to protect her reputation, especially as one of the wealthiest young men in the region was courting her.

Edmund Chelmsford was a lucky man to have caught the eye of so fascinating a woman. Would Chelmsford value her intelligence? Charlie tried to imagine the man enjoying the thrill of spotting clues on a corpse – a ludicrous proposition.

Not that it was Charlie's concern. He shut out the memory of Grace, bending over the corpse with intense concentration, and turned his thoughts to the mysterious gentleman at Wains Hotel. By the time he had reached the grand entrance, not far from the bottom of High Street, he was no further advanced as to whom the gentleman might be.

The doorman opened the doors with a flourish at his arrival and showed him into a small parlour, where the gentleman was already seated with tea and crumpets. He looked quintessentially English, but when he spoke, there was no doubting that the man was born north of the border. No surprise there, as Scottish immigrants outnumbered all others in this part of New Zealand.

The gentleman welcomed him with an appraising nod, before waving a hand towards an ornate armchair. He bent forward to pour another cup of tea, sliding the cup and the plate of crumpets across to Charlie. "Thank you for coming, Constable Pyke. Did Miss Penrose tell you why I asked to see you?"

"She refused to say a word, sir."

"Is that so? An impressive young woman, Miss Penrose. Intelligent, skilled, and able to keep her mouth shut when asked to do so. I am very tempted to recruit her to my cause. Perhaps you could persuade her?" He pushed a card across the table.

Charlie read the man's name and leapt to his feet, forgetting the teacup balanced on the arm of the chair. He lunged forward and snatched the cup in mid-air, before snapping his hand up into a salute. "Detective Inspector Stewart, an honour to meet you, sir."

After a moment, he caught the amused look on the Stewart's face and sank back into the armchair. "Are you to be our new District Inspector, sir?"

"I've been assigned to a special operation. Squeezing the last ounce of blood out of me before they force me to retire, I expect. The Premier is concerned about the state of unrest amongst the working classes, particularly in view of the upcoming Royal Commission into sweatshops. He's concerned at reports that some members of the police force are turning a blind eye to labour violations, especially child labour and excessive hours."

Stewart paused to sip his tea. "Naturally, the Commissioner of Police wants to ensure that this is not the case before the Sweating Commission begins its investigation in three weeks' time. The child's death in a factory could not have come at a worse time."

Charlie's heart sank into the pit of his stomach as piercing grey eyes met his. Had Sergeant Lynch somehow found a way to make him the scapegoat? Surely the Detective Inspector must have noted his willingness to investigate Miss Penrose's claims, when he was at the station yesterday morning.

Stewart sat back in his armchair and sipped his tea, as if he had all the time in the world for this meeting with a disgraced third-class constable. "You have been stood down from duty, Constable Pyke."

"Yes, sir." Charlie's heart continued its downward slide, coming to rest in his freshly polished boots. Surely the police did not bring in a renowned Detective Inspector like Stewart just to sack a lowly constable?

Stewart let his words sit between them for long seconds. "Tell me, Pyke, what did you hope to achieve when you joined the police force?"

The unexpected question startled him into admitting the truth. "I hoped to be a detective one day, sir, like yourself." More chance of flying to the stars than becoming a detective after yesterday.

"Miss Penrose informed me – quite forcibly I might add – that you have the makings of a good detective. She was most impressed with your deductions regarding the unidentified man's cause of death."

Charlie's heart inched back up towards his knees. "In truth, sir, it was Miss Penrose who provided much of the insight. I realise it was an appalling breach of protocol to allow her to be present during the recovery of a missing corpse."

"She claims she gave you little choice, as I can well imagine. I had a word with Professor Scott, who agreed with Miss Penrose's assessment of your aptitude and your conclusion that the death was suspicious." DI Stewart put the empty cup down with not even a hint of a rattle. "Scott has sent the body to the police surgeon, and I will ensure the local detective team takes over the case. It is no longer your concern."

"I'm pleased to hear that the man's death is to be investigated, sir." Charlie wished Stewart would get on with telling him his fate.

Detective Inspector Stewart continued to watch Charlie's every muscle twitch, which made him twitch all the more. "I met your father some years ago, Constable Pyke, when you were a wee bairn in your mother's arms."

"You've met *both* my parents, sir?" The twitch turned to a minor muscle spasm.

"They both impressed me with their dedication and good sense. Policing the goldfields is a hard job. Takes a man of courage and principle, with a fine woman by his side."

"Thank you, sir. I hope to live up to my father's high standards." His muscles relaxed again. If Detective Inspector Stewart, who was a legend in the force, was unruffled by Charlie's Chinese ancestry, perhaps there was hope.

Stewart buttered a crumpet and cut it into precise quarters. "I am concerned about rumours of corruption in the local police force. Money changing hands to turn a blind eye to illegal activity. Would you know anything about that, Constable Pyke?" He popped a piece of crumpet into his mouth, chewing with agonising slowness.

Charlie knew he was being tested, but he needed time to find the right words. He would never have a better chance to unburden his conscience, yet there was still the unpleasant fact that ratting on a fellow officer would put paid to any chance of a career in the local force. Before he could speak, Stewart answered for him.

"Your hesitation tells me all I need to know."

"I have never taken a bribe, sir, and never will," Charlie said.

The grey eyes were unwavering, but not unkind. "I don't doubt it, Constable. Tell me, did Sergeant Lynch complete the required paperwork to formalise your stand-down?"

The change of tack caught Charlie off guard. "Paperwork, sir? Not that I know of. He told me I was to take a week's leave while he investigated. But I have little doubt that I will be dismissed."

"Which means you are officially on leave, rather than under sanction. As it happens, I'm in need of a man on the ground, Pyke. If I can convince the local Inspector, I wonder if you would be interested? My role gives me the power to second a man as an acting Detective Constable. Only temporarily, mind."

"Interested, sir? I would walk over hot coals for a chance to assist you, even for a day. But, sir, there are constables with far more seniority than me who would give their first-born for such an opportunity."

"A few of us at police headquarters feel that young men of merit should not be overlooked in favour of plodders, even if the plodders have served more time." Stewart picked up the last piece of the crumpet. "Take my advice, lad. Seize the opportunity and show me what you are capable of." The grey eyes flicked up again, with crinkles around the edges. "Neither hot coals nor first-borns are necessary."

"Yes, sir. It would be an honour." Excitement overcame Charlie. He jumped to his feet and saluted again, taking care to set the cup aside first. His heart felt as if it was zinging around the room, ricocheting off the disapproving face of Queen Victoria, framed in thick gilt, and bouncing off the chandelier, before thudding back into his body.

Amusement rippled across Stewart's face. "Not such a great honour, I assure you. It's only for a few days and I have already been informed that the district has no other constables to spare, given the massive crowds and surge of crime accompanying the New Zealand and South Seas Exhibition."

"Nevertheless, I thank you, Detective Inspector Stewart. I promise I won't let you down."

"Before you even know what I want you to do?"

"I should like to hear it, sir, but I can assure you my enthusiasm will be undiminished if you assign me to investigate a rash of stray dogs. I will retrieve my uniform from the barracks and report for duty immediately."

"Plain clothes will be best, Acting Detective Constable Pyke. I'll put in a formal request for your secondment now, while you make a start on this appallingly large pile of unsubstantiated complaints." Stewart pointed to a desk in the corner of the room, which was a foot deep in files. "See if you can spot a pattern in these files of worker complaints made against various factories. And do have something to eat. I have a feeling it will be a long day."

"Yes, sir." Charlie took the outstretched hand and gave it a vigorous shake.

"I ought to warn you, Pyke, that the life of a detective is not nearly as glamorous as you might think. Long hours of fruitless surveillance, days of chasing dead-end leads, piles of paperwork. You will be resented by the uniforms, distrusted by the public, and shown no mercy by the criminal classes. Popular fiction may be rife with detectives who solve cases in a trice, based on trifling evidence, but the reality is not nearly so neat. Wilkie Collins has a lot to answer for."

Stewart left the parlour, leaving Charlie to tackle the files and remaining crumpets, with scarcely a twinge of regret that he would not be involved in the murder investigation. Compared to yesterday, his future was looking decidedly rosy, for the short-term, at least.

The complaints listed in the files were not nearly so rosy. Each incident report had been stamped as "closed", with a scrawl of script indicating the outcome of the investigation, almost all being "accident" or "unsubstantiated". Several resulted in the complainant being charged with laying a false complaint, after which there was a marked decrease in the rate of reported incidents, no doubt counted as a success.

Grace's paperwork wasn't in the file, despite the serious nature of the incident, which either meant it was under investigation or it had been used as a fire-lighter. He certainly would not want to be the one who told her, if it was the latter.

After an hour, Charlie stopped reading and attempted to get his thoughts in order for DI Stewart. As he looked around the room, with its embossed wallpaper, Oriental carpets, and mahogany furniture, the incongruity of Stewart's accommodation struck him. Perhaps the fact that the Premier himself had instigated the investigation explained the luxurious surroundings.

"I hope you're not planning to steal that Wedgewood jug, lad?"

"No, sir." Blimey, Stewart moved as silently as a cat, even though his leg was obviously giving him pain. He would have to keep his wits about him. "Not a lot of Wedgewood crockery at the barracks, sir."

"My current task requires a certain degree of discretion and independence. And my aged body cries out for a little comfort. Fortunately, I have private means, so I chose not to stay in the fleapit hotel my employers were willing to pay for." Stewart eased himself into the armchair. "The good news is that Sergeant Lynch has been persuaded to release you, against his rather emphatically expressed better judgement. Now, lad, what have you found?"

Charlie glanced at his hastily scrawled summary. "Some factories have had no issues at all, others just the odd one or two, while a small number have been the subject of repeated complaints, most often laid by the unions on behalf of the workers. The usual issues: underpaying the rate set by the union, being forced to take piecework home after hours, insanitary conditions, apprentices working for no wages for months at a time, excessive holding back of wages to pay for damages. As you will know, sir, the current law does not provide sufficiently clear guidance on the required standards, allowing the more unscrupulous factory owners to bend the rules."

"Any prosecutions for using underage workers? Or charges involving dangerous workplaces?"

"Several cases reported of both, sir, but rarely substantiated and almost never prosecuted. Underage children seem to vanish when the police attempt to investigate, while injuries are most often written off as accidents. And so they might be. But it seems to me that such accidents might never have happened if proper safety standards had been in place. The Inspector of Factories has limited power and even less time than the police, except in cases of the most serious violations."

Stewart curled a finger around his moustache, tweaking the ends around and up into symmetrical curls. "Hmm. If the underage workers are not there when the factories are inspected, then the factory owners must have inside information on when an inspection is being conducted. Go on, Pyke."

"The more serious complaints pertain to a handful of factories, most especially to the premises of Mr Kendall, where the boy died yesterday morning. A flood of complaints, in fact, but nothing seems to change. Rather the opposite, in fact. The number of complaints against him has dropped markedly in recent months, after Kendall accused several complainants of making false allegations. If the Sweating Commission

78

admonishes the actions of the police force, I'll wager it'll be down to Kendall and a few others like him."

"I checked with Sergeant Lynch about the boy's death," Stewart said. "He has written the incident off as an accident. The factory foreman said a worker accidentally knocked the machine into gear while the boy was still under it. A Mrs Lily Wu. I'd like to hear her account of the incident, but she has disappeared, so that would appear to be a dead end."

Charlie felt his cheeks burning, but he sensed that his future would be at stake if he didn't tell the full truth, right from the start. "She was not the cause of the accident. Mrs Wu tried to rescue the boy. She heard him scream and tried to help him, injuring herself in the process. One of the factory girls, Bess Todd, can vouch for her."

Stewart maintained the poker face to be expected of one of the force's most experienced detectives, betraying his feelings only by a slight twitch in one eyelid. "Constable Nolan interviewed Bess Todd yesterday and claims she saw nothing."

"I can only say that Miss Penrose gave a completely different account of what Bess told her, sir. It was Bess who took Miss Penrose to tend to the injured Mrs Wu."

Stewart drummed his fingers on the arm of the chair, letting the silence sit for a moment. "A pity this worker, Mrs Wu, cannot be located. Constable Nolan reported she was not at work nor at her boarding house. He believes her sudden disappearance indicates a guilty conscience."

With his eyes fixed on Stewart and his back straight, Charlie took a deep breath and continued calmly, pushing down his simmering anger. "I must inform you that Mrs Lily Wu is my aunt, sir. After the incident, they left her outside on a pile of rubbish, unconscious. Thanks to Bess, Miss Penrose rescued her. Mrs Wu is currently staying with Miss Penrose's great-aunt, Mrs Macmillan, who runs a refuge for women."

The finger-drumming stopped abruptly. "Is that so? When Miss Penrose recounted the incident to me yesterday afternoon, she failed to mention your relationship to Mrs Wu or her location."

"I believe Miss Penrose did not wish to make my situation worse than it already was."

"The Police Force has no rule banning constables with Chinese ancestry, Pyke."

"As you say, sir, there is nothing written in the regulations."

Stewart was the first to blink. With a sigh, he said, "And what does the redoubtable Miss Penrose plan to do about the incident?"

"She has given up on the police, I regret to say, and is taking it up with Miss Morison of the Tailoresses' Union as we speak. Mrs Wu is also willing to give evidence, regarding both the boy's death and an earlier incident where she witnessed the passing of a large sum of money between Mr Kendall and Constable Nolan. However, I fear she is unlikely to be believed against the word of the owner and foreman, especially if Bess Todd has been coerced into changing her account."

Stewart began drumming his fingers again. "The union will no doubt bring it before the Sweating Commission. I would like to pre-empt that, if possible. I believe the best course of action is for us to conduct further investigations. Even if the boy's death was an accident, rather than wilful negligence, the subsequent actions of the factory owner or foreman towards the boy and Mrs Wu are unacceptable. Add to that your findings regarding possible suppression of past incidents, and we may have a case."

"It won't be easy, sir. The child's body was dumped, and the factory cleaned of evidence. The foreman, Mr Fergus Duncan, may be our best bet. If we could persuade him to give evidence, we might have a shot at a conviction."

"If nothing else, I wish to show that the police are willing to take action. It is the potential for an accusation of corruption that most worries the Police Commissioner." Stewart stood up and put on his coat. "Your relationship to a crucial witness complicates the situation. I need to satisfy myself that Mrs Wu is in no way culpable, before I allow you to do any more on this case."

Missing Militants

Grace watched Charlie disappear down the hill that morning under the inquisitive gaze of Mrs Patterson, before returning to her preparations for the day. She had no time to waste. Anne had given her leave to take further action on the child's death, but the waiting patients at Lavender House needed her attention too.

Twenty minutes later, Grace entered the offices of the Tailoresses' Union, which was already buzzing with activity and awash with paperwork. The lilt of an Irish accent emerged from an adjacent room, followed by a sturdy woman, wearing a no-nonsense dress in dark grey with a softer edge of white ruffles under the high collar. She strode over to Grace and thrust her out.

"You'll be Miss Penrose. Mrs Macmillan sent me a message to expect you. I'm Harriet Morison."

Grace took the offered hand, wincing at the firm grip. "A pleasure to meet you, Miss Morison. I've come in relation to the death of an underaged worker at Kendall's clothing factory yesterday. The poor lad was dragged into a malfunctioning loom."

Miss Morison called across the office to a young woman, not much older than Grace. "Get me the Kendall file please, Molly."

"Which one?"

"The current one. Seems we have yet another complaint to add. This one a death."

While Molly rummaged through files, Miss Morison gestured Grace to a chair. "What action has been taken so far?"

"Nothing by Kendall, other than to dump the body and scrub the blood off the floor. I reported the incident to the police, but I have little hope of any action being taken. At least, not by the uniformed branch. There is a Detective Inspector nosing around who seems much more amenable to taking action, if only to forestall embarrassment to the police force with the upcoming labour inquiry."

"That's news to me. Good news, I hope. We could certainly do with the support of as many factions as possible at the Royal Commission on labour conditions, which they're calling the Sweating Commission. And what do you wish me to do?"

"My great-aunt tells me you are giving evidence before the Sweating Commission soon. I thought you could raise the boy's death as an example of dangerous practises."

"Aye, it'll raise more than eyebrows, for sure. Conditions at Kendall's are bad enough. A death might well be the lever we need to force them to abide by the regulations or close the place down."

The young woman arrived with a bulging file.

"Miss Penrose, meet Miss Molly Sugden. I'm afraid I have to attend another meeting. Molly will take the details. Thank you for taking the time to bring this to our attention. 'Tis a bad business, a child dying."

By the time they had set down the details of names, events and witnesses, Molly and Grace were on first-name terms and heading down the path to a friendship forged by kindred spirits.

"The critical issue will be to get credible witnesses to give their testimony to the Sweating Commission," Molly said. "You'd think it would be simple, but I have spent weeks and weeks trying to recruit enough workers brave enough or militant enough to speak out. Several have dropped by the wayside under threat of losing their positions, while others have been offered inducements to say how good their conditions are. And, of course, most workers are just ordinary women, desperately trying to make ends meet, who don't have the time or energy to do anything but accept their lot and plough on regardless."

"Mrs Wu is an excellent speaker," Grace said. "She would be highly credible to anyone not prejudiced against the Chinese community. You might persuade young Bess Todd to give evidence, although I fear their intimidation has silenced her. Constable Pyke is talking to the Kendall factory foreman today, but I expect Mr Duncan will value his job too highly to speak out."

Molly sipped her tea, which was so strong it was a wonder the spoon didn't dissolve. "This Constable Pyke, is he on the take, like the others?"

"Not at all," Grace said, with rather more emphasis than she intended. "I don't doubt his integrity. He's an excellent man … policeman."

Molly grinned. "There are few enough excellent men around. Better keep a tight rein on him, Grace. For official purposes, of course."

Another young woman came up behind Molly and gave her a playful swat on the head with a file. "Don't you be teasing the lass, Molly Sugden. Miss Molly thinks she the queen bee ever since she nabbed a bright young man for herself."

"Get away with you, Agnes. I think no such thing."

The two women chuckled as they teased each other, reminding Grace how much she had missed the companionship of bright young women since arriving in a new city.

"Agnes, this is Miss Grace Penrose, a fellow campaigner against injustice."

"Good to hear it, Grace. Do come along to our meeting tonight." Agnes put a pamphlet on the table in front of her. "Eight o'clock tonight at Temperance House. Harriet Morison puts on a rousing show and Molly is giving a talk."

"I would love to attend." Grace studied the pamphlet, her senses tingling, though she couldn't pin down why. "If not tonight, then definitely another night."

"Now, Agnes," said Molly, "was there something you wanted to see me about or were you merely interrupting for the pleasure of it?"

All traces of Agnes' light-heartedness vanished. "I've bad news, I'm afraid. I've been following up your list of the women who were to testify at the Sweating Commission."

"Please don't tell me that someone else has withdrawn," Molly moaned.

The frown lines deepened to furrows across Agnes' brow. "Not just one, Molly. All of them."

83

Molly's jaw fell slack as the words hit home. "All of them! How is that possible? Some of them were champing at the bit to give their testimony."

"They've all disappeared. Taken up new positions out of Dunedin, from what little I could gather." Agnes squeezed her friend's shoulder. "I hate to be the bearer of grim tidings, love."

Molly slumped forward, resting her head on the table and letting out a groan. She pushed herself upright again and thumped her fist on the pile of files. "Get me the list of their addresses, Agnes. Wherever they are, I will drag them kicking and screaming to give their testimony, if I have to."

"Mind if I go with you, Molly?" Grace asked.

Half an hour later, Molly stopped in front of a tiny wooden cottage with an alarmingly saggy iron roof. The word "hovel" sprang to mind, as it did so often around here. The council had condemned most of the houses in the area as unfit for human habitation, not that it made a jot of difference. A leaking roof was better than no roof at all.

"Clara Green, one of our staunchest supporters," Molly read from the notes. "Kendall's clothing factory. Originally employed for six months without pay as an apprentice, now an experienced knitter earning around eleven shillings a week, plus an extra shilling or so by taking work home in the evening. And that's before the factory owner takes out money to pay for breakages and cleaning, up to a shilling a week."

Grace stared at her new friend. "How can she survive on eleven shillings a week? That cannot be enough to cover her board and lodging, surely?"

"Most of the girls live at home. Their pitiful incomes are needed to keep the family above the breadline." Molly consulted her notes again. "Aside from the criminally low wages, Clara was going to testify that the factory is poorly ventilated, freezing in winter, boiling in summer, with one filthy closet for thirty women. They threatened Clara with dismissal if she joined the union. Never seen a factory inspector visit."

"Clara is a brave woman to testify, given the circumstances."

Molly knocked on the door. "The Sweating Commission is supposed to guarantee anonymity, but I have my doubts whether they can keep such a promise."

The door opened a crack. "Who are you?"

"Miss Molly Sugden to see Miss Clara Green."

The crack narrowed. "She don't live 'ere no more. You can scat. We don't want no trouble."

"Good day to you, Mrs Green," Grace chimed in. "It's Miss Penrose from Lavender House. Would you like me to see to the bandage on Jimmy's arm?"

"Oh, it's you, Miss Bones. Come in then."

Grace pushed open the door and entered a tiny, cluttered room. An older sister had taken Jimmy to Lavender House with a burn on his arm, so she hadn't seen inside his home before. As she examined and re-bandaged Jimmy's arm, she kept up a chatter of conversation, gradually easing around to the absence of Clara.

"Got 'erself a right good position out of town, she did," crowed Mrs Green. "All clean and well run, with full board provided."

"She be a lucky cow," added a sister. "Half the town fallin' over themselves for that job."

"She's happy then?" asked Grace, as she tucked the end of the bandage under.

"Not heard a word, it being so far away, but Clara reckoned on sending us a shilling or two a week. It'll be a godsend if she does."

Grace and Molly walked away from the cottage in silence.

As they turned the next corner, Molly said, "Did you see all those grog bottles stacked up?"

"And the bruises on the mother and children. The oldest of the boys could scarcely move without wincing. I dread to think how Jimmy got that nasty burn."

Molly huffed out a frustrated sigh, but marched resolutely onwards to the next addresses on the list.

By the time they knocked on the door of the final missing militant, the story had an all too familiar ring. Better position, happy mother, envious sisters. Not all showing evidence of beatings, but all the families were desperately poor, living in rundown, damp, overcrowded houses.

The father was home at the last address, half-drunk already, and venting his anger on them. "Flamin' shit-stirrers, you unionists," he yelled at their retreating backs as they hurried out of the house. "Taking men's jobs, going against what the Good Lord intended womenfolk to do. You mark my words, my wilful slut of a daughter will end up selling herself on a street corner if she don't mend her ways."

As they left, Molly turned to ensure he hadn't followed them. "Blimey, I'd rather live in a sewer full of rats than come home to that man. The demon drink has a lot to answer for around here. With their husbands drinking away their pay, it's no wonder the children go out to earn or steal whatever they can."

The grim weight of reality drained Grace's spirits and dragged at her shoulders as they trudged back towards the centre of town. "At least the missing daughters have found good positions."

"I truly hope so, Grace."

"You doubt it?"

"I don't doubt that is what their mothers believe, but it worries me that not one of them has heard from her daughter."

The anxiety in Molly's voice stopped Grace in her tracks. "What are you not telling me?"

Molly was clearly reluctant to speculate, but eventually she said, "There are plenty of shady characters lurking on the streets, attempting to lure girls away from unhappy situations, with false promises of higher wages and better conditions far from their homes." She must have seen the horror on Grace's face. "Not all for prostitution. Some go to domestic positions that are hard to fill or into the countryside to slave on farms."

Grace felt sick to her stomach at the wickedness in the world. If that was the case, they could only pray that the girls would escape and find a way home.

It was Molly who finally broke the silence. "I'll just have to find other women to testify. We still have three weeks before the Sweating Commission begins hearing testimony."

"If anyone can do it, it'll be you, Molly. Miss Morison has great faith in you." Grace hoped rather than believed it to be feasible. If Molly had spent many weeks convincing these militant young women to talk, was there really any hope that she could replace them with less willing volunteers within so short a time?

"So, you're Miss Bones?" Molly said, with forced cheeriness, in an obvious attempt to change the subject. "However did you learn to be a doctor?"

"I'm not trained yet, but I hope to be accepted into medical school soon. You could apply to go to university too, if you wanted, Molly."

"Me? Yeah, and rainbows have pots of gold at the end."

"You're clever, Molly, and good at what you do."

"And happy as I am. Though it's good to know that women like you are bringing about change."

As they neared Lavender House, Grace racked her brain to find something positive to say before they parted company. "My great-aunt and I are going to the New Zealand and South Seas Exhibition tomorrow evening. Would you care to come with us, Molly?"

"That would be marvellous. I've been dying to go, but my young man has been too busy with his work."

Grace departed with a merry wave, her delight at meeting a woman of her own age and with a similar outlook on life taking the edge off her anxiety over the missing women, temporarily at least.

Lavender House

Charlie Pyke and Detective Inspector Stewart found none of the ladies at home in High Street. The maid told them that Mrs Wu was feeling better and had gone to Lavender House with Mrs Macmillan.

Lavender House was humming with activity. Anne was in the pink room, tending to a scalded arm, while Lily was so busy in the waiting room, taking details of injuries and ailments, that she failed to notice the two policemen. Charlie's spirits lifted at the sight of his aunt in her element, working with brisk efficiency despite her bandaged head and injured arm.

As he moved forward to help her, Stewart raised a hand to stop him, gesturing to two empty chairs in the corner. "Always take a moment or two to observe the situation, Pyke, if you can. You learn more from people's actions than their words."

Lily took one look at the limp body of a baby, clutched in his mother's trembling arms, and led her straight into the pink room for Anne's immediate attention. Next, she examined a nasty gash on a toddler's leg, replacing the blood-stained rag the mother was holding against the wound with a clean dressing and sending him and his mother to the seat outside the pink room. That left a family of five newly scrubbed, skeleton thin urchins, who were scratching their scalps so vigorously, the rasp could be heard across the room.

"Jam tonic, if you please, Miss Newland," Lily called to the lady on the reception desk. She bent down to examine their hair, one by one.

By the time Lily had bundled several bottles into a bag and talked to the children's mother, Miss Newland had returned with five jam sandwiches, which disappeared into five mouths with ferocious speed. The family departed with sticky lips and contented smiles.

Lily turned to see who else was waiting, noticing them for the first time. "Charlie! What are you doing here?"

"Detective Inspector Stewart would like a word with you, Aunt Lily, about Alfie's death."

Lily watched Stewart limp across the room. "That foot been giving you trouble long, Detective Inspector?"

"What? Oh, injured it a few weeks back, never came right. These cursed Dunedin hills aren't helping. Is there somewhere we can talk in private, Mrs Wu?"

"Not before I look at your injury," Lily replied, with steely resolve in her sing-song voice. "Nobody leaves here in pain if we can help it. I'll just wash my hands. Those wee kiddies could mount several battalions of nits between them."

Stewart hobbled obediently after Lily, leaving Charlie in awe. Detective Inspector Stewart was renowned for his success in tackling the toughest cases, and infamous for not meekly following orders. Everyone in the force knew he had been injured when Callum Evans had flung him against a brick wall. Evans was a serial bank robber with a vicious streak and the build of a battleship. Stewart had got his man though. Hurled a loose chunk of brick at the fleeing robber's legs, bringing him down in a whirl of limbs and oaths. That would teach the lout for risking the wrath of one of the finest spin-bowlers in the country.

The next thing Charlie knew, the sound of a door banging against the wall behind him jerked him awake. Anne's voice could be heard giving instructions, then the front door closed.

Anne appeared in the waiting room, glancing around at the empty seats in disbelief. "Your aunt is a treasure, Charlie. She's only been here a few hours and already I cannot imagine how we ever managed without her."

"I haven't seen her so happy in a long time, Mrs Macmillan. Aunt Lily was wasting her talents working as a seamstress."

"Think what the world would be if all talented women could follow their vocation. Speaking of which, here comes my great-niece, with a bee under her bonnet by the looks of it."

The door swung open. Light, but vigorous, footsteps whisked down the corridor. Charlie could have picked Grace Penrose out from a crowd, based on her lively tread alone.

"I'm back, Auntie. I'll have a quick bite to eat, then head out on my rounds." Grace poked her head around the door. "Oh, hello Charlie. If you're interrogating Anne, give up while you're ahead. You'd sooner get a smile out of Queen Victoria than a confession out of my great-aunt."

"Don't you go giving Constable Pyke the wrong idea about a harmless old lady." Anne prodded her gently with the end of her walking stick. "I was just about to tell him what I found out this morning. Perhaps you could bring a tray of tea and shortbread to my office? This detecting lark is leaving me parched."

Grace gave her great-aunt a quick peck on the cheek before disappearing. By the time Anne and Charlie were settled in Anne's office, Grace was back with the tea.

"Before you start, Aunt, I'm dying to know how Charlie's meeting with Detective Inspector Stewart went." Grace turned her inquisitive blue eyes on him and raised an eyebrow.

"Couldn't have gone better, thanks to you. I've been transferred to his service for a few days. Acting Detective Constable – it's a dream come true for me."

Her smile was pure delight. "The Inspector must have seen the potential in you."

"He told me you were a force to be reckoned with on my behalf. How can I ever repay you, Grace?" Charlie accepted the offered cup, reflecting that he had never drunk so much tea in his life. Back at the police station, he was lucky if he had a spare minute to swill some water from the tap.

"After what you said about me to Professor Scott, it's the least I could do to return the favour. Besides, you're overestimating my influence. Detective Inspector Stewart had his eye on you from the start. He only wanted to meet me to get the details of Alfie's death."

"You underestimate yourself, Grace. Stewart will be offering you a job before you know it."

"Over my dead body. Or, better yet, over his dead body," Anne said. "Grace was born to be a doctor, not a detective."

"Quite right, Mrs Macmillan," Charlie agreed. "Can't have your great-niece putting the rest of us ordinary coppers to shame. Now, what was it you wished to tell me?"

Anne put her cup down and settled into the deep cushions of her chair. "While I was on my rounds this morning, I had a word to the Reverend Waddell about Bess and Johnny Todd. The children are only working because their father was laid off from his job and they are desperate for money. Waddell said they are a lovely family, doing their best under difficult conditions."

"Bess struck me as a kind-hearted girl," Grace added. "She was terrified she would lose her position if she helped Mrs Wu, but she still did it."

A knock at the door interrupted them. "Room for two more conspirators?" Without waiting for a reply, Lily squeezed into the small office, followed by Stewart.

Charlie gave his seat to his aunt. "I'll fetch another for you from the waiting room, sir."

"No need, lad. Against my better judgement, I allowed your aunt to stick needles into my foot. I felt the oddest buzzing sensation, then the pain simply vanished. Darndest thing I've ever witnessed." He looked across at Lily with an expression halfway between reverence and astonishment.

"Glad to hear it, sir. My aunt is a wonder with the acupuncture needles. Mrs Macmillan was just telling us about Bess Todd, the girl who witnessed the incident at the factory."

Stewart turned to his hostess and bowed his head. "Mrs Macmillan, a pleasure to meet you. Your reputation precedes you."

"Detective Inspector Stewart, I presume. You must be a brave man to enter Lavender House if you know my reputation. Luckily for you,

you smoke the same type of pipe tobacco as my late husband. One whiff of that aroma and I'm as contented as a cat before a fire."

"I am honoured that you have admitted me to the sanctum, Mrs Macmillan, even if it is solely because of my choice of tobacco."

"A police officer with a sense of humour. What an unexpected pleasure." Anne crossed her hands on the desk and glanced around her audience. "I expect you have no time to waste, so let's get to the matter at hand. I dropped in to have a chat with Mrs Todd to see if Bess was in trouble at the factory. According to her mother, Bess retained her position only on the condition she agreed to say nothing about the 'accident'. She said Bess was distraught, having to choose between her position and the truth, especially after all the Lily had done to teach her the trade."

"Would Bess Todd be willing to corroborate Mrs Wu's version of events if the police laid charges?" Stewart smiled at Lily again. "I might add that I am fully satisfied with Mrs Wu's innocence and grateful for her willingness to testify. However, the more witnesses we have, the better."

"I'm sure Bess would help, especially if I could find her a position in another factory," Anne replied. "Now that her father has a job, there will be less pressure for the children to earn money."

Grace sat up. "Mr Todd found work at last? That's excellent news, Auntie."

"Waddell told me the man can turn his hand to anything, so I offered him a position as our new gardener, learning under the old gardener's tutelage." Anne sat back with a look of smug satisfaction. "Which rather neatly solves the problems of his employment, my home's incipient takeover by wilderness, and the availability of Bess to testify."

"You sly old bird. Well done, Auntie."

"A little more respect for your elders please, Grace dear. Old indeed. I'm barely past seventy."

"I expect you'll outlive all of us. What about Johnny Todd?"

"Johnny has had his arm twisted to go to school, while continuing his various business ventures in the afternoon. That lad has more gumption than half the so-called pillars of society at the Dunedin Club."

"Business ventures? Dare I ask?"

"No need to ask. Here he comes now."

Charlie looked out the window in time to see Johnny "Sticks" Todd arriving with an extraordinary conveyance, which appeared to be a chair on top of a set of wheels. An old woman was sitting in the chair, clearly having the time of her life, being pulled along by an enormous boy with bulging muscles. They stopped outside. The lad lifted the old lady out of the chair with gentle ease.

"What on earth is that contraption?" Stewart asked.

"Lily told Johnny about a wheeled chair called a rickshaw," Anne said. "Johnny and his father knocked one together overnight and voilà! I've agreed to pay him for each delivery, as we will save a great deal of time if the elderly and incapacitated patients can come to us."

"Who is the Goliath pulling it?"

"I believe he is known as Tiny Tim," Lily replied. "Johnny says he used to be an enforcer at a gambling den, but he is much happier escorting the aged and infirm. I had a wee chat to him earlier, and he appears to be an absolute sweetheart."

Charlie shook his head. "After the last couple of days, nothing could ever surprise me again."

Anne waved her hands like a conductor gathering her orchestra for the finale. "With Lily helping at the clinic, and a delivery service, we can handle twice as many patients, leaving you free to go to medical school, Grace."

Grace threw her arms around her great-aunt and hugged her tightly. "I know I say it every day, but you never cease to amaze me. I'm so glad fate threw Lily into our path."

"As am I," Lily added, "although I would have been happier to make your acquaintance without resorting to concussion."

They hastened outside to examine the rickshaw. Before they could satisfy their curiosity, a pair of young children of indeterminate gender, with matching shocks of red hair, burst into sight, yelling incoherently.

Anne snapped to attention. "Looks like Mrs Campbell has gone into labour. Last time I visited, the baby hadn't turned and Mrs C was looking like a stranded whale."

"I'll get your bag." Lily fled up the stairs, cradling her injured arm.

Anne pointed to the taller of the two panting children with her stick. "Ada, tell me slowly and clearly about your mother."

"Ma's been screaming half the night, Missus. Gran said to tell you to hurry."

Johnny effected a sweeping bow. "Your carriage awaits, milady."

Tiny Tim helped Anne into the seat of the rickshaw as Lily threw her medical bag up beside her.

"Grace, you come with me. Lily, you hold the fort here." Anne banged on the front of the rickshaw with her stick. "Tally ho, Tiny Tim."

Lily disappeared into Lavender House with their newly delivered patient, while Anne and her convoy jogged and wheeled down the street, leaving the two policemen standing on the pavement in stunned silence.

Stewart stared after them with his mouth agape. "I feel as if I have been sucked up into a whirlwind and spat out again in a foreign land."

"You got that right, sir. They're a formidable bunch of women."

"Let us pray they never turn to crime." Stewart dragged his gaze away from the peculiar procession. "Right, I'm heading back to the hotel. Pyke, I'd like you to see if you can catch this Duncan fellow on his lunch break. Sound him out, see if he shows any remorse, but don't scare him off."

"Yes, sir."

Charlie watched Stewart head down the street, noting that his limp was far less pronounced than before. With a swell of pride, he set off to conduct his first interview as an acting Detective Constable. It being a little too early for Duncan's lunch break, he figured he might as well satisfy his curiosity on the way. No one else need know of the detour.

Grace Under Pressure

Tiny Tim was more than capable of pulling the rickshaw by himself. Indeed, he took off at such speed, it seemed as if he hardly noticed the extra weight behind him.

"The rickshaw was a brilliant idea, Johnny Sticks," Grace said, as she and the lad trotted along behind.

"My name's Rickshaw Johnny now, Miss Bones."

"What about the kindling barrow?"

Rickshaw Johnny shot Grace a cheeky grin. "I done hired it out to Kenny Duncan. Kindlin' Ken, he calls himself."

"Would that be the son of Mr Duncan, Kendall's foreman?"

"One of 'em. With nine bairns and the da in hock to his eyeballs, they need every penny to put food on the table."

Grace spent less than a second debating the ethical issue of questioning a juvenile about another family's problems, when justice for a dead child was at stake. "Do you know why Mr Duncan owes money, Johnny?"

"He's a drinker and a gambler. I dunno who he owes, but I can find out."

Grace put a hand on his shoulder to stop him, crouching down to his level and giving him a hard stare. "You must promise me you will do no such thing. Such men are dangerous."

"Yes, Miss Bones," Johnny replied, although his words came with a contradictory shake of his head. "I was only going to ask some of the other lads working the streets. They see what others don't. Nobody would be the wiser, honest."

"I mean it, Johnny. How would I be able to face your folks if something happened to you? I'll take it from here. Come on, your friend Tiny Tim is miles ahead."

They caught up with the rickshaw as it pulled to a halt outside a neat little weatherboard cottage. The screams pouring through the open window had drawn a small crowd of silent onlookers, who parted like the Red Sea as Anne sailed through.

Mrs Campbell lay supine on the bed, her pallid, lifeless face appearing tiny behind her enormous belly. The other three women in the room looked at Anne with terror in their eyes.

"Greetings, ladies." Anne plumped her bag down and issued her commands in a calm but firm tone. "You, one basin of hot water, one of cold. You, clean towels. You, a couple of those bricks from outside. Grace, check her vitals."

Anne took a moment to brush Mrs Campbell's hair back from her dripping brow. "How are you, Mrs Campbell? We'll have you and the bairn right in no time. Let's see what the wee one is up to." With practiced hands, Anne assessed the situation. "Still not turned. No wonder the little mite is stuck."

"Pulse elevated and weak, but regular," Grace reported. She did her best to emulate Anne's calm, although she was well aware of the seriousness of a breech birth, with the lives of both the baby and the mother hanging in the balance.

The women returned with their assigned items. Grace followed Anne's lead and washed her hands thoroughly.

"Ladies, can we have the end of the bed elevated on the bricks, please? After that, I need everyone out so we can have some peace."

Once her commands had been executed with hushed efficiency, Anne's voice dropped an octave as she addressed the mother-to-be in a soothing murmur. "Mrs Campbell, I would like you to take some deep breaths and try to relax your muscles as much as you can between contractions. Grace, you must assist her with breathing."

Anne soaked one towel in cold water, the other in warm water, before wringing them out and laying them above and below the baby bump. "Sometimes the baby will turn itself to put its head to the warmth, especially if gravity is in its favour." To Grace, she whispered, "A prayer or two wouldn't go amiss either."

With Grace holding Mrs Campbell's hand and demonstrating the breathing pattern and Anne providing a haven of professional reassurance, the expectant mother relaxed and regained a little of her normal colour, in between the agony of contractions.

Under the inducements of gravity, heat and gentle massaging by Anne, the baby took the hint and slid into the correct position. Anne appeared to take it in her stride, but not before Grace noted a fleeting expression of fervent relief.

The rest of the birth proceeded relatively smoothly. Which is to say, with the usual heart-rending mix of groaning, panting, sweating and swearing. Before long, Grace had the absolute pleasure of handing a squalling, healthy baby boy into his exhausted mother's arms. A loud cheer drifted in the window from the waiting crowd.

Mrs Campbell's face transformed instantly from drooping weariness to a wreath of smiles. "Thank you," she whispered, through a flood of tears. "Our firstborn son."

Grace gave her patient's face a final mop with a square of muslin. "He's a grand one, Mrs Campbell. Must be nine pounds at least and perfect in every way. With lungs like that, he'll be playing bagpipes before he can walk."

"You can go now, Grace, if you want to. I'll wait for the afterbirth and finish up here." Anne patted her shoulder. "Well done, my girl. You handled that like a seasoned midwife."

"Thanks, Auntie. Can you and Lily manage for the next hour or so while I make some house calls? I'd like to visit the Duncan household this afternoon, as wee Robbie has a nasty cough."

"Duncan? Kendall's foreman? What a coincidence." Anne raised a single eyebrow and leaned forward to whisper in her ear. "Trying to impress someone with your detective skills, Grace?"

"Not at all. With nine children living in a rundown three-bedroom cottage, there's always one of the little blighters who is sick."

Grace felt light as air as she made her way back to Lavender House for a quick wash and a fresh apron. Achieving a successful result in a difficult birth was reward enough. Praise from her great-aunt was icing on the cake.

And, much as she hated to admit it, she felt an added dollop of relief at leaving Mrs Campbell in good spirits. Not to mention seeing the ancient Mr Jones on her way back, looking hale and hearty as he dug over his vegetable patch with vigorous thrusts of an equally ancient spade. Two deaths were more than enough to cope with in one week.

In the Devil's Heart

Charlie looped around the block so that he might pass by the alley where the murder victim's body had been found, in the heart of the Devil's Half Acre. In a single block, he passed five hotels, a gambling den, two sly-grog shops, an opium den, and incongruously, what appeared to be a saddlery shop, lit with a red lamp, even in the middle of the day.

On closer inspection, he realised his mistake, judging by the items arrayed beside the riding crop that had first caught his eye. He dared not speculate what some of the devices were, but it was clear that the leather harness on display was never intended for a horse.

A dark and pestilent alley ran alongside the buildings. Curiosity overcame common sense as he spotted a narrow spiral staircase descending from an upper storey window at the far end. When he got close enough, he could see a smear of blood on the lower step. Flakes of rust came off on his fingers, matching the victim's head wound.

He crouched down to examine the filthy cobbles, but far too many boots had passed this way to make out individual footprints. A length of rusty metal lay underneath a pile of rubbish. He checked it carefully, but blood appeared to be the one substance absent from the grime, so he used it to poke through the debris lining the alley, working his way back toward the entrance.

Several yards down, under a half-rotten flour sack, Charlie found a woollen scarf. From the relative lack of dirt, it was a recent addition to the charms of the alley, and a fancy one at that. A gentleman's scarf, of fine wool, which felt soft to the touch and smelled faintly of whisky. He examined it, then folded it and tucked it into his pocket. With any luck, it might be a match for the fibres found in the victim's nose. A pity it was not conveniently monogrammed. In fact, even the maker's label had been removed.

Charlie walked back up to the stairs, kicking a stray tin can so hard it smashed against the wall. How the devil had Constable Nolan been so careless, or lazy, as to report the case as an accidental death of a drunk? Like a swallowed bone, it stuck in his gullet that his own investigation of the facts had got him stood down, while the man who had passed his beat in a grog shop, then failed to spot a murder under his nose, was probably now snoring his way through the day shift on full pay.

With a grunt, he hurled the metal bar, hitting the iron stairs with a clang that would have awakened the dead. The dulcet tones of a female foghorn, coming from above his head, cut his internal rantings short.

"If it ain't Constable Pyke. Knew you'd drop by sooner or later. Come on up, laddie. Show me what ya got under that pretty suit."

The prostitute he'd met at Lavender House thrust the top half of her body out of the window, giving him a preview of her wares. The red dress was gone, replaced by black lace that breached every law of decency in Queen Victoria's Empire.

Knowing he was sure to regret it, he scaled the stairs, which swayed alarmingly. There was, after all, a chance that she might have seen the murderer on Monday night. And maybe he was just a little intrigued by what he would find inside. He may have grown up on the wild goldfields of Central Otago, but being a policeman's son had kept him firmly behind locked doors at night.

The structure gave an ominous creak as he squeezed through the window into a room furnished in an explosion of red satin and black lace, which almost – but not quite – diverted the eye from the threadbare carpet and sagging bed. At close quarters, the prostitute was a match for her surroundings. The provocative costume thrust up a wrinkled bosom, while a thick layer of face paint couldn't entirely disguise the ravages of time and disease.

Thankful for the surfeit of red to hide his blushes, he tried for nonchalance. "No leather?"

"That's 'er next door. It's only the wilting willies as goes for bondage. Strapping lad like you'd do better with a real woman, like me." She stepped forward and ran her hands down his body, purring. "What is it you like, Constable Pyke?"

Charlie took a step back, knocking down an erotic statue of a voluptuous woman in his haste. He would have picked it up again, but he didn't quite know where to put his hands on it. "I am here for answers, madam, not services. What is your name, please?"

She smiled suggestively at him, baring a row of rotten teeth. "Lady Victoria Queensbottom."

"I see. Well, Lady Victoria, were you here on Monday night?"

"C'mon, a good-looking lad like you." She eased the shoulder of her flimsy garment down and blew a sultry kiss his way. "Show me what you got in them breeches and I might do you for the pleasure of it."

He gave her what he hoped was an authoritative glare. "Monday night, please, Lady V."

She flopped down on the bed. "Might have been 'ere. Hard to remember, the nights being all the same."

He showed her the sketch of the dead man. "Did you have a visit from this man? Short, slim, no facial hair, thin face, short reddish-brown hair, dressed in a good quality worker's clothes?"

"Don't ring no bells, but I tries not to look at them."

"Did you see anything unusual happening in the alley outside?"

Lady Victoria picked up a hairbrush, stroking it through her long auburn hair, her face a mask of pious contemplation. "Reckon you mean the body being dumped at the bottom of the stairs."

Well, well, perhaps it was worth the trip up those hazardous stairs after all. "*Dumped* at the bottom? Not a man who fell on the stairs?"

"Dumped is what I said, copper. Too dark to see the cove what done it, afore ye ask. Just gone eleven o'clock it was going by those damnable church bells. Drive me half crazy, they do."

"Did you see anything before the body was dumped?"

"Heard 'em coming. Quiet night, Monday, so I watched the two of 'em weaving up the alley, one of them so drunk he couldn't stand. He slipped, or maybe got pushed, then the other one crouched down beside him. Thought he were helping, so I kept my beak out of it. It went all quiet for a while, then there was an 'orrid noise and the stairs shook. The other cove ran like his breeches were on fire. Don't know no more'n that."

"Can you tell me anything about the man who did it? Tall, short, gentleman, navvy, limping, wearing a hat, … anything at all."

"Sorry, love. Too dark and misty down there to see more'n shapes that night. The one that died musta been smaller, cos the other cove was holding him up. Or perhaps he were just bent over."

"And why did you not report this?" Charlie asked without hope of an answer. Around here, those with any sense of self-preservation averted their eyes and kept their mouths closed.

She stopped brushing her hair and gave him a withering look. "Who d'ya reckon sent the urchin to the grog shop to rouse up Constable Sticky-fingers from his drunken stupor?"

"I see. And did you tell Constable Nolan what you told me?"

"He never asked, love, an' I were busy by the time he got here."

Charlie paused to consider whether he needed to ask her anything else, but it was Nolan who needed to be interrogated, not her. "Thank you for your assistance, Lady Victoria."

"Ain't you a polite one? Sure you wouldn't like to learn a few new tricks while you're here? Your missus will thank you for it."

"I'll leave you to your paying customers." Charlie climbed out the window and down the swaying stairs to the safety of the ground.

She sat by the window, watching him. "You're a rum customer, Constable Pyke. I'd be offended, only I reckon it's Miss Bones you want to rattle your bones with."

Shrieks of laughter followed him down the alley. The surge of blood to his face was nothing to do with Lady Victoria's parting shot, he assured himself. She must have known that Grace Penrose was destined for a better man than him. Besides, he was rather looking forward to taking the shopgirl to the South Seas Exhibition tomorrow evening. If only he could remember her name.

Right now, he was just thankful that nobody had seen him coming out of the brothel, even if he was only doing his job.

An Accident Waiting To Happen

Grace had to take a second and then a third look down the alley before she trusted the first. What in the name of Aphrodite was Charlie Pyke doing, climbing out of the window of one of the city's most notorious brothels? The woman at the window was certainly not in any fit state to be seen in daylight, but it didn't stop her laughter from floating down the alley after him.

She waited at the corner, catching him gawping into a shop window filled with … paraphernalia of the trade. Whatever it was, it was most definitely not a shop that her mother would want Grace to be within a mile of.

"Enjoying a break from work, Detective Constable Pyke?"

Charlie spun around, then staggered two steps back, clutching his chest. If his face had been red before, it was flaming now, with an interesting undercurrent of white-hot shock. "Grace, what the hell are you doing here?"

"What am I doing here? Walking home after saving the lives of a mother and baby. More to the point, what are you doing here? Not having a heart attack, I hope?"

"Investigating," he muttered.

"Find out anything interesting?"

"It's not what it looks like, Grace." Charlie slunk out of the alley with a furtive glance behind. "This is the alley where the murder victim was found. The window of the brothel overlooks the spot. That woman actually saw it happening, at least as far as being able to confirm that two men walked in alive and only one walked out."

"I trust you didn't have to work too hard to get her confession? Fanny Snoot isn't known for giving anything away without adequate compensation."

Charlie finally allowed his gaze to rise to meet hers, taking in her barely suppressed grin. "On the contrary, Miss Penrose, the lady was most accommodating, without resort to payment of any kind."

"No doubt your charms overwhelmed her," Grace said. "I commend your dedication to duty, Detective Constable Pyke. Indeed, I am rather cross that I did not think to visit Fanny myself."

He pursed his lips, but did not waste his breath giving her a lecture on appropriate behaviour. "If you will excuse me, I am off to interview Fergus Duncan."

"Excellent, I'll come too. I want to meet the man before I interrogate his wife."

"Grace, please be reasonable. You cannot come. This is police business."

"Fine. I won't come with you. Although, as it happens, I have another reason to visit Kendall's factory. I'll just trot along behind you, shall I?"

He loomed with all of his intimidating size and glared down at her. She was sorely tempted to provoke him, to see how he would react. Instead, she smiled and picked a fragment of black lace off his sleeve, holding it out as a memento.

His diaphragm contracted as his shoulders slumped, pushing a deep sigh from his chest. "Must you examine me as if I was a specimen on your dissecting table? It's unsettling."

She held up her hands, demonstrating the lack of a scalpel. "My apologies, Charlie. I wasn't aware that I gave that impression." It wasn't the first time she had been guilty of studying his anatomy, but never with a scalpel in mind.

He turned and set off up the road at a fast pace, forcing her to scramble to keep up.

Entering the clothing factory was like breaching the gates of the underworld. Screaming machines, a choking haze of dust and wool fibres, the stench of coal smoke, oil and sewage, and so gloomy that all Grace could see were rows of knitting and sewing machines, tended by rows of pallid, perspiring girls. The only light and air came in through a high row of small windows, which utterly failed to keep the steamy heat at bay.

They didn't see anyone who looked like a foreman, but they did see an ancient loom tucked away at the far side of the factory, so hemmed in that she doubted Charlie would have been able to manoeuvre around it. No wonder they had to use the young boys. The loom was silent and the floor under it was the cleanest spot in the entire factory, by a country mile.

Several women looked up as they passed, but none would catch her eye.

"I'm looking for Mr Duncan, the foreman," Charlie said into the gloom.

"He's having his break. Reckon he's gone to St Andrew's again."

Charlie nodded his thanks and turned to leave. Grace held up her hand, nodding her head at the small girl working at the sewing machine at the end of the row. "Two minutes," she mouthed.

He wandered over to examine the loom, while Grace edged her way around the mass of machinery to see Bess Todd.

"Hello, Bess. Glad to see you kept your job."

Bess flicked a glance in Grace's direction before scanning the room. "I can't speak to you, Miss Bones." Her voice was tight with fear.

"I'll be quick, I promise. Two questions. Was Duncan near the loom before Alfie died and would you tell the police what you saw, if I could guarantee you another job with better pay?"

Her voice quavered, but her words were resolute. "Yes, to both questions."

Grace signalled to Charlie. They hurried out of the factory. Grace gulped fresh air and said a silent prayer of thanks that she had never had to work in such a place. They walked in silence to the end of the lane, but she could sense his mood from the tension in his shoulders.

"If I had known my aunt was working here…" Charlie growled.

She stepped around in front of him, forcing him to stop and look at her. "I understand how you feel, Charlie, but you must realise Lily kept

107

her situation from you for a reason. She is a proud woman who wanted to make her own living. She loves you too much to risk your career."

"If I thought less about my work and more about my loved ones–"

She put a finger to her lips and whispered, "Someone's coming out of the factory."

Charlie assessed the situation in an instant. He used his body to shield her and stepped sideways, guiding her into the doorway of a neighbouring building. She glimpsed a rotund man standing at the factory entrance, padded with enough fat to keep an elephant seal cozy, before he was lost to view.

A testy voice yelled, "Stop! I want a word with you."

Charlie turned and inclined his head politely at the man. "Good morning, sir. Would you be Mr Kendall?"

Now that the two men were intent on each other, Grace risked a peek. Charlie strolled down the lane with calm authority, in marked contrast to the near-apoplectic state of the factory owner.

Kendall thrust his tomato-red face out from his bull neck. "Who might you be, entering my factory without permission?"

Before Charlie could reply, Kendall dropped his gaze to take in the gentleman's suit. Taking a step backward, he deflated, visibly drawing his temper under control, replacing anger with a mask of affability.

"Please excuse me, sir. We've had some troublemakers around here lately. I apologise for my rude welcome. You are a customer looking for one of our fine woollen garments, perhaps? None better in the colony, I assure you. We supply our goods to the best retail establishments in Dunedin. I would be happy to provide you with directions."

"That is most obliging of you, Mr Kendall," Charlie said, in a voice that sipped from cut crystal. "I was looking for Mr Duncan. I am sorry to hear you have had troublemakers. Not thieves, I hope?"

"Only militant unionists and disgruntled workers. Nothing for you to fear, sir. I won't have them on my premises."

"Perhaps the police could help. I hear they know which side their bread is buttered in this town."

Kendall shot him an appraising glance. "I'm sure the police do a fine job of maintaining order, sir. If you'll excuse me, I have work to attend to. Good day to you."

Kendall disappeared inside. Grace stepped out from the doorway as Charlie strolled past. "Charming man."

"His foreman will be a tough nut to crack if he is under the thumb of Mr Kendall."

Grace thought he was probably right, but it was worth a shot. "If Mr Duncan is spending his lunch hour at a church, perhaps there is still hope. No man of religion would rest easy at the death of a child on his watch. Especially not one under the pastoral care of the Reverend Waddell."

As they trudged up the hill to St Andrew's Presbyterian Church, Charlie said, "I have read Waddell's speeches in the newspaper. He seems to be a champion of workers' rights."

"The Sweating Commission would never have been established, but for the public outcry set off by his rousing sermons on the 'Sin of Cheapness'. His good works are so extensive, I wonder the man has time to sleep. Poverty, temperance, workers' rights, education, prison reform – there is no cause of social injustice Waddell has not thrown himself into wholeheartedly. Even Anne is in awe of him."

"I look forward to meeting the man in person. Given his reputation, I have a picture in my mind of a barrel-chested firebrand."

Grace smiled to herself. Charlie was in for a surprise.

The church was not far, but the steepness of the hill and the summer sun quickly worked up a sweat. Entering the cool of the church was like stepping into a slice of paradise. Charlie took his hat off and waited, clearly unwilling to disturb the quiet discussion between the two men seated in the front pew, with their heads bowed low.

Grace slipped past him and took a seat at the far end of the pew, to let him know she would not get in his way. All she wanted was to watch Duncan's reactions, to get a sense of the man who ran Kendall's factory.

While Charlie sat and waited, he got out his notebook and started sketching.

After a while, curiosity got the better of her – as it always did – so she walked behind him to pick up a hymn book from the stack by the door. On the way back, she lingered by his shoulder to look at his drawings. Kendall's portly figure stared with pompous bluster from the page, opposite a sketch of Nolan that was distinctly unflattering, except perhaps to a desperately lonely female ape.

She leaned down and whispered in his ear, "I hope you haven't been turning your satirical talents to me as well."

Charlie dashed off a sketch of a woman with her face, transplanted on to a limpet body, with the ears of a mule and the snout of a pig.

She flicked his head with her hat. "For heaven's sake, don't show that to Anne, or she will want a copy to send to all my friends and family. I'll never hear the end of it."

Grace smiled and slipped back to her seat. How pleasant it was to take the weight off her feet and just sit still, eyes closed in silent meditation, surrounded by cool tranquillity.

After several minutes, the smaller of the two men noticed Charlie. The man patted the other on the shoulder with paternal care, before moving down the aisle in silence. With his slight body and lack of clerical garb, the Reverend Waddell looked nothing like a barrel-chested firebrand.

Waddell leaned towards Charlie. "What can I do for you, my son? You'll have to speak up. I'm a little hard of hearing."

Grace knew those kind brown eyes and the soft Irish lilt, just as she knew that anyone within their vicinity would feel that they might safely confess any secret.

"I am Acting Detective Constable Pyke. I was hoping to find Mr Fergus Duncan here."

"He is here." The Reverend gestured towards the man in the front pew. "You are here about the poor boy who died at the factory, Alfie Watts? I thought the police were not interested in a dead orphan."

"You know about the boy?"

"Mr Duncan brought his body here. He is a good man, who has been taken down a false path by the evils of drink. He is seeking a way back to the light."

"Did he tell you how Alfie died?"

"You will have to ask Mr Duncan. I can only say he did the right thing by bringing the lad here, instead of dumping the body. We have him laid out, ready for burial."

"May I see him?" Charlie flicked a glance to the end of the pew. "May *we* see him?"

Waddell looked over at her and smiled. "Ah, Miss Bones. I had heard a rumour that you were now an official medical expert assisting the police force. What a busy life you lead, young lady."

She returned his smile and failed to correct his misapprehension of how official her role was. Charlie rolled his eyes, but looked amused rather than annoyed.

Alfie's body was so small and skinny, it scarcely elevated the heavy cloth draped over him. Waddell murmured a brief prayer before lifting the cloth. One half of the lad's face was reminiscent of a cherub, with blond curls falling on chubby cheeks. On the other side, his injuries were gruesome.

Charlie laid a gentle hand on her arm. "Do you feel able to do the medical examination while I take notes?"

Gruesome or not, she was going to have to get used to this. She began with a few general comments on his condition, noting that he looked reasonably well-fed and in good health. A bonnie lad. Then, she started at the top and went down his body methodically, reciting the name of each broken bone and listing each contusion, break and crush wound, in a voice as quiet and reverential as the atmosphere warranted.

Charlie wrote quickly, in between glances to confirm each injury. When they had finished, Grace pointed to several coloured threads, and a broken piece of shuttle, which were imbedded in the worst of the wounds. These he wrapped in a clean handkerchief. Having gathered the required evidence, he gently laid the cloth back over Alfie's body.

"I believe you said he was an orphan, Reverend Waddell."

111

"Only in that his birth parents are dead, Constable. Mr and Mrs Watts took him in and cared for him like one of their own. They were good people who made sure he had food and clothes, as well as love. Our Alfie was a lovely lad and very clever at school. If he had been born into other circumstances, I know he would have made a success of his life."

"Took care?" Grace queried. "Are both Mr and Mrs Watts dead?"

"Mrs Watts is still of this world, though her mind has strayed into the next. They were of advanced years when they took him in, but they did their best by him. If you wish to know any more about him, I suggest you talk to Mrs Thomson of the St Andrew's Church Friendly Aid Society. She sees that Mrs Watts is cared for."

"I also need to talk to Mr Duncan," Charlie added. "May I do that here?"

The Reverend nodded. "I think it would be best."

Charlie slid into the pew beside Duncan, while Grace sat two rows back, far enough away that she wasn't blatantly eavesdropping, but close enough to get the gist of their conversation. She bowed her head low and buried her nose in the hymn book.

Charlie allowed a few seconds for the foreman to register and accept his presence. "Mr Duncan, I am Acting Detective Constable Pyke. Thank you for bringing Alfie Watts here."

"It wouldn't have been right to deny the poor laddie a proper burial."

Duncan's voice was so soft, Grace had to lean closer to hear the words. They were in luck. She had been expecting Duncan to be full of bluster and denial, but the man in front of her spoke with anguish and regret.

"Can you tell me what happened to Alfie?" Charlie continued, using the gentle purring voice he used to seduce the unsuspecting to reveal their secrets.

"It was the old loom, a beast of a thing. Mr Kendall only bought it because it came with a lucrative contract to make tartan to meet the local demand. The previous owner had to close down because of ill-health, so he was willing to let his experienced weaver come with the loom, as part of the deal."

"And then?"

Duncan sighed. "The weaver took one look at the factory and turned his toes toward greener pastures. Showed me how to use the loom before he left, but weaving is a skill that takes years to master. The tarnation thing constantly jammed. It was so old and unstable that the slightest bump could knock it into gear and set the rollers turning."

"Was no attempt made to fix it?"

"Mr Kendall engaged an engineer to fix it and install a safety catch. The engineer passed it as fit to use."

"Yet the boy got caught up in it," Charlie said, his rising tone making it a question.

"Alfie must have crawled under the loom to clear out the tangled threads without anyone noticing." Duncan's head dropped into his hands, stifling a sob. "I don't know how it jumped into gear. I wasn't near it when it happened. The steam engine rattles the floor that bad, it might have been as simple as that. A terrible accident, but an accident nevertheless. Worst moment of my life, hearing his scream. Just the one long scream, then silence."

"It must have been terrible for you," Charlie murmured, allowing Duncan a chance to regain his composure before gently asking the next question. "How did Mrs Wu get injured?"

"She was quicker on her feet than anyone else. Tried to rescue him."

In the same beguiling voice, he risked a more probing question. "Who asked you to dispose of Alfie's body?"

Duncan flinched. "No one. I brought him here, as you can see." He turned red and pleading eyes on Charlie. "Please, I have nine children. I cannae lose my job. Mr Kendall promised it was all squared away with the police."

Grace held her breath to stop a gasp from escaping. The interview was worth their time for that admission alone. DI Stewart would be pleased, as long as he could persuade Duncan to testify. For a moment, she thought Charlie would leave it there, as Duncan was getting twitchy, but he continued in a reassuring tone, as gentle as a lullaby.

"Did you know Mrs Wu was left out in the courtyard?"

"No! That's not what I was told. She was taken to the hospital before I got back from the church. Mr Kendall is a respectable businessman – a tight focus on profits, to be sure, but not a bad man."

"Then why is the factory employing underaged workers?"

"You don't know how it is for these people," Duncan said. "Young lads, and lasses too, come begging for work. Their mothers and fathers – if they have them – have been put out of work in these hard times. If the children do not bring in a few shillings, the family starves. I'm sure you've seen the children scavenging for dropped coal around the rail yards and rifling through the rotten vegetables discarded at the market. I always ask their age, of course, and they always say 'fourteen, sir', bold as brass. What more can I do?"

"I understand, but it is still against the law to have underaged workers."

Duncan showed he had some fire in his belly, after all. "Should it be legal for families to starve? We only ever took on the older ones, no less than thirteen years old, and made sure they worked reasonable hours."

"Depends what you consider reasonable, especially in a filthy, unventilated factory."

"It may not look much, but the owner has to make a living, same as they all do. Margins are tight and he cannot afford to spend money on fripperies."

"Fripperies like fresh air and properly maintained equipment?"

"We have a row of windows that open. And, as I said, Mr Kendall engaged a local engineer to make the loom safe. Mr Finlay. Mr Kendall was determined to get the loom running, as he had a contract to supply tartan to one of the local pipe bands. Mr Kendall was furious that Finlay's failure to fix the loom caused the death of the lad, not to mention putting the contract at risk."

Grace suspected that it was the contract Kendall was more worried about, not the boy, but Charlie didn't comment on it.

"He viewed the accident as Mr Finlay's fault?"

"There was a right barny about it," Duncan said. "Mr Kendall refused to pay the engineer and Finlay threatened to sue for payment. If you ask me, Finlay is soft between the ears if he thinks he can threaten a man of Mr Kendall's importance, not to mention temper. Kendall would crush that chit of a lad under his thumb with no more regard than a cockroach, if he tried to sue."

"And if the police charged Kendall with negligence, causing a death?"

Duncan looked at Charlie with an expression of total disbelief. "Don't be daft. You're a Dunedin copper. You ought to know Kendall's untouchable." He reached out and patted Charlie's arm. "Honestly, you seem like a decent lad. I swear to you it was just a tragic accident."

Grace could sense that Charlie didn't want to push the foreman any harder today. He had done well to extract as much as he had, especially from a man with a great deal to lose by telling the truth. If they got any charge to stick, it might be for employing an underaged worker. A big "if", given they would have to prove Alfie's true age. As an orphan, it was unlikely anyone would know when he was born.

As Grace rose quietly to sneak out, hopefully without being noticed, Charlie leaned back into the pew again.

"Thank you for your honesty, Mr Duncan. I don't suppose you know Mr Finlay's whereabouts? The police will need a statement from him as to the condition of the loom."

"I believe he's got premises in Bond Street. But you'll not find him. Kendall went to talk some sense into him yesterday and he'd scarpered. Smart move if you ask me, especially a weedy young runt like him, trying to threaten Kendall."

Grace saw the tiny jerk of Charlie's head and the tightening of his shoulder muscles. What was he thinking? She heard a rustle of pages as he opened his notebook.

"Might this be Finlay, Mr Duncan?"

"A fair resemblance, although I couldn't swear to it."

She sat back with a squeak of wood as the connection triggered. A weedy runt? Threatened by a powerful man with a disturbing reputation for getting his own way ... and now vanished? An engineer certainly fit the bill of a professional man who might also wear grease-smeared working clothes. And Bond Street was fairly close to the alley where the body was found.

"I'm afraid I must get back to work, Constable. Mr Kendall wouldn't want me to be late, with so much to do."

Grace slid quickly out of the pew and behind a stray lectern, while Duncan rose and turned for the door. Charlie took the time to add a sketch of the foreman to his notebook.

Grace slipped in beside him. "Brilliant work, DC Pyke. Am I right in thinking he identified our corpse?"

"Tentatively identified. It seems the boy's death and the murder in the alley may share a common element – a link with Kendall's factory. I've been warned to stay away from the homicide case, so I'll have to pass this information on to the detective in charge." He snapped the notebook closed and turned bright eyes on her.

"I may not have known you long, Charlie Pyke, but I can read that expression like an open book. You are up to something."

His nostrils flared for a fraction of a second, then a smile stole across his lips. "I thank my lucky stars you are not my commanding officer, Grace. I was merely thinking that it would be remiss of me to report a possible identification of the victim without confirming it."

"Naturally, you would not wish to waste the time of another detective. How terribly thoughtful of you."

"Besides, if this engineer fellow is not the murder victim, then I must interview him as a witness to the dangerous conditions in the factory and the state of the loom that killed Alfie." Charlie paused. "And I suppose you will follow me like a shadow?"

"Alas, much as I am honoured to be in the shadow of a brilliant detective, I have other things to attend to. Happy hunting."

Charlie picked up Grace's hat from the floor and leaned over to place it on her head at a jaunty angle, whispering, "It won't be half as much fun without you."

She watched him walk down the aisle with the natural grace of a dancer. As she lingered in the cool of the church, waiting for her heartbeat to return to normal, she reminded herself that she had come to Dunedin to attend medical school, not for amusement. Helping Anne in any way she could and getting justice for Alfie were worthy additions to the agenda, but everything else was a distraction.

A Corpse Unmasked

Charlie cursed softly once he was outside the church grounds. Picking up a fallen hat was a matter of courtesy, but there was no earthly excuse for doing more than simply handing it back. Was it the sudden change in his circumstances that was making him so reckless when, more than ever, he had everything to lose?

He put the impossible thoughts to one side and headed down into the nearby cluster of commercial offices and warehouses, which filled the strip of reclaimed land behind the docks. On Bond Street, he found Jack Finlay's office without too much trouble.

Inside, a woman of advancing years was staring helplessly at a heap of telegrams and letters, her curly grey hair coming askew from the tight coil pinned to her head.

"How may I help you?" Her words were laced with forced pleasantry, edged with frustration.

"Good morning, madam. I am Acting Detective Constable Pyke." Would he ever tire of saying that? "I am trying to locate Mr Jack Finlay."

"As are we all," she replied, putting down the letter in her hand with a harrumph. "I am his secretary, Miss Abercrombie. Mr Finlay left on Monday morning for a work engagement out of town. I have not seen him since. I inquired of the livery stables, who said he returned his horse on Monday evening, so I presume he has been engaged in urgent business about town, as he often is."

"Would he usually inform you of his movements, Miss Abercrombie?"

"Ordinarily, although he gets immersed in his work and forgets the passage of time. Never for this long, however."

"His work being?"

"My employer runs a small engineering and foundry business." Miss Abercrombie glanced at a portrait on the wall, her face softening for an instant. "His father would be proud of him. Young Mr Finlay is making a name for himself, designing devices to make factories safer."

Charlie got out his notebook, flipping to the sketch of the unidentified body. "Would this be Mr Finlay, Miss Abercrombie?"

"A strong likeness of him, certainly." Her face crumpled as the implications struck home. "I…I hope nothing untoward has happened to him."

Seeing her distress, he softened his voice, hating to be the one to impart bad tidings. "A body was found late on Monday night, which we have had some trouble in identifying. I regret to say that I believe it may be Mr Finlay."

Policing had given him ample experience of sudden grief. Reactions were always impossible to predict. The toughest man might collapse in tears, while the frailest lady might stiffen her spine and carry on as if nothing had happened. Miss Abercrombie was a talker.

"Oh, no, I pray you are wrong. The poor dear boy was so young and talented. A good man. Very pleasant tempered, a good Christian and rarely a drop of the demon drink. Thank the Lord his dear father is no longer alive to see this day. Was it a fall from a horse, perhaps? He insisted on riding rather than hiring a buggy, even though he had little experience of horses. Oh dear, and now I have spoken ill of the dead…" A sharp intake of breath cut off her words, before being ejected in a heart-rending sob.

Charlie fetched a glass of water. "I'm truly sorry, Miss Abercrombie, but his death was not an accident. Is there someone I can contact to look after you?"

The secretary pulled her spine straight with visible effort. "No, thank you, Constable. I will be perfectly fine." She rummaged in a card file. "You will need the address of his mother and solicitor." She wrote the directions in neat script, despite her shaking hand. "And the location of the foundry, as well as my details."

"Thank you, Miss Abercrombie, you are most efficient. The first requirement will be to have his body formally identified by someone he knew well. Would his mother be up to the task?"

"I fear not. His mother, poor lady, is addled with age. She does not recognise him any longer, but he is still ever so good to her. I'm afraid I don't know his friends or his sweetheart."

"Is there no other family member?"

"Only a brother." The secretary looked as if she had been force-fed a lemon. "You'll not get an ounce of sense out of that monster. The devil struck him down at birth."

"Does the brother have the mental capacity to identify Mr Finlay's body?"

"I couldn't say. I won't have him in the office, for he scares me half to death. If you wish to see for yourself, you must visit the foundry just down the street, where his charitable brother gave him work." She pulled a lace handkerchief out of her sleeve and dabbed her eyes. "Lord knows what will become of him and their mother, if dear, kind Mr Finlay is truly gone."

Charlie gave her a moment, then continued in a gentle voice. "Perhaps there is someone else who could identify him?"

"His solicitor, or any of the factory owners or foremen he has worked with. Mr Kendall could do it, although perhaps he might not be the best choice. They had a falling out. Mr Kendall threatened to 'knock Mr Finlay's block off if he continued to demand payment for his shoddy work'. I don't wish to speak out of turn, but Mr Kendall can be extremely intimidating."

Charlie suppressed a smile. She might look like a straitlaced old lady, but Miss Abercrombie had a wicked skill at mimicry. She would make an excellent witness if the detective could nail Kendall for killing Finlay. Perhaps the boy's death might be avenged, indirectly, after all.

"Was this altercation on Monday?" Charlie asked.

"Last Friday. But Mr Kendall came in again on Monday morning, while Mr Finlay was out of the office. He apologised to me for his previous outburst and said he would be back later to apologise to Mr Finlay. He didn't return before I left at my normal time."

"Did Mr Finlay have many clients?"

"At present, only two. Mr Kendall and Mr Chelmsford. I can make a list of his previous clients if required. What with being on his own, now that his dear father has passed, and developing his inventions, he has little time to spare. Mr Chelmsford, in particular, kept him busy, with designs for a new woollen mill, incorporating his safety devices. Very proud of it, Mr Finlay was, and rightly so."

Charlie scribbled down the names and closed his notebook. "I expect his solicitor will be the best person to identify him. I thank you for your time and candour, Miss Abercrombie."

"But what am I to do?" The shrill note in her voice, as she waved her hand over the piles of paperwork, warned Charlie that her professional façade was cracking.

"I suggest you inform his solicitor. The police will have to see him anyway, to ascertain the beneficiaries of his estate."

The stiff upper lip held, albeit with a tremor. "There's no secret there. Will Finlay is his brother's sole heir, with provision for the support of his mother. I believe there is a small token for me as well, given my long service to Mr Finlay and his father before him."

"You have an impressive knowledge of the business, Miss Abercrombie."

"Is it any wonder, after nearly forty years' service to the family?"

Charlie knew he had already gone several leagues beyond his mandate, in a case that was explicitly not his to investigate, but he couldn't seem to stop asking questions. Oh well, in for a penny, in for a pound. "This must be a terrible shock for you. Would you prefer to go home now, or may I ask a few more questions?"

"Please proceed, Constable. I will do whatever I can to assist."

"Mr Finlay was not married?"

"He was very much in love with his sweetheart. I helped him choose a ring for her only last Friday. He had been planning to propose to her this week." She dabbed her eyes again.

121

"Was the ring valuable?"

"Mr Finlay said it was more than he could afford, but less than she deserved. Oh dear, do you think someone might have robbed him for the ring?" Miss Abercrombie hurried over to the inner office, reaching up her hand to knock on the door, before withdrawing it sharply. She pushed open the door.

Charlie looked over her shoulder, seeing a neat office with all the signs of a busy, but organised, occupant. "Is anything missing or out of place, Miss Abercrombie? Take your time and have a good look around."

Finlay's secretary allowed her discerning gaze to travel slowly around the room. "The visitor's chair is not in its usual location, the papers on his desk are not in the place I left them on Monday, and the ring is gone. It was right here on the edge of his desk." She turned to Charlie, fear in her eyes for the first time. "Might someone have broken in?"

"If so, he left the place a great deal tidier than the average burglar." Apart from a few papers knocked to the floor and an overturned wastepaper basket, there were no indications of a struggle. "Was the outer door locked?"

"Yes, everything was as it should be when I arrived on Tuesday morning."

Charlie was not surprised, as Finlay had apparently gone willingly with the other man into the alley. Presumably, if the killer drugged him, Finlay had let his killer in, despite the lateness of the hour. Someone he knew and trusted. Charlie looked around for a bottle of whisky, but saw nothing besides papers, drawings and instruments.

"Miss Abercrombie, does your employer ever drink alcohol?"

"Rarely. Perhaps a wee dram at Hogmanay or a mouthful on special occasions, when the drinking of a toast is customary."

Charlie opened the desk drawers. A ring box, holding a beautiful garnet ring of a rich red hue, was in the top drawer, where even the most slapdash of thieves would have found it.

"What a relief," Miss Abercrombie exclaimed. "May I put it in the safe?" At Charlie's nod, she took the box and went to the wall safe. "That's odd. The safe is unlocked. I'm certain I put the patent file in there after Mr Finlay left on Monday morning and I always double-check the …" Miss Abercrombie let out a restrained squeak as she flicked through the papers in the safe. "The patent file is missing."

"Patent file?"

"He was about to apply for a patent for a brilliant design, making weaving looms more efficient and safer for the workers. He was sure it would make him a fortune."

A fortune? Nothing like greed as a compelling motive. "Can you see if the file is one of those on his desk, please?"

She searched through the files with commendable efficiency. "It's not here. But someone has split water on the desk. This stain was not here when I left on Monday night."

Charlie bent over to smell. Not water, but whisky. He dropped to his knees, checking under the desk and cabinets, but found no signs of a discarded glass or other evidence. The killer had been careful, but not careful enough.

"Miss Abercrombie, I don't wish to alarm you, but it may be best if you lock up the office and go home. I will hand this investigation over to another detective, who will contact you for the key."

Charlie waited until she had locked up, then saw her safely on the horse-drawn tram.

A dozen lines of inquiry jostled for space in his brain. Kendall, the brother, anyone wishing to profit from a valuable patent – all before the investigation was even properly underway. But not his investigation.

He knew his priority must be to inform Detective Inspector Stewart and pass the intelligence he had gathered on to the Detective Inspector of the Dunedin District. More's the pity. It might be an awful thing to admit after a man had been murdered, but Charlie had never felt so alive.

His only consolation in handing over the evidence was that Nolan was going to be in a cesspit of trouble.

Wives and Mothers

Grace left St Andrew's church with a resolute step and a mental list of people who might help their investigation.

Her first port of call was the St Andrew's Church Friendly Aid Society, to see the lady who looked out for Mrs Watts, as their best chance of achieving justice for Alfie lay with proving that he was under the legal age for factory work. Besides that, Grace wanted to assure herself that Mrs Watts was coping with her ward's tragic death.

As luck would have it, Mrs Thomson was one of the half-dozen women bustling around the hall, sorting donated clothes and blankets with quick hands and lively chatter. When Grace explained her interest, Mrs Thomson added her stack of neatly folded blankets to a box and took Grace into a back office, where she flicked through the files with deft fingers.

"Here he is. Alfred Watts. Parents unknown. Date of birth unknown. Transferred to this parish six years ago in order to attend school, by which we can infer that he was probably around twelve years old, give or take a year, at his tragic death."

"You don't know where he came from?" Grace asked. "Or who cared for him for the first six years?"

Mrs Thomson ran her finger down the card, then flipped it over to read the back. "I regret to say there is nothing on record and poor Mrs Watts is now too senile to help. As I recall, Mrs Watts said at the time that he was found on the church steps as a baby. Her daughter took pity on him and raised him, but she couldn't cope, as she had children of her own. The daughter is married and lives up-country somewhere, too far away to visit. No address for her recorded either."

"Does Mrs Watts have any other children who might provide more information?"

"She had another daughter, who was in service. Sadly, she passed away many years ago." Mrs Thomson's head tipped to the side as she searched her memory. "Hannah Watts was her name. A lovely lass, pretty as a picture, with rosy cheeks and blonde curls, and always with a bright smile. All the local lads used to moon over her, including my son, but she wasn't interested in the boys around here."

Grace sifted through the new information. Unless they could find the living daughter, there was little chance of an exact birth date. Her other deductions would remain her own, there being nothing to gain by airing unwarranted speculation.

Mrs Thomson was watching her deliberations with interest. "I know what you are thinking, Miss Penrose, and you wouldn't be the first. Little Alfie, with his blond curls and cherub face, was becoming more and more like Hannah Watts as the years passed. What better way to disguise an unwanted pregnancy to an unwed mother than to leave town and pass the baby to a married sister to raise? But Mrs Watts stuck to her story that Alfie was a foundling and no one but the gossips had the heart to say otherwise. Whether or not Hannah was his birth mother, the important thing is that Alfie grew up loved and cared for."

"You are absolutely right, Mrs Thomson," Grace said. "The great tragedy was not his birth, but his death. May I have a direction for Mrs Watts, so I that I might pay my respects?"

"That's kind of you, my dear. I was about to visit her myself, if you would care to accompany me. I must warn you though, she lives in another world these days."

Mrs Thomson's words were prophetic. In body, the lady was spritely enough, given her advanced years, but her mind was floating in the clouds. Grace couldn't decide whether it was fortunate or desperately sad that Mrs Watts was unaware of Alfie's death. Indeed, she didn't so much as blink at the sound of his name.

As is often the way with those whose minds are slipping, Mrs Watts dwelt in the past, not the present. Her daughter Hannah had obviously been the light of her life, at least within the fantasy world of her head. Mrs Watts rambled at length about her, although her tenuous grip on reality was obvious from her words. At one point, she referred to

Hannah as a princess in a castle, set on a rock above the sea, where giant birds circled and mermaids sang, like something out of the Brothers Grimm.

"I'm sorry, Miss Bones," Mrs Thomson said as they left. "Poor dear Mrs Watts wasn't having one of her better days."

"At least she has happy memories of her daughter."

"Heart-breaking that she must live in a world of fairy tales, instead of having her lovely daughter by her side in her old age. I pray times will change, so that no other poor girl dies needlessly in childbirth."

"Amen to that, Mrs Thomson." Grace noted the unconscious slip, admitting the girl's real cause of death, but did not comment.

Grace's next stop was not far away, within the crammed-together cottages of the working class. A boy of about three years old, with a dripping nose and no shirt, opened the door.

"It's Grace Penrose, Mrs Duncan," she called out, over the boy's gape-mouthed silence.

"Come in, Miss Bones."

Grace followed the sound into a cramped kitchen. Mrs Duncan was in the corner, feeding a baby. The poor woman had bags under her eyes as big as a pair of dried damson plums. Four more children were at the table, devouring fresh bread scraped with jam. Last time Grace had been here, there hadn't been a crust in the house. Now, a rich, meaty aroma drifted from a pot over the fire. A new pot, by the look of it.

"I came to see about Robbie's cough, but I can see that he is feeling much better."

Mrs Duncan managed a tired smile. "Right as rain, our Robbie. Mr Duncan brought home some medicine." She flicked her head at a bottle on the windowsill.

Grace picked up the bottle. Dr Freeman's Chlorodyne, a mixture of chloroform, morphine, hemp and goodness knows what else, sold as a cure for every imaginable complaint, from cholera to coughs to insomnia. "This medicine is awfully potent, Mrs Duncan. If you must use it at all, please be extremely careful with the dosage and only give it as an absolute last resort."

Mrs Duncan waved her concerns away. "That medicine is a godsend, is what it is. Cured our Robbie in no time and put him to sleep for a good twelve hours. I tell you, I was sorely tempted to give the lot of them a dose, so I might get a decent night's sleep myself. Not cheap mind. Over two shillings a bottle. Luckily, my Fergus won big at cards for a change. Things is looking up for us, Miss Bones, and no mistake."

Grace bit back her retort. With nine children, who wouldn't crave a peaceful night now and then. "I'm delighted to hear it, Mrs Duncan. I'll see myself out."

After a long day on her feet, Grace was aching to get home for a long, hot bath and her own peaceful night's rest. But there was one more call she wished to make, which required a quick wash and a change of shirt, at the very least. Fortunately, she had what she needed at Lavender House, which was on her way.

Before long, she was rapping an ornate brass knocker on the door of a gracious two-storey house in the upper reaches of High Street. The house resembled a larger version of the Macmillan home, in that it had beautiful filigree rails and decorative bargeboards, but they showed to better effect, with precisely trimmed box hedges rather than rampant undergrowth.

Grace gave her card to the butler, apologising for calling on Mrs Kendall at such an unsociably late hour without an appointment. Somewhat to her surprise, the butler showed her to the drawing room. While she waited, Grace appraised the elegant, high-ceiling room with a pretty bay window. The room was over-stuffed with bulky armchairs, spindly side tables, assorted lamps, needlework samplers and enough china figurines to open an antique shop.

Everything was at least a quarter of a century old, presumably dating from the family's arrival in New Zealand. One might have thought the outdated style was simply a matter of taste, had it not been for the carefully draped armrests, concealing fabric worn through to the stuffing. Evidently, the Kendall's business was not thriving.

The door opened, admitting a small, rounded woman of middle age, wearing a frilled bonnet and a high-necked gown of the same vintage as the furniture. "Miss Grace Penrose?" The lady was far too polite to

128

add, "who are the blazes are you and what do you want", but the question hovered in the creases around her down-turned mouth.

"Mrs Kendall, how good of you to see me. I am from Lavender House, an institution that cares for the needs of–"

Mrs Kendall's frown cleared. "Ah, you would like a donation." She waved to the man standing by the door, who withdrew a small coin-purse from his pocket.

Grace was about to refuse, when she realised this was a far better reason for her visit than her own hastily assembled excuse. "That would be most kind of you, Mrs Kendall." She received the sixpenny piece with what she hoped was a beaming smile of gratitude. "I believe I have seen you before, Mrs Kendall. Was it at the recital on Monday night?"

"You have me mistaken for another, Miss Penrose. My husband never goes out in the evening between Sunday and Friday. He works so hard, you see, and needs his rest."

Mrs Kendall hovered uncertainly, waiting for her uninvited guest to either leave or declare her intentions. When neither happened, good manners overcame her indecision. She waved in the general direction of an over-stuffed chair, upholstered in an unpleasant dark red and pink fabric, which looked like swirls of blood on skin.

Grace ignored the tepid welcome and settled herself into the uncomfortable chair. "I apologise again for visiting without an introduction, but I happened to be passing and felt a sudden urge to meet you, after hearing the Mayor speak so eloquently of you and Mr Kendall as pillars of the local community. I am quite new to this town, you see." The mayor had mentioned Kendall in a speech reported in the newspaper, so she was stretching the truth rather than blatantly fibbing.

"The Mayor? How kind of him to single us out for such a compliment." Mrs Kendall sat a little straighter and favoured her with a gracious smile. "My husband is well known in the business community. I flatter myself that I have lent constant support to his many endeavours, leaving me little time to spare for other charitable work."

A not-so-subtle hint that the lady of the house might spare sixpence for Lavender House, but she was not about to have her arm twisted further. "Naturally, Mrs Kendall. I expect you are both particularly busy, given the imminent commencement of the Royal Commission on labour conditions. It must be a great burden to factory owners, who have so many other calls on their time."

Two dots of red appeared high in Mrs Kendall's cheeks and spread rapidly. "Young lady, I pray you refrain from mentioning that abomination in this household. Workers' rights? It is outrageous. What about the owners' rights to make a profit in these difficult times? It is shameful the way the government allows shoddy imports to undercut the hard-working local manufacturers."

"I couldn't agree more, Mrs Kendall. If we all paid a few pennies more for local goods of good quality, I'm sure businesses would be better placed to thrive and an honest man could make a decent living." Grace failed to add her own view that the extra pennies should go towards wages, not profit.

"Quite so, Miss Penrose." Mrs Kendall cast her gaze around the outdated furnishings in the room with a sigh. "Of course, low-quality imports are not the only drain upon an honest living. Unscrupulous contractors undercutting legitimate industry, women working for a pittance in their homes, the extortionate prices for wool demanded by the big run-holders – well, it keeps my husband awake at night, I can tell you."

The ease with which this list of grievances rolled off Mrs Kendall's tongue suggested she was the frequent recipient of comprehensive tirades from her husband on the subject.

"My father is the same, Mrs Kendall. He finds it terribly hard to sleep soundly with all the worries that beset a man of business." Grace crossed her fingers behind her back as she told this falsehood. Her father often fell asleep in his chair before going to bed and regularly woke up at dawn with an annoying level of refreshed vigour after a sound night's sleep.

"Your father might like to try a sleeping draught. A few drops in a glass of whisky before bed and his insomnia will vanish. Mr Kendall swears by it."

From the tinge of pink in her cheeks, Grace thought that Mrs Kendall might make use of the sleeping draught too. Now that she had seen the ample figure of her husband, she felt certain he would have a snore of equally ample proportions. "An excellent idea, Mrs Kendall. What is it that your husband uses, if I might be allowed to ask such an indelicate question?"

"I'm afraid I have no idea. The pharmacist makes it up for him."

Grace was about to thank her and bid her good day, but Mrs Kendall had built up a head of steam and was not about to be stopped in the face of a captive audience.

"My husband's considered opinion is that the Royal Commission is an egregious waste of time and money. The 'Sweating Commission' – the very name is an outrage to impugn our reputation by implying that factory owners run sweatshops, when we are doing our best to give the wretched workers a living. And are the workers grateful? No, they are not. These young girls flit off without a by-your-leave, leaving Mr Kendall short-handed at a critical time. No sense of duty at all."

"What is the world coming to?" Grace couldn't think of anything else to say without compromising her principles, so she nodded sympathetically. She contemplated bringing up the boy's death, but she felt sure that Mr Kendall would not have troubled his wife with such a distasteful event. Instead, she exchanged a few platitudes, then said, "I fear I have taken enough of your time. Thank you for a most enlightening discussion, Mrs Kendall."

A mixed success, she decided, as she strode down the street. Kendall used a sleeping draught, but he did not go out on the night of the murder, according to his wife. Thus, means, but not opportunity. On the other hand, he had a strong motive, given the apparently precarious financial state of his enterprise.

An Arrest

Detective Inspector Stewart listened to Charlie's summary of his investigations without interrupting. After a few terse questions about the evidence, he lapsed back into silence.

"Wait here, Pyke. I need to convey your discoveries to the local inspector immediately."

Charlie relaxed back into the comfort of the armchair and basked in the novel feeling of being a valued member of a team. While Stewart had not openly praised his efforts, nor had he scoffed. After working for Sergeant Lynch, simply having his work accepted was a boost to his morale.

Within half an hour, a local Detective Constable, a middle-aged man in a tweed suit, arrived at the Wains Hotel. No wonder Stewart had a reputation for getting things done, if he could conjure this rapid reaction from the police force.

"Pyke, is it? Seen you around, but we haven't met. Detective Constable Richards."

Charlie shook the outstretched hand. "Pleased to meet you."

"Your Sergeant Lynch asked me to pass on his best wishes. What was it he said? 'Tell Pyke that I won't forget what he did and look forward to having him back under my command.' You're lucky to have his support, Pyke. When I started out, I had a right ogre as a sergeant."

"How kind of Sergeant Lynch," Charlie muttered. Lynch's implied threat no longer concerned him. Indeed, his only reaction was regret that he hadn't acted against the man sooner.

"I hear you have stumbled across the identity of the corpse found in the alley," Richards said. "My governor is thrilled. Damned newspaper man has been snooping around, digging out all the grisly details. The whole of Dunedin will know there is a murderer on the loose once the evening paper hits the streets. Come on, you can brief me on the way. The chief is keen for an arrest as soon as possible."

"What's the hurry?"

"The Police Commissioner is anxious, what with all the dignitaries in town for the South Seas Exhibition and the police force in a state of disarray with our District Inspector gone. He doesn't want people to be worried about a homicidal maniac on the loose as well."

"Why a maniac?"

Richards gave him a withering glance. "Has to be a maniac to bash a man's skull in with a metal pipe. Let's get the body formally identified first. At least then we'll have something to feed to the hungry maw of the press."

Charlie strode along beside Richards, heading toward the solicitor's office. He outlined everything he had found out so far, including the inconsistencies in the stated cause of death and the potential suspects. The detective constable pricked up his ears at the mention of Finlay's brother.

Richards veered off down Water Street, heading for the commercial district near the wharves. "No point looking for a convoluted cause of death, when the man has a ruddy great dent in his skull and a monstrous brother. Whereas a gentleman like Mr Kendall would hardly stoop to murdering a man in a seedy alley."

"But–"

"Pyke, I commend your enthusiasm. However, once you have more experience, you will realise that murder is most often a straightforward affair. Money, envy, greed, trivial family arguments that get out of hand. You mark my words, the brother did it. The secretary called him a monster and won't have him in the office. His brother was a success and about to make a fortune. And the brother will inherit the entire business now, but perhaps not in a year's time, when his brother might have a wife and son. Open and shut case."

"Before the body has been formally identified?"

Richards tapped the side of his nose. "Watch and learn, Pyke. We get the brother to answer a few questions and identify the body, watching his reaction like a hawk. Then, we nab him. After a few days stewing in gaol on suspicion of murder, he'll be falling over himself to talk. If he is guilty, we'll soon know the truth. Simple and efficient, home in time for steak and kidney pie."

Charlie fumed inwardly on the brief journey down the hill, frustrated with his colleague's rapid leap to a conclusion and growing doubt at his own deductions. Had he been too quick to see an intriguing mystery when a simple solution was staring him in the face?

The foundry was silent when they arrived. At the far side, a lonely figure was sitting on an anvil staring at a wall lined with dozens of tools and stacks of iron. The man was enormous, with muscles a blacksmith would be envious of.

When the door banged behind them, the lone man looked up hopefully. Richards let out a startled gasp at the sight of his twisted lower jaw, with bones so overgrown and misshapen that eating and talking must be difficult.

Richards stopped near the door and called out, "Mr William Finlay?"

"Will. Thas me. Wha' ya want?"

"Can't understand a word he's saying," Richards grunted. "A brute and an imbecile. Now tell me he ain't the killer."

Will Finlay must have heard the first sentence at least. He rose from the anvil, pointing at his twisted jaw. "Naw stupid."

To Charlie's ear, Will's words were slurred, but comprehensible. Despite the insult, his tone was more resigned than angry. Charlie crossed the foundry, sizing up the man as he went. Will Finlay made no aggressive moves, not even tensing his muscles. He watched Charlie with intelligent, but wary, eyes.

Charlie extended his hand to Will. "Good afternoon, Mr Finlay. We are here about your brother."

Will brightened. "Jack? Where's 'e?"

The man hadn't so much as twitched. Unless he was a consummate actor, he did not know of his brother's fate. "When did you last see him?"

"Mondee night. Jack only came by to say 'lo."

Charlie wanted to make sure he had heard the slurred speech correctly. "Your brother Jack dropped by briefly to say hello on Monday night?"

The giant man nodded. "Sh'd be 'ere yes'day. Lots o' work to do."

"You expected him to be here yesterday? That is, Tuesday?"

Will Finlay nodded again, but now worry lines were deepening on his massive forehead. "Wha's happened?"

Richards strode across to join them. "Did you argue with your brother on Monday night?"

Will shook his head. "Naw–"

"But you don't deny seeing him?"

Will Finlay took a step towards Richards, looking undeniably intimidating, even if that was not what he intended. "I...did...not...argue...with...Jack," he enunciated as clearly as he could.

Richards took two steps back. "I would advise you to keep your temper under control, Mr Finlay. Tell me, do you ever get so angry that you want to strike someone?"

Will shook his head at the confusing attack, looking at Charlie for help.

"William Finlay," Richards intoned, "I'm detaining you for questioning with regard to the murder of your brother, Jack Finlay."

"Murda? Jack's dead?" Will stumbled backwards, his muscled bulk crumpling as shock took hold.

Charlie drew Richards away from the grieving man. "We haven't even formally identified the body as Jack Finlay."

"He can do that on the way to the lock-up. Open and shut, Pyke, open and shut. Chief will be over the moon."

Charlie knew it was pointless to argue. Indeed, it would be another black mark against him. But if his career was disappearing down a sewer, at least it wouldn't take his honesty with it. "I'm not convinced Will killed his brother. You can see how surprised he was."

"And your assessment is based on what, Pyke? All your decades of experience on murder investigations? Or the fact that you're so darn clever you've been stood down? Remind me, does Will Finlay stand to benefit from his brother's death?"

Charlie could hardly deny it. "I believe he is his brother's sole heir. You'd have to confirm it with his solicitor."

"There you are then. In my experience, it's usually someone close to the victim, especially if that person stands to benefit from the death. Once you have a motive, you need only look at timing, means and aptitude. The brother admits to seeing the victim, works close to the location of the crime, has access to plenty of metal bars for bashing in a skull, and is obviously both mentally deficient and physically more than capable of killing a small man. Case closed. If we're quick, news of the arrest will make the next edition."

Charlie stood by and watched with clenched fists as Richards escorted Will Finlay out of the building. The giant man turned at the door and stared at Charlie, his twisted mouth silent, but the desperate look in his eyes pierced through Charlie's flesh, into his heart.

Two hours later, back at the Macmillan home, Charlie could still feel the burn of Will Finlay's plea. Whichever way he churned the evidence over in his brain, his gut told him that Will was innocent. The question was, how could he prove it when the case was not his to investigate? Much as he hated to admit it, he might well have to rely on Grace Penrose's unerring ability to extract information out of the people he could not interview himself. Ironic that he might end up as her shadow, rather than the other way around.

He glanced at the mantelpiece clock. Where was she? The stab of worry he felt at her late return to the house was the downside to having an extra pair of eyes and ears. Trouble seemed to find her, or vice versa, with a regularity that did his blood pressure no good at all.

The front door banged open and rapid steps pattered down the hall, stopping only to thump a heavy object on the hall table. Her medical bag, no doubt. The door to the drawing room swung open with a liveliness that threatened the hinges.

Anne looked up from the card table, where she and Lily had been chattering away like long-lost friends, despite their thirty-year age difference. "Grace, home at last. You look like something the cat dragged in."

"It's been a long day, Auntie," Grace said. "One of the Potts' boys fell out of a tree as I was walking home. Fortunately, he escaped with a sprained ankle and a few scratches, but I had to pull him out of a blackberry patch."

"Looking after this neighbourhood is a Sissyfussian task ... I mean a Sisyphean task," Anne agreed.

Grace picked up the half-empty bottle of sherry, which was sitting amidst a debris of plates, glasses and scattered cribbage pegs, boards and cards. She had heard their cackles of laughter from the far end of the hall. "I can see you two ladies are having a fine old time. I hope you are not leading Lily astray?"

Lily giggled, a tiny tinkle compared to Anne's raucous laugh.

Grace rolled her eyes, although she was secretly delighted to see her great-aunt so merry. "I'm ravenous. What's that heavenly smell?"

"Lily made some delicious little savoury dumplings to serve with drinks before dinner. At least, that is what they were supposed to be for, but I fear I may have eaten more than my share."

"I set some aside for you, Grace, in the kitchen." Lily put down her cards. "I'll get them."

Charlie jumped to his feet. "No need. I can show Grace where they are."

He led the way down the hall to the kitchen, seating Grace at the scarred wooden table and setting the plate of dumplings, still warm from the range, in front of her.

Grace studied his face. "What's happened, Charlie? I've seen happier expressions on the terminally ill." She got up to get an extra fork and pushed the plate of dumplings into the middle of the table.

"On the whole, it was one of the best days of my life. The chance to show my worth as a detective, a successful first interview, the boy's body found and our missing corpse identified." Charlie stabbed a dumpling, missing Grace's fork by a whisker as she went for the same one. "Oops, sorry."

Grace extracted her fork and used it to divide the dumplings into two equal piles. "Not bad for your first day as a detective. Keep that up and Stewart will make sure it's not your last. Was the murder victim the engineer?"

Charlie nodded. "Jack Finlay, designer of safety equipment and machinery. His secretary confirmed the argument with Mr Kendall."

"Do you think that is why Finlay ended up dead in a sleazy alley? I know Kendall isn't going to win any popularity contests, but I'd hate to think he was capable of murder."

"With the Sweating Commission due to start hearing evidence in three weeks, I suppose the factory owners are all desperate to stifle any trouble. Everyone is capable of murder if put under enough pressure, Grace."

"These dumplings are so good, I'm tempted to murder you right here and now, so I don't have to share." Grace speared another of the fragrant delicacies. "Is there any damning evidence against Kendall?"

"Not as far as I know. If his foreman hadn't identified Finlay from the sketch I drew, I'd be none the wiser." Charlie's fork hovered over the plate, but he deferred to her greater need. "The Finlay investigation is being handled by the local detective branch now. DI Stewart told me to keep out of it. I have no authority to inquire into Kendall's motive or whereabouts on Monday night and I'll eat my uniform from cap to boots if the officer in charge so much as looks in his direction."

"I have news on that front, both good and bad," Grace said. "Kendall appears to be under significant financial strain. But Mrs Kendall said her husband was home on Monday night. They went to bed early, after taking a sleeping draught."

"Interesting. Chloral hydrate?"

Grace shrugged. "She didn't know. So, what is the problem, other than being excluded from a murder case you deserve to investigate?"

"Kendall is not the only suspect. Or rather, he is not a suspect at all. The detective detained another man on the flimsiest of grounds, and I don't think he did it."

"Let me guess – anything to avoid the unpleasantness of charging a so-called pillar of society."

"Exactly. Jack Finlay has a giant of a brother, who has a motive in that he will inherit the business." Charlie flipped open his notebook to the sketch he had made of Will Finlay.

"Poor man. Looks like a birth defect rather than an injury."

"Will Finlay is certainly strong enough to overpower his brother without the need of a sleeping draught. Even so, I doubt he would have been detained if he wasn't so monstrous in appearance. He finds it difficult to speak clearly, but he is not an imbecile or a killer. I can't help but feel responsible for leading the detective to him. If only there was something I could do to prove his innocence."

"You gave them all the evidence, as you were required to do. It's not your fault the detective jumped to the wrong conclusion."

"They wanted to make a quick arrest to look good. Can't have a murderer running around with so many important people in town, can we?" Charlie jabbed at another dumpling, screeching the fork into the plate. "What else have you found out?"

"Harriet Morison says Kendall's factory is the subject of a huge number of complaints. Her assistant, Molly Sugden, has spent weeks cajoling seamstresses to give evidence at the Sweating Commission, but suddenly, they've all vanished."

"Vanished? That sounds ominous. This case is getting more complicated by the minute."

"The workers who were going to testify have taken desirable jobs elsewhere." Grace showed him the pamphlet advertising the meeting at Temperance House. "This is giving me tingles and I can't think why."

Charlie examined it, feeling that jolt of excitement he got at each new clue. "The design in the corner matches the fragment of paper we found on the dead body. Looks like Finlay planned to meet someone there at eight o'clock. Would it be this meeting, or do they have meetings most nights?"

"Temperance House buzzes like a beehive day and night. Many community groups hold meetings there."

Charlie read the meeting topics listed on the pamphlet. "I can't imagine it was tonight's meeting he would have attended. Tips for soothing colicky babies, followed by the rights of women in the workplace, to be given by Miss Molly Sugden. Neither topic is likely to interest a young male engineer."

"It might still be worth going to the meeting and asking around, in case someone recognises Finlay."

"I agree. Right now, I could use a few fresh leads to untangle this mess. I'll escort you."

"I appreciate the thought, Charlie, but it might be a little difficult to ask discreet questions with a six-foot detective at my side."

"The citizens of Dunedin ought to be eager to bring a killer to justice, although I concede you might have the advantage in questioning any young men present. Regardless, I will accompany you. No woman is safe on the streets alone at night. Even you, Grace."

By which Charlie meant, especially you. Trouble with a capital T.

Deliberations

"I hope you two aren't planning on going anywhere this evening," Anne chimed in from the doorway. "We are having a dinner party. Don't look so surprised, Grace. When I heard Detective Inspector Stewart was on his own, I sent him an invitation to dine with us."

Grace looked around the kitchen, which showed no signs of activity aside from the empty plate of dumplings. "It's Mrs Brown's night off. Who will cook?"

"A problem delegated is a problem solved, my dear. I have arranged with the Grand Hotel to deliver a feast, thanks to Lily knowing the head chef. You've time to freshen up, if you hurry. I've asked Sadie to lay out some clothes for you that are free of bloodstains, since we have company."

Half an hour later, Grace came down the stairs with a scrubbed face and hands, neatly coiled hair and a fresh set of clothes. The dark blue gown emphasised her best features, according to Sadie, and Grace hadn't had time to argue the point. Her own view was that her best feature was her brain, but, short of drastic cranial surgery, that was not on display. The guests would have to make do with the larger than usual expanse of chest exposed by the chill-inducing neckline.

"You look lovely, my dear," Anne said. "Doesn't she, Charlie?"

Charlie looked up from pouring three glasses of whisky. The amber liquid spilled over the edge of the glass as he gave a fair impersonation of a startled deer. "Mmm," he mumbled, as he bent to mop up the wasted drops of a fine single malt.

Anne picked up two of the glasses, and, with a twitch of her lips, crossed the room to place one of them on the mantelpiece next to a portrait of her husband.

"A nightly ritual. Anne doesn't like Uncle Gordon to miss out on the entertainment," Grace explained to Charlie, who was watching

Anne engaging in a conversation with her beloved. "She misses him deeply."

"Mrs Macmillan told me that Doctor Macmillan was the perfect husband, willing to accept her for who she was and encourage her to be what she could be. One would hope all marriages would be like that."

"If only that were true." Grace sighed. "I have spent far too much of today seething over women and children who were at the blunt end of the drunken rages of the man of the house. Or, to be more precise, the blunt, sharp and burning ends."

"I expect you'd like a stiff drink? A large whisky, perhaps?"

"A dribble of sherry would be better. Any more than a few sips and I'll be out like a light." Grace clinked her glass against Charlie's. "I think I'll leave the detecting to you in future."

"Very glad to hear it. I wouldn't sleep at night if I thought you were out hunting down dangerous criminals. Shall we see if my aunt needs rescuing from Stewart or vice versa?"

Lily and Detective Inspector Stewart were deep in conversation on the sofa with their bodies turned to each other as they conducted an animated discussion. Their glasses of sherry went untouched.

"They don't look like they need rescuing," Grace said. "They are well past pleasantries about the weather."

Anne returned from her devotions to Gordon. "I think that you two should leave them to enjoy their conversation. Lily has seen little enough of life's pleasures in recent times."

At this, Charlie nodded and drifted away to stand by the window. Although his eyes were directed at the view, Grace had the impression his thoughts were directed inward.

Grace turned back to her great-aunt. "I wonder what the pair of them find in common that so absorbs their attention?"

"Lily and Stewart are discussing literature, Grace," Anne replied. "Dickens, to be precise."

"Are they interested in his fiction or the social commentary he provides, which bears a sad resemblance to the situation of many in this fair city?"

"Both, from what little I overheard as I walked past them. It would appear that Detective Inspector Stewart no more conforms to the perceived norm of a thick-skulled copper than Lily does to the ridiculous notions that society has of Chinese immigrants."

Both women looked over to where Charlie was staring out the window.

"Is he uncomfortable with his aunt talking to Stewart, do you think?" Grace asked. She knew him well enough to know that it would not be a matter of race, so perhaps it was the awkwardness of seeing his superior officer in a social situation.

"No, I do not believe so," Anne replied. "Charlie has a lot on his mind, between worrying about his future and concern for his aunt. I suspect he feels ashamed that he was not aware of his aunt's situation. Lily told me she was too proud to admit that she was struggling to make ends meet. She and her husband had good jobs in the kitchen of a hotel, with accommodation provided in the basement. When her husband died, Lily lost her position and her home. With nowhere to live and no employer willing to give a middle-aged Chinese widow a job, she had limited options."

"Why would Charlie blame himself when his aunt kept the truth from him?"

"It is not a matter of logic, Grace. We all regret the questions we never thought to ask. Family is very important to him, I think, and he is an honourable young man."

Grace glanced at Lily, who was holding her own in a debate with Stewart. "Lily is a bright and capable woman. Why do you think she didn't turn to Charlie for help? They seem to care a great deal about each other."

"Lily was afraid she would jeopardise his career if she let him help her. He only transferred to Dunedin a few months ago, and she knew he was having a terrible time of it. As the constable who was making

Charlie's life hell was also taking bribes from the factory Lily worked at, she kept her head down and only saw her nephew away from any of the places someone might recognise them."

"No wonder he was so devastated when he heard of her injury in Kendall's factory."

"Enough of this retrospection. We have every hope for their futures and a dinner party to attend to in the present." Anne caught the eye of the maid, who was waiting by the door for her signal, and clapped her hands. "Time to go through to the dining room, everyone."

Charlie was by his aunt's side in an instant, offering her his arm.

Anne nudged Grace with her elbow. "How lovely to see a young person who respects his elders."

"I trust you are not implying that I lack respect for you, dearest aunt? Why, only the day before yesterday, I respectfully allowed you the honour of attending to the boils on Mr Cobb's arm."

"Mr Cobb, the collector of night soil. What an honour that was."

"Ladies, may I escort you through to the dining room?" Stewart inclined his head politely and held out an arm to each of them. "And may I reiterate what a pleasure it is to be invited to your home, Mrs Macmillan. Since my wife passed, I have dined out only at my club, which is a mighty dull proposition when compared with your household."

"My husband always maintained that we learn more from people who differ from us than from the like-minded. Although, to be honest, I have always thought his insistence on assembling a diverse group of diners was driven by his wicked sense of humour. Seating a conservative Member of the House of Representatives next to a militant unionist is far livelier than listening to a group of conservatives drone on in full agreement with one another."

"Did sparks fly, Mrs Macmillan?" Stewart asked.

"I always insisted on a reasonable degree of decorum and respect," Anne replied. "As I recall in that particular case, the politician and the unionist discovered a common interest in fly-fishing and talked of nothing else all evening. Exceedingly dull. Who knew there were so many types of flies? Ironically, it was the vicar and his wife who almost came to blows that night, over the degree to which that gentle man of God slurped his soup."

They sat down at the table and continued this amiable conversation over the soup, taking care not to slurp.

When the maid cleared the soup and brought out the roast goose, Stewart took up the carving knife. "Well, Mrs Macmillan, this is most delightful, but I suspect you didn't invite me to talk about the weather. Is it time to pay the piper?"

"I assure you I had no ulterior motive, Detective Inspector Stewart," Anne replied with an air of injured innocence and a twinkle in her eye. "However, since you mention it, I am sure we would all be interested in hearing more about this murder."

"Only if you think it a fit conversation for dinner, Mrs Macmillan," Charlie said, although he was leaning forward as expectantly as the rest of them. "Besides, Detective Inspector Stewart and I are not involved in that case. The detective in charge has detained a suspect for questioning."

Stewart sliced through the tender meat with deft strokes. "And what is your opinion of the brother's guilt, Pyke?"

"I don't think he did it, sir. His brother's death came as a shock to Will Finlay."

"I'd be interested to hear your thoughts, lad. Purely as an academic exercise, of course."

Charlie was eager to oblige. "For a start, there are other men with a motive. Mr Kendall and Jack Finlay had a heated argument over poor workmanship. Kendall was at Finlay's office on Monday and said he'd be back. However, without further investigation, I wouldn't care to discount other offenders or other motives, such as robbery, personal vendetta, or a spurned lover."

"What's your pick?"

"Greed. A valuable patent application was taken from Finlay's office the night he died, but an expensive ring was left behind. Finlay was about to patent a design for making weaving looms safer and more efficient. Worth a fortune, according to Finlay's secretary, who is a first-class witness."

Stewart leaned forward, unaware that he was dragging his cuff in the gravy. "Take us through it, Pyke, for the benefit of the ladies."

"I think it is probable that Finlay let someone he knew into his office late on Monday night, accepting a glass of whisky laced with some form of sedative. Although Finlay rarely drinks, there was whisky spilt on his desk. After that, the murderer must have lured his victim to the alley, where his body might not have been noticed. Fortunately, a witness saw a man supporting the victim, who appeared to be weaving unsteadily up the alley. Cause of death still to be determined, but Miss Penrose identified fibres in his nostrils, suggesting suffocation. I found a gentleman's fine woollen scarf discarded in the alley, which might be the murder weapon. None of that evidence points to the brother."

Stewart passed the last of the plates, while scrutinising his constable. "An impressive amount of information, considering this is not your case."

Silence descended on the dining room as all eyes focussed on Charlie, who was sitting so upright, it was a wonder the chair did not fall over backwards.

"I was following up the boy's death with Mr Duncan, as requested. Duncan mentioned Mr Finlay and provided a possible identification of the victim. The alley was on my way and I felt it was important to visit Finlay's office as well, so that … so that …" Charlie stuttered to a halt.

"So that the police force would not be subjected to the additional awkwardness of an incorrect identification," Grace continued. "In addition to the embarrassment of wrongly assigning the case to misadventure, getting the cause of death wrong, and possibly arresting the wrong man." She favoured Stewart with an angelic smile. "Would you be so kind as to pass the gravy, please?"

Stewart pursed his lips, attempting to look stern but failing. "I intended my words as a compliment, not a criticism. Pyke has made excellent progress in a short time." He passed the gravy before continuing his interrogation. "Did your witness give any description of the perpetrator, Pyke?"

"Too dark and drizzly, sir. Taller than Finlay was all she could say, which was no help at all. Finlay was shorter and slighter than all the potential suspects."

"Patents worth a fortune?" Grace murmured. "Hmm. It may be a coincidence, but the foreman at Kendall's factory recently came into a significant sum of money. Won at cards, his wife said. Duncan had a gambling debt and needed money desperately to feed his nine children."

Charlie gave her a grateful nod. "Duncan also knew the alley, if the prostitute was telling the truth about his visits to her. We'll have to find out if he knew about the patent. If he got the money so quickly, he was likely paid to steal the patent, presumably by his boss, Kendall. Duncan identified Finlay with no sign of distress, which means he was either a talented actor or he was not the killer."

"Dare I ask how you found out about Mr Duncan's vices, Grace?" Anne asked. "Or is it better that I remain ignorant in case your mother wishes to know what you have been up to?"

"I merely had a word with Johnny Todd, who knows all the lads who work the streets. They have eyes and ears everywhere, but no one notices them, except to shoo them away." Grace heard a Charlie's intake of breath and didn't wait for his admonishment. "Before you tell me off for putting a young boy's life at risk, Constable Pyke, let me assure you I gave Johnny explicit orders not to approach any of the criminal lowlifes."

"I remember a time when women and children did what they were told," Stewart sighed, but he said it with a twinkle in his eye.

"We women will be able to vote soon," Anne countered. "Then we'll be telling men what to do."

"I am already determined to recruit Miss Penrose if she does not get accepted to medical school," Stewart declared. "The instinct for detective work is a rare talent. Mind you, Professor Scott looked none too pleased when I told him so."

"She'll be an even better doctor," Anne replied. "Go on, Grace, we might as well hear what Johnny found out."

"One of the street lads is paid to keep a lookout for coppers outside the gambling den. It seems the whole area is given over to purveyors of vice at night. The lad knows Fergus Duncan by sight. A hard man to mistake, given his three missing finger tips."

"Did he say where the gambling den is? There was one near to where the body was found."

"You'll have to ask him, Charlie … er, Constable Pyke."

Charlie glanced at Stewart, who drummed his fingers on the table while he worked through the ramifications. "No harm in making a few inquiries. If someone else saw who took Jack Finlay into that alley, then Will Finlay might be exonerated. Keep on with the other inquiry though, Pyke. And for heaven's sake, be discreet. I will liaise with the local Detective Inspector, should you confirm a link between the boy's death that we are investigating and their homicide case."

Charlie let out an audible sigh of relief. "I'm not sure what more I can do on the death of Alfie Watts, sir, unless I can get Fergus Duncan to make a formal witness statement. He claims he wasn't near the loom when the accident happened, but I'd wager he is terrified that he'll be blamed."

"You have my statement," Lily interrupted, "And Bess will support me, if she can find another job away from Kendall's. My memory is that Duncan had been fiddling with the loom, not too long before the boy was killed."

"Bess Todd also implied that Duncan was by the loom," Grace chipped in.

"We appreciate your help, Aunt Lily," Charlie continued, "but I fear it might not be enough without evidence from Mr Duncan."

"Don't look so downhearted, Charlie," Anne said. "I hear that the Tailoresses' Union is gathering a group of stalwart young women to testify at the Sweating Commission. Kendall may not be charged over the boy's death, but his factory could be shut down anyway."

Grace dropped her fork with a clatter. "I'm afraid I have bad news to report on that front. It appears the young women who were to testify have all vanished."

Everyone turned to stare at her, forks suspended in mid-air, mouthfuls going unchewed.

Stewart was the first to swallow. "Vanished? As in missing under suspicious circumstances?"

"Word is, the seamstresses have left to take up new positions," Grace replied. "Their mothers appear pleased and their sisters are envious, so it is fair to say they think the girls have done well. However, Molly Sugden, of the Tailoresses' Union, reminded me that there are unscrupulous men who lure young girls away with promises of a better life that is anything but."

Stewart didn't blink an eyelash, but the muscles in his neck tightened into hard cords. "Have other young women gone missing, or just the ones who were due to testify at the Sweating Commission?"

"Molly was most concerned about the loss of her best witnesses, but I'm sure she would have mentioned it if other girls were missing too. Regardless, it is an extraordinary coincidence to lose all of them at the same time."

"I have no doubt there will be many factory owners delighted by their disappearance," Charlie chipped in, "so close to the start of the commission's investigations."

"There may be a perfectly innocent explanation," Anne said. "Sterling Chelmsford has recently opened a new factory, which is said to be a model of health and efficiency. I expect he will have employed a considerable number of young women. Indeed, he told me he had applications from half the workers of Dunedin."

"Still, rather odd that Chelmsford would choose to employ only the more militant union girls. Rather the opposite, I would have thought, unless perhaps the other owners made it worth his while."

"Constable Pyke and I can find out more tomorrow." When Charlie's brow wrinkled, Grace added, "Have you forgotten that we are touring the Chelmsford factory tomorrow?"

"My apologies. It had slipped my mind," Charlie said. "I won't be able to go now that I am working for Detective Inspector Stewart."

Stewart dabbed his napkin across his mouth and moustaches, then tweaked up the ends into symmetrical curls. "I think it might be a good idea for you to go. I don't want any surprises in the lead up to the Sweating Commission. The thought of a substantial number of critical witnesses all vanishing in a short space of time makes me ill at ease."

"It would certainly be a significant blow to the truth if the Sweating Commission did not hear testimony from the few workers brave enough to testify," Grace said. "Harriet Morison said that some other girls have reported being coerced into giving favourable testimony or threatened with dismissal if they give damaging evidence."

The clang of the bell by the front door interrupted their deliberations. A few moments later, the maid came to the door of the dining room. "Message for Constable Pyke, ma'am."

The maid paused to flutter her eyelashes at Charlie, but he had his eyes on the letter. "Redirected from the police station, to Wains Hotel, to here. I hope it wasn't urgent."

Charlie sat down at the table again and slipped a knife under the seal. "It's from Miss Abercrombie, Finlay's secretary."

"Charlie, what is it?" Grace asked. "You've gone as pale as frost."

"She has remembered that there was another family member of Finlay's living in Dunedin. The excellent Miss Abercrombie has provided the full details. The man is a distant cousin, court-martialled out of the army in England, and sent to New Zealand for a fresh start. He worked briefly for Mr Finlay's father, but showed no aptitude for engineering either. Mr Finlay's father dismissed him when the two young men came to blows over a girl. The cousin claimed he saw her first, but young Mr Finlay was the one who won her heart. A sum of money went missing when he left, but the elder Finlay took no action."

Charlie's jaw clenched so tight, she thought his teeth might shatter. Grace rested her hand on his shaking fingers. "Did the secretary name him?"

"Bartholomew Nolan. Known to us as Constable Bart Nolan."

"Ah, the pugnacious Nolan." Stewart let out a low whistle. "Am I right in recalling that it was Nolan who had to be roused from a grog shop near the alley to deal with Finlay's body?"

"The very man who reported the death as a simple case of misadventure to a drunken vagrant with no family. Nolan surely must have recognised his own cousin."

"And Nolan is also taking bribes from Kendall," Lily added.

"Well, well, this web of intrigue gets more tangled at every turn." Stewart folded his linen napkin with military precision. "Mrs Macmillan, that was the finest meal and most enjoyable company I have had in a very long time. I hope you will excuse my hasty departure. Miss Penrose, Mrs Wu, a delight to see you both again."

Anne rose with him. "I trust that we might have the pleasure of your company again soon, Detective Inspector. And I pray you will succeed in cutting this festering canker from the police force."

Charlie rose too. "May I be of assistance, sir?"

"No need, Pyke," Stewart said. "This requires an old-timer with enough authority to overcome the inevitable reluctance to investigate one of the police's own men. Excellent work, Pyke, by the way. A constable who combines intelligence and initiative can go a long way, if he avoids stepping on too many toes." Stewart bowed to his hostess and left.

Charlie blew out a puff of breath and sat back in his chair, basking in the compliment and the delighted smiles of the three women at the table. "Mrs Macmillan, my apologies for being the unwitting cause of breaking up your dinner party. I thank you again for your generosity at having myself and my aunt at your table."

"The pleasure is all mine, young man," Anne said. "Meals is this house have always been a communal event to be shared with all who are staying beneath our roof. Except the Browns, who steadfastly adhere to the usual rules of service. If you will forgive a much-told story, I like to be reminded of the lively communal meals the passengers took together while sailing from London to New Zealand.

What an exciting adventure that was, aside from the rather too frequent occasions when death knocked at our cabin door."

"I would like to hear the full story one day," Lily said. "The voyage from Australia seemed interminable to me. I cannot imagine what it must have been like to have sailed halfway around the world."

Grace silently thanked her great-aunt for the change of topic. "It is the stuff of family legend. My grandparents met and fell in love on board the ship."

"The high-society ladies on board dismissed George Penrose as a country quack, but your grandmother and I saw through that in an instant, to the fine man he really was." Anne dabbed her lips with the napkin, failing to wipe off a nostalgic smile as she looked around the table. "They were made for each other, those two, regardless of their different backgrounds."

Grace studied her great-aunt, detecting a hint of scheming in the tone of her voice. She had certainly noticed how much Lily Wu and Detective Inspector Stewart were enjoying each other's company. "I, for one, am grateful for the shipboard romance, or I would never have been born."

Anne cast her one of her all-knowing smiles. "Charlie and Grace, would you gratify an old lady by collecting up the dishes and bringing out the dessert? All this stimulating talk of villainy has made me uncommonly hungry."

Charlie hastened to gather up plates and glasses. "I feel as if I couldn't eat another morsel after double helpings of goose."

A statement he rapidly amended when the maid appeared with jam roly poly and custard.

Corruption

Charlie woke up before dawn on Thursday morning from force of habit. The wonderfully soft linen and down pillow were a sore temptation after a disrupted night's sleep, but he had work to do.

His first task was to track down Johnny Todd. Fortunately, Johnny was at home, wolfing down porridge.

"Breakfast for you too, Constable?" Mrs Todd gestured, with obvious pride, to the bubbling pot.

Charlie knew that Anne had paid Mr Todd a week in advance for his new job as her gardener. It did Charlie the world of good seeing the family well fed, knowing that tomorrow and the day after would be the same. "Not for me, thank you, Mrs Todd. If I stay at Mrs Macmillan's house much longer, I'll be waddling around like a prize porker. Can I have a word with Johnny?"

The two of them sat on the step, watching Mr Todd sharpening his hoe and hedge clippers with deft strokes.

"You'll be off to school this morning, Johnny," Charlie said.

"Suppose so." Johnny tossed a stone against the fence with a sigh. "Unless you got a better idea," he added hopefully.

"Nothing beats education, lad. But I wouldn't mind some help after school. You know where the dead man was found on Monday night?" A sharp nod. "Ask around and see if anyone saw who was with him in the alley, or between the alley and Bond Street. Ask your friends, I mean. No dealing with crooks and rogues."

Charlie handed over a small pile of copies of the sketches he had made of the dead man and the various suspects, along with some coins. "Anything you can find out about these men in particular, but remembering it might be none of them."

"Consider it done," Johnny replied with a cheery grin. "Was there something else, Copper Charlie?"

Charlie hesitated, wondering how much he could ask of a boy so young. "Just … look out for yourself. Don't go poking a stick into a rat's nest."

"Aye, me mam would have me guts for garters otherwise." Johnny flipped a coin in the air and caught it again. "Reckon I'll keep half an eye out for Miss Bones too. Wouldn't want her getting into no trouble neither, would we?"

Had the boy read his mind? He reached for his purse again, but Johnny waved it away.

"We all look out for each other round here. The ones that matter anyhow." Johnny got up and gave Charlie a salute. "Catch the stinker what did for Alfie Watts, Copper Charlie. He was a good kid who'd had a hard life."

Charlie nodded and saluted back. He'd have promised, if he thought he had a better than even chance of achieving justice for Alfie.

The rapidly rising sun warned him to get a move on. He dropped in to Wains Hotel, where Detective Inspector Stewart was already at work, reading through a stack of papers over a cup of tea and a plate of discarded bacon rinds floating in egg yolk. On any normal day, the sight would have Charlie salivating. Today, the waistband of his trousers was feeling unusually tight.

"Morning, sir. Any word on Constable Nolan?"

"Unfortunately, Constable Nolan is rostered for two days off," Stewart said. "I have notified the Chief Inspector of his relationship to Finlay, with an altogether satisfactory reaction. Nearly blew his boiler when he heard Nolan hadn't declared his relationship to the victim, let alone failing to identify him as Jack Finlay and reporting his death as an accident. The Chief Inspector assured me Nolan has become his number one priority."

"Do you think Nolan might be our killer, sir?" Charlie was careful to keep his face devoid of expression. After Sergeant Lynch, Bart Nolan had been the man who had given him the most trouble during his time in Dunedin. Nothing would give him greater pleasure than to

154

see Nolan get what he deserved, whether by disgraceful discharge or any other means.

"No proof of that on the evidence we have, but he is firmly on the list of suspects."

"I would be happy to assist the investigation in any way you see fit, sir. Or should I visit Chelmsford's factory, as planned?"

"Keep to the plan, I think, Pyke. There is still the matter of the missing militants who were to testify to the Sweating Commission. The local investigation team has not asked for our help on the murder, although they are grateful for any information that might come our way as a result of our other inquiries."

Stewart pushed his plate away. "May I ask you a question in confidence, Pyke?"

"Of course, sir."

"What is your opinion of Sergeant Lynch?"

Charlie took the time to gather the right words. "A stickler for discipline. I find him a hard man to read, if I'm honest. Half the time I have no idea why he is disciplining me, but that may be my own fault, sir."

"Have you ever heard rumours that Lynch takes bribes to overlook illegal activity?"

Heat rose up Charlie's neck setting up a nasty itch under his starched collar. Time to choose between his old life and what he hoped might be his future. "I have personally witnessed it, sir. We raided a gambling den on Monday night, but Sergeant Lynch called it off when a wad of cash changed hands."

"Why didn't you report this?" Stewart asked the question with resignation, rather than anger.

"I'm ashamed to say that I failed to put my duty above my concern for my position, sir."

"Did Lynch threaten to have you dismissed if you reported him?"

Charlie nodded. "Not in so many words, sir, but the implication was clear."

"And was that the only occasion you witnessed Lynch accepting a bribe?"

"Yes, sir. Although I had my suspicions when packages arrived at the station for him. I happened to see that one of them contained a bottle of whisky. The enforcement of licencing hours is not a popular activity amongst the local force. From various comments he has made within my hearing, Lynch has given me to understand that he feels it is his duty to allow men to drink when and where they wish, rather than to stick to the letter of the law."

"And Constable Nolan?"

"All I can say for sure is that Nolan is close to Lynch and seems very sure of himself. Lynch never punishes him, although everyone knows Nolan drinks and sleeps his way through night duty, and day duty too, on occasion. And we have Mrs Wu's account of him leaving Kendall's with money. A couple of weeks ago, I overheard him boasting about his plan to purchase a small cottage, which seems decidedly out of keeping with the pay scale of an ordinary constable. Of course, it is possible he has received an inheritance or other windfall."

"Thank you, Pyke. I appreciate your candour. Better head off, lad, so as not to keep a lady waiting."

When Charlie had his hand on the doorknob, Stewart called after him. "Watch your back, son. When Lynch and Nolan realise I am barking at their heels, they might turn nasty."

Charlie hung onto the door and threw caution to the wind. "I want you to know that I will give evidence against Lynch and Nolan even if it costs my position."

"I don't doubt it, Pyke."

Charlie raced back up High Street again with little time to spare before Chelmsford arrived. He sprinted past Grace and up the stairs, two at a time.

"Anne has laid out your clothes," Grace called after him.

The hint of amusement in her tone should have been a warning sign. He flung open the attic room door to see what Anne had in store for him and skidded to a halt. Lucifer would be serving ice cream in hell before he agreed to wear the outfit laid out on the bed.

Grace's voice followed him up to the attic. "Better hurry, Charlie. I see the carriage coming up the hill." Then, as if she could see his scowl from the bottom of the stairs, "Please can you put the clothes on, for my sake?"

With a defeated shrug, he flung his working clothes to the floor and pulled on the white shirt, brocade waistcoat, and morning suit. He was halfway to the door, struggling with the braces essential for keeping the trousers from falling off, when he remembered to grab his notebook. Dressed as a gentleman or not, he was still a detective at heart.

Grace was waiting at the bottom of the stairs with a top hat in her hands and a smirk on her lips. "Goodness, what a transformation."

He glared at the top hat. The tall silk folly of it was a step too far for an honest working man. "Absolutely not. I'll look like an idiot."

"No more than any of the rest of them." She plonked the hat on his head and removed the silk tie from his fist, securing it around his neck with a few deft twists. "You look perfect, aside from the scowl. Think of it as a disguise, Charlie. A very effective one at that. I would have walked past you in the street if I hadn't been forewarned."

Belatedly, Charlie realised he wasn't putting on a creditable show as a gentleman. He wiped the scowl off his face and took her arm with a slight bow. "My dear Miss Penrose, allow me to escort you to your conveyance. And remind me to thank Mrs Macmillan for taking so much trouble on my behalf. Did she choose your lovely outfit too? Dark green suits you very well."

A snort was the only reply he got, but Grace allowed him to escort her to the door. Out on the street, a handsome barouche stood waiting. There was no need to ask to whom it belonged, with a stylised "C" in gold paint on the side.

The liveried coachman raised his top hat. "Good morning, Miss Penrose, and to you, sir. Mr Edmund Chelmsford sends his apologies and his regrets at being unable to call for you himself."

Charlie helped Grace up onto the soft leather seat. "Don't see many of these around the streets of Dunedin. Edmund Chelmsford clearly wishes to make a good impression on you."

The coachman turned to ensure they were settled. "On such a lovely day, I have taken the liberty of folding the roof down, but please let me know if you wish it to be raised, Miss Penrose."

"It would indeed be a great shame to waste a perfectly splendid day," she replied.

"There is a parasol under the seat if you would care to use it, Miss Penrose." The coachman sent the whip flicking above the flanks of a matched pair of dapple-grey horses, who stepped out in perfect synchrony.

Grace leaned back into the padded seat with a small sigh. "Makes a pleasant change from trudging up hills on shanks' pony."

They passed the journey by dissecting the evidence they had accumulated over the last two days, as the horses clip-clopped downhill and up again. They had made no further progress by the time they arrived at the corner of Royal Terrace, where a row of mansions looked down over the city. In the distance, the long teal-hued tongue of the harbour snaked between the green mouth of hills on either side. The sight of the sea still thrilled Charlie, after growing up in the rock-strewn hills of Central Otago.

Grace broke the silence. "Charlie, might I ask a favour?"

"Of course, anything."

"When we are with Chelmsford, could you perhaps be a little less …" She struggled to find the right words.

Several options flashed through his mind, none of them pleasant. Less rough around the edges? Less like a plodding country copper? Less like a wretched imposter in a top hat?

"Less like a shrewd detective," Grace said.

A grin spread across his face at the unexpected compliment. "You wish me to play the role of a daft aristocrat instead?"

"That might be a little too much to ask of your acting skills, although I confess I should love to watch you try. Perhaps you might aim for an innocuous gentleman of leisure instead?"

"As you wish, milady." Charlie dipped his head in a sweeping bow, almost losing the top hat.

"It's just that my great-aunt wants to keep the Chelmsford philanthropy flowing and she has made me promise to be nice to them."

"I can be nice. Occasionally."

Grace tweaked his hat until it sat straight. "You can also be awfully daunting when you start asking questions."

Daunting? Even better as a compliment, although Charlie knew he had a long way to go before he could emulate Stewart's adroit interviewing skills. "I'd wager you are not intimidated by me in the least, Miss Penrose."

"You have no idea. The first time I met you, I was shaking like a blancmange. Fortunately, having five brothers means I have learned to hide my fear."

"I would never have guessed you were the least bit intimidated that day. The way you put Sergeant Lynch in his place was inspiring. Anyway, I give you my word that I shall put away my thumbscrews and talk about nothing but how dreadfully changeable the weather has been lately and how frightfully delightful his pretentious mansion is."

Grace suppressed a chuckle at his impersonation of a daft aristocrat, as the barouche had pulled up outside a two-storey, double-bay house, guarded by a stout hedge trimmed with military precision.

The house rose above the road like a majestic white wedding cake, laced with a decorative balcony and an arched porch, and topped with carved finials. Charlie found it hard to imagine living in a house with twice as many bedrooms as inhabitants. A far cry from the mean lean-to shacks and weatherboard cottages of the poorer parts of Dunedin.

He took Grace's glove-covered hand, marvelling at how small it seemed in his own, and helped her down from the carriage. Edmund

Chelmsford appeared on the porch and bounded down the steps, all but knocking his hand away as he greeted Grace with the enthusiasm of a schoolboy vying for a rare treat.

"My dear Miss Penrose, what a delight to see you again. I do apologise that I could not call for you myself. Always work to attend to, as you may imagine."

Edmund hovered his lips over her glove, before glancing up and deigning to notice Charlie. "But where is Mrs Macmillan?"

"I'm afraid she could not come," Grace said. "Allow me to introduce Mr Charles Pyke."

Chelmsford thrust out his hand and pumped Charlie's with enough vigour to shake a lesser man. "Mr Edmund Chelmsford. You look a little familiar, Mr Pyke, but I cannot place you."

Charlie wasn't about to let on that he was last seen as the "tradesman" carrying a canvas bag and a box into the Macmillan house. He held his head high and answered in an upper-class drawl. "Delighted to meet you, Mr Chelmsford. I know you only by reputation, not by any closer acquaintance."

Chelmsford retained a puzzled frown. "You are not a member of the Dunedin Club, perhaps?"

"I have not yet been accorded that honour, sir. Perhaps you have seen me at Wains Hotel, which has become my temporary office of late?"

"A fine establishment," Edmund conceded. "Are you are a visitor to Dunedin, Mr Pyke?"

"I am a relatively recent arrival, compared to your own family, Mr Chelmsford. I do hope you will forgive me for imposing myself upon your company. Miss Penrose tells me you have made significant innovations to improve efficiency in your factories and insisted I see them for myself."

Chelmsford turned to Grace, tucking her arm through his. "Dear Miss Penrose, how kind of you to sing our praises to your visitor."

"Mr Pyke is the nephew of a dear family friend. I hope you will not mind that I brought him with me, but my great-aunt was unavailable and Mr Pyke has an interest in factory design."

"Miss Penrose, your wish is my command." Chelmsford escorted her up the steps, looking back over his shoulder for a moment. "I don't believe I am aware of any factories operating under the name Pyke. Do you make medieval weaponry perchance?" He chuckled at his own joke as he guided Grace into a corridor the size of most ordinary houses, leaving Charlie standing on the path.

Charlie tried to keep his annoyance in check at Chelmsford's condescension, not to mention his repellent fawning over Grace Penrose. With a valiant attempt at mimicking Chelmsford's superior attitude, he hurried after them and said, with as much disdain as he could muster, "I do not engage in business, Mr Chelmsford. I am merely a keen observer of recent developments in a variety of fields, industry amongst them."

"Quite right, sir. A gentleman must always have a wide variety of interests, while a businessman has only one. I myself spread my time between the everyday work of managing a thriving business and more pleasurable activities, such as breeding champion racehorses. I think of it as a contribution to society, as no civilised nation can do without horse racing."

Grace discreetly rolled her eyes at Charlie before turning back to Chelmsford. "While I am more interested in seeing this magnificent mansion. The décor calls to mind paintings of the grand houses of England."

"You have a fine eye, Miss Penrose. All the furniture is oak and walnut, manufactured in London to special order, although the gilt mirrors are from Paris and the carpets are from Belgium and Turkey. Come, my dear, I shall give you a tour, then we will take tea in the drawing room. Mr Pyke, would you care to amuse yourself in the library?"

Thus dismissed from their presence like a superfluous servant, Charlie whiled away the minutes, learning that the Chelmsford family preferred cabinets of liquor and displays of antiques to actual books in

161

their library. The only two bookcases contained a set of leather-bound classics, whose pristine spines showed no sign of use, and a selection of works of non-fiction, largely on horse breeding and manufacturing. He couldn't help but recall his parents' small but well-thumbed assortment, which spanned a range of topics from science to art to philosophy and fiction.

As the books held little interest, Charlie got out his notebook and sketched the two Chelmsford men, using the sole family portrait on the wall to supplement his memory. The pencil refused to capture Edmund's fine features, resulting in beady eyes and a prominent chin, not to mention a nose angled rather higher in the air than in real life.

As the minutes dragged by, he added a drawing of Grace in the blue gown she had worn last night. This time, his pencil ran true, capturing her expressive eyes and mischievous grin perfectly. He was just pondering the exact curvature of her cleavage when the lady herself appeared, with Chelmsford right behind her, pawing at her back.

He snapped his notebook closed and swallowed his pride, plastering an inane grin back on his face.

Utopia

Grace caught a fleeting expression of guilt as Detective Constable Pyke tucked his notebook into his pocket. What he had been scribbling so furtively?

The shrewd detective evaporated, and Mr Charles Pyke rose from the armchair with a foppish wave of his hand. "A charming library you have here, Mr Chelmsford. One can always be sure that a man's library will be a true reflection of his character."

Edmund Chelmsford searched Charlie's face for hidden meaning, before his smile declared his satisfaction that the unwanted guest intended it as a compliment. "Would you care to join us in the drawing room for tea, Mr Pyke?"

Grace allowed the two gentlemen to precede her so that she might take a quick look around the library. Within a few seconds, she concluded Chelmsford was a fool if he thought this library spoke highly of his character. She hurried out as he held the door open for her, flashing a perfect row of pearly whites. After the rotten teeth and gap-filled mouths of Devil's Half Acre, his dazzling smile looked almost inhuman.

The drawing room matched the style of the library, with heavy velvet curtains, a surfeit of ornate armchairs and walls full of pictures, including a cluster of photographs of Sterling Chelmsford with various politicians and other worthies.

With a start, Grace realised that there was not one portrait of Sterling Chelmsford's wife and son amongst them. Indeed, no women at all adorned the wall of fame. She racked her brain for a memory of anyone mentioning his wife with no success. One of the upstairs rooms was laid out as a ladies' sitting room, but it had an air of disuse. No flowers, no traces of scent, no cards or needlework or books left out.

"An impressive collection of photographs, Mr Chelmsford," Grace said.

"I expect we will add to the photographic record soon. My father and I attended a reception on Monday night, given by the Mayor, Mr Roberts, for several important dignitaries who are visiting the New Zealand and South Seas Exhibition."

"Monday night?" Charlie said. "How splendid. Where was the reception held, Mr Chelmsford?"

"The Grand Hotel. I cannot recall when I last saw so many influential people in one place. A marvellous night. The speeches and dancing went on so long, it was well after midnight when we arrived home. It is a great shame I did not meet you until the following day, Miss Penrose, for I went unaccompanied."

Grace and Charlie exchanged a glance. Unlikely as the Chelmsford men were as suspects, at least now they could exclude two people from the list of possible killers, assuming they really were at this reception. Not something Edmund would lie about, with dozens of witnesses.

Edmund Chelmsford gestured for Charlie to take a seat at the far side of a low table, where a maid had left a tray of tea and a tiered cake stand set out with miniature cucumber sandwiches and petit fours. Grace, naturally, was guided to a two-person sofa with a crested back and curved arms. Edmund sat beside her, angling his body to give her his full attention.

She raised her eyebrows at Charlie, who appeared to be untroubled at playing the silent gooseberry to this overly cozy arrangement. Before she could lift the silver teapot, the door opened and Sterling Chelmsford strode in, presenting the very picture of a busy man honouring them with a moment of his precious time.

"Welcome to my home, Miss Penrose. What a great shame your charming great-aunt could not come too."

"She sends her apologies, Mr Chelmsford. I am sure she will regret not having taken the opportunity to visit your lovely home."

Sterling Chelmsford nodded, but his mind was clearly focussed elsewhere.

"Would you care to join us for tea? I was about to pour, unless your wife will be joining us too."

"My wife is abroad at present, Miss Penrose, recovering from illness on the Continent. The cold winters of Dunedin do not sit well with her delicate constitution." Chelmsford took the large armchair facing the fireplace, as befitted the head of the house, and cast a glance in Charlie's direction.

Grace dismissed her uncharitable thought that Mrs Chelmsford must be experiencing markedly chillier weather in Europe, it being summer here and winter there. "May I introduce a family friend, Mr Charles Pyke."

Charlie rose from his chair and shook hands with his host. "You have a fine residence, Mr Chelmsford. Your photographic gallery is most impressive. To have one's image captured alongside Henry Atkinson, John Ballance and the Earl of Onslow, amongst others of note, must surely be a rare achievement."

Sterling Chelmsford gave a satisfied nod at the compliment. "I have been fortunate enough to gain acquaintances on both sides of the House, Mr Pyke. My natural sympathies, as you might imagine, are more aligned to the Premier than with the liberal views of Mr Ballance. Although I dare say Mr Ballance was grateful for my support of the Royal Commission investigating labour conditions."

"I'm sure both sides of the House would value the opinions of a man of your considerable experience, sir."

Charlie accepted a fine porcelain cup from Grace with a slight lift of one eyebrow. He held the delicate china with the tips of his fingers, his littlest finger elevated in a parody of fine manners. Grace dragged her gaze away to stop herself from laughing. If Charlie lost his job as a copper, he might well find a new career on the stage.

"Kind of you to say so, Mr Pyke," Sterling said. "It is no great secret that I have been asked to stand for parliament myself. Much as I respect the traditions of the Old Country, I believe that here in New Zealand we have an opportunity to create a utopian paradise for workers and owners alike."

"A bold vision, sir," Charlie replied. "How would you balance the desire of workers for better conditions against the need for owners to achieve the greatest profit?"

Edmund started to speak, but his father overrode him. "An excellent question, young man. Unlike most people, I do not see the two as mutually exclusive. Are you familiar with the endeavours of Mr Edward Akroyd and Sir Titus Salt?"

"I must admit that I am not, Mr Chelmsford," Charlie drawled.

Sterling Chelmsford made himself comfortable in his chair, as one does when beginning a favourite story. "Both men of vision in the textile industry. They are building model villages around their mills and factories, out in the countryside, where the air is clean and the temptations of vice are absent. The workers are provided with high-quality housing, communal amenities for education, moral instruction and recreation, and excellent working conditions, far from the city slums. Thus, the employer gains a healthy, productive, morally pure workforce and all parties are winners."

His son broke in, to the obvious annoyance of his father. "We have established the first of its kind in this colony. A woollen mill and village on the plains around Mosgiel, surrounded by the farmland where we will raise sheep–"

The father took over again. "Are you familiar with the concepts of Mr Charles Darwin?"

"*On The Origin Of Species–*" said Charlie.

"*By Means of Natural Selection,*" added Grace.

Sterling Chelmsford gave them another satisfied nod. "I commend you both for your knowledge of the latest science. By careful scientific breeding, I intend to create a breed of sheep with the highest quality wool. Combine that with the very best of technology at the mill and exceptional finishing, and I can proudly state that the final product will be of unprecedented quality."

"And the workers?" Charlie asked. "Will you create a superior breed of them as well?"

"A splendid idea, Mr Pyke. Would that I could." The father gave a light-hearted chuckle, but his eyes did not join in the mirth. "Jesting aside, I have put a great deal of thought into creating the safest and most agreeable conditions possible for the workers. Natural light and ventilation, the latest safety features designed right here in Dunedin, with strict rules governing working and living arrangements. Every worker in this city is clamouring to join my workforce."

"I can only repeat Mr Pyke's observation. A bold vision indeed, sir. Ross and Glendinning must be quaking in their boots." Grace set her cup on the tray and dusted confectioner's sugar from her lips with a monogrammed linen napkin. "One day, I should love to visit the mill. Today, your son has been kind enough to offer us a tantalising preview at your finishing factory in town."

The father glowed at her compliment, which he acknowledged with a royal wave. "Yes indeed, Miss Penrose. I look forward to showing you around. It is a rare pleasure to find a charming young lady with a curious mind and an interest in science and industry. The clothing factory is a modest accomplishment next to my new woollen mill, but I know you will be impressed, nevertheless."

Sterling Chelmsford put his cup and unused plate down and rose from his chair. He offered Grace his arm, cutting off his son. Anger flashed across Edmund's face, before he rose too and placed a firm hand on his father's arm.

"Father, I'm sure you must be extremely busy. Perhaps I might escort Miss Penrose on the tour?"

His father glanced down at the hand with surprise, then the light dawned and he gave his son a playful nudge on the arm. "Yes, yes, by all means, Edmund. Far be it from me to interrupt your time in the company of the lovely Miss Penrose."

Edmund hurried Grace towards the door, leaving Charlie to thank and farewell their host.

The coachman had turned the barouche around and was waiting outside. After Edmund helped Grace into the seat, he turned to Charlie with a meaningful look. "I expect you must have business to attend to, Mr Pyke."

"On the contrary, I am very much looking forward to viewing your father's factory, Mr Chelmsford, after hearing him speak so eloquently."

"*Our* factory," mumbled Chelmsford, as he climbed up to the seat beside Grace, barely waiting for Charlie to follow before telling the coachman to proceed. Charlie settled into the rear-facing seat, raising one eyebrow fractionally at Grace, as the other man pretended he was not there.

Edmund Chelmsford took Grace's arm as they began the steep downward journey into the heart of the commercial centre of Dunedin.

Grace struggled to keep a straight face. Small talk seemed appropriate to fill the silence. "You must miss your mother, Mr Chelmsford. Has she been gone long?"

"What a sensitive soul you are, Miss Penrose. You are quite right. I miss her terribly, even though she has been gone more than a dozen years."

Good heavens, how could a mother be away from her son for half his life? "She must find the weather on the Continent very much to her taste, if she can bear to be away for so long."

Incomprehension clouded his face for a moment, followed in quick succession by understanding and bitterness. "My mother has passed on to a better place, I'm sorry to say. My father remarried within a year of her death. It is my step-mother who is abroad."

Grace wished she had stayed silent. "My condolences. I apologise for my thoughtlessness. May I be so personal as to inquire whether you have brothers or sisters?"

"None who lived."

Grace filled the oppressive void that followed Edmund's terse statement with polite chatter about the merits of Chelmsford House. She felt like cutting her tongue out for asking such an insensitive question. Two wives and only one child. She had no problem imagining what a terrible disappointment that must be for a man like Sterling Chelmsford. It was a wonder he was not more considerate to his only heir.

168

Fortunately, the finishing factory was not far away.

Grace let out a low gasp as they entered the work area. "My goodness, Mr Chelmsford, there is so much natural light and ventilation, one can scarcely smell the smoke from the engines."

Long rows of women bent over long rows of sewing and knitting machines. The machines were well spaced and operated with less of a deafening clatter than most factories. Compared to Kendall's factory, this was indeed a paradise of a workplace. "Your father is a man of vision, Mr Chelmsford."

"Indeed, he is, Miss Penrose. A paragon of virtue shining so bright, all else is blinded."

Grace watched Edmund's face carefully, noticing an initial flick of sourness, quickly replaced by a wry grin.

"Father plans to build a great empire, controlling every aspect of production from the sheep's back to the gentleman's back. The woollen mill, being in the countryside, will allow plenty of space for expansion, as well as a ready supply of our own wool. The mill itself will scour, card and weave the wool to produce the best quality fabrics, from which we create clothing of distinction in this factory." He guided her to a display of finished articles, taking care to ensure she kept her skirt away from the machines.

Grace ran her hand over the fine worsted. "Beautiful fabric and marvellously precise seams. You can be rightly proud of the quality you produce here. I declare myself most impressed. May I ask your role in the enterprise, Mr Chelmsford?"

Again, she noticed a slight hesitation, followed by a hearty response.

"I am his right-hand man, Miss Penrose. Father intends to put me in charge of the mill, once it is running to his satisfaction. I also oversee the breeding programme for the sheep, given my experience in horse breeding."

"A considerable responsibility for one so young."

"I will turn twenty-five next year, Miss Penrose. More than old enough to make my way in the world."

169

"Tell me, Mr Chelmsford," Charlie asked, "do you share your father's passion for the manufacturing industry?"

Chelmsford's mouth turned down. "My own preference would perhaps lean more towards horse breeding and racing. However, as the only son and heir, I know I must take my place at his side."

"I do hope you will be able to achieve both," Grace said. "My family are great believers in allowing everyone – son or daughter – to follow their passions. I have five brothers and not one of them expressed the desire to become a doctor, like my father and grandfather."

Edmund Chelmsford looked at her as if she had admitted that the Queen had decided to abdicate to become a brothel madam. "Was your father not bitterly disappointed?"

"Perhaps a little disappointed at first, but each of my brothers has found a calling and happiness, so my father is very content."

Charlie came up beside her, slipping his arm through hers. "Miss Penrose is too modest. Her father is delighted that he has a daughter with the enthusiasm and aptitude for medicine. As are all her friends and family."

Chelmsford shot him a sullen look. "Miss Penrose is a woman of rare insight and sympathy. Any father would be proud."

Edmund turned at the footsteps behind him. "Ah, here comes McIntyre, my foreman. I will get him to show you the workings of the factory, Mr Pyke, while I show Miss Penrose the variety of finished garments we produce."

An Unsuitable Man

Charlie felt like a sapling beside this tree trunk of a man.

Mr McIntyre's hooded eyes and clenched jaw stood out from behind the cover of a bushy red beard. "I dinnae wish to interrupt ye, sir, but I need to know when the engineer be coming in. Supposed to be here this morning."

Chelmsford let out an annoyed grunt. "How am I to know, McIntyre? I am not the man's keeper."

"I'm sorry, sir, but it be urgent." McIntyre waited a fraction of a second before turning away. "Och, ne'er mind, I will send a messenger to yer father."

A deep flush rose up Edmund Chelmsford's neck and face. "McIntyre, I would like you to show Mr Pyke the workings of the factory. Just a quick tour mind, we've all got important work to do."

"Come with me, sir." McIntyre jerked his head in the direction of the engine room, muttering "Sassenach bampot" under his breath as he stomped away.

With a start, he realised Charlie had followed him and was close enough to overhear. "Mr Pyke, is it? Ye'll be a friend o' Mr Chelmsford?"

"Far from it," Charlie replied. "I am here for only two reasons. To find out more about the factory and to protect the honour of Miss Penrose, who is a dear friend. With the latter being the priority."

McIntyre let out a snort of laughter and slapped Charlie on the back. "Cannae blame you laddie. She's far too fine a lass for that wastrel. Now, what it is you'd like to know?"

"For a start, I'd like to know the name of the engineer you are waiting for."

"We have our own engineer in the factory, but we also use a local lad, Mr Jack Finlay, for specialist design work."

"In that case, I am sorry to be the bearer of bad news. Mr Finlay died on Monday night."

"Died? Well, that's a dreadful shame. A good man, unlike some. A real loss. Must have been an accident, with Finlay such a young man."

"We believe it to be a suspicious death, Mr McIntyre. I must admit that I have not been completely frank with Mr Chelmsford. I am with the police." He showed the foreman his badge. "Can you tell me when you last saw Jack Finlay?"

The big Scotsman chewed on a stray strand of beard. "Cannae rightly say. More than a week, probably closer to two weeks. Finlay only did the odd bit of work here. He was mostly involved with fitting out the new woollen mill near Mosgiel, although that work is now complete."

"He specialised in new designs for safe and efficient machinery, I understand."

"Aye, a clever laddie. Mr Sterling Chelmsford might know more, him being in charge of the business and working closely with Finlay."

"And the younger Chelmsford?"

McIntyre blew a huff of air out of his nostrils. "Wanders around giving orders when he can be bothered." His gaze sharpened on Charlie. "Ye'll not be entering that in yer notes, I hope."

"Not a word. But I thank you for your honesty." Charlie handed him one of DI Stewart's cards. "If you recall anything else that might be relevant to Finlay's death, I'd be grateful to hear it."

"Aye, I'll do that." He flapped an enormous, red-knuckled hand in the direction they had come. "Reckon you might want to return to the lady, sir."

Charlie followed the line of his gaze to where Chelmsford was draping samples of ladies' hosiery over Grace's outstretched arm. His lips were so close to Grace's ear that Cupid would have been hard pressed to shoot an arrow through the gap.

172

Charlie hastened back to Grace's side. "Miss Penrose, the day is advancing rapidly. I'm afraid we will have to leave."

Chelmsford gave him the evil eye, before turning a simpering look on his quarry. "I was about to ask Miss Penrose to dine with me."

"My apologies, but I have another engagement." Grace neatly folded a pair of fine wool stockings and laid them on the pile. "Thank you for reminding me, Mr Pyke. And thank you, Mr Chelmsford, for a fascinating morning."

As they strolled towards the exit, Grace said, "Have you considered inviting the commissioners of the Sweating Commission to visit, Mr Chelmsford, so they may see an example of what is possible and desirable in a factory?"

"An excellent idea, Miss Penrose. I see you have a good head on those dainty shoulders. I shall look forward to dining with you on another occasion." Edmund dipped his head to kiss her hand. "Soon, I hope."

"How kind, Mr Chelmsford. Although, I'm afraid I have a great many calls on my time at present."

Charlie took Grace's arm and all but shoved her out the door.

"What's got into you, Charlie?" Grace asked as they strolled across town. "Has your impersonation of a daft aristocrat become too much of a strain? Or have you found out something important?"

He refrained from telling her that he'd had more than enough of Chelmsford's ill-disguised superiority, both father and son. "McIntyre said Finlay worked closely with Sterling Chelmsford, mostly at the new woollen mill. And you?"

"I managed to have a quick word with a couple of the working women, while Chelmsford went in search of his finest stockings. The women were both thrilled to be working at the factory. So much so, they saw no need to join the Tailoresses' Union, like most of the other women here. The pay is no better than the union rate, but at least they can work without choking on coal smoke."

"And how did you find the obsequious Edmund Chelmsford? McIntyre didn't think much of him. He indicated that the younger Chelmsford had little to do with the real work of the business."

Grace gave him a sharp look. "I can see you don't like Edmund, Charlie. But I have to say, I feel sorry for him."

That was the last thing he expected to hear. "Why in the Realm of Hades would you feel sorry for him? Edmund Chelmsford is wealthy, handsome, well-connected, and being handed a thriving business on a plate, as sole heir, if he can be bothered to take it."

"He also appears to be under a great deal of pressure doing a job he is unsuited for, working for a controlling father with high expectations, who is sparing in his praise and quick with a disparaging word. And all with no mother to lavish him with the attention he so desperately craves."

Charlie could see from her furrowed brow she was genuinely concerned. "Forgive me, Grace, perhaps you are right. Your kindness does you credit, as ever."

"Did you notice how the father dominated the conversation, as if his son wasn't even in the room, and talked of *my* business, while the son referred to *our* business?"

"It was hard to miss." Charlie couldn't resist adding, "Although, I wonder, if the son worked a little harder, perhaps he would be praised more often."

"Mr Chelmsford's father is a hard man to read. On the surface, he appears to be a visionary and philanthropist. Yet, I got the feeling that the workers whose lives he seeks to improve are looked on as no more than a cog in the process of making him more money. A cog that needs to be well-oiled and looked after for efficiency, rather than for a greater good."

"Like his sheep. Fed and tended for the sole purpose of being fleeced to add value to the business."

"Indeed. Sterling Chelmsford is a rather unnerving man." Grace was walking at a fast pace, with her head down, obviously deep in thought.

Charlie held her back from crossing the road as a horse and cart clattered past. "I'm not sure I would like to be stuck in the middle of nowhere, with every aspect of my work and private life governed by his rules and morality." He realised he had slipped back into the role of a suspicious copper. He nudged her arm and added, "But he does show excellent taste, in approving of you as a match for his willow-spined son."

"Do stop teasing me, Charlie. The notion is ridiculous. Edmund Chelmsford was forced into the acquaintance, yet he has been more than civil to me, with none of the condescension of his father. But there is no earthly way his father would see a woman of such inferior status as me as a match for his only son. Besides, Edmund Chelmsford and I are as different as water and fire, by every possible measure."

"Grace, I assure you I am deadly serious." The words came out more sharply than Charlie intended, so he softened his tone. "The fact that you are so completely different is exactly the point of attraction. Sterling Chelmsford needs a daughter-in-law of determination and intelligence, since he finds those characteristics so lacking in his son. Certainly, the son approves his choice."

"I hope you are wrong." Grace sighed. "I suppose one might equally say that Edmund would act as a calming influence on my impetuous nature, but that still doesn't mean that I wish to be anything more than acquaintances. What can I do? I promised Anne that I would be nice to him until Chelmsford's much-needed donation to Lavender House is in the bank."

"With all due respect to Mrs Macmillan, you ought not to marry for donations alone."

Grace stopped abruptly, causing the man behind them to swerve, almost hitting her with the sack of flour on his shoulder. "I'd sooner become a nun than marry Edmund Chelmsford. Indeed, I have no intention of marrying at all until I have my medical degree, and certainly not for money."

"Forgive me, Grace, I am being boorish. No doubt you will meet many men of intelligence, charm and wealth at medical school, who would leap at the chance to claim your fiery heart when you are good and ready to give it."

Grace laughed. "Another doctor? Heaven forbid. I need a court jester to prod me away from serious matters and bring joy to the match. Or a dancer, so I might know joy without having to think at all."

"Now it is you who is teasing me." Charlie lapsed into silence, trying to clear the Chelmsford men from his mind so he could concentrate on his job. It might have been easier without the warmth of Grace's arm threaded through his own.

"Penny for your thoughts, Mr Charles Pyke, Esquire?"

"I was … I was thinking I ought to send a telegram to Mosgiel to find out if the missing girls are at Chelmsford's new factory. The coincidence of him taking on new workers and the girls disappearing is hard to overlook. And I, for one, would welcome a simple solution to at least one of our mysteries."

"An excellent idea, Detective Constable Pyke. I admit to feeling considerable disquiet at their disappearance, no matter that their mothers are happy about it." Grace removed her arm from his. "Thank you for escorting me and defending my honour, not to mention providing me with the exceptional amusement of your impression of a daft aristocrat."

He looked up to find they were outside Wains Hotel, with the carved figures of Neptune and his mermaids grinning down at his distraction from the imposing black and white stone façade.

"It was an interesting outing. I do hope you will excuse me for being overbearing at times, Grace. Suspicion and distrust come with the job, I'm afraid. I must learn to conceal it as well as Detective Inspector Stewart does."

"You are never overbearing, Charlie. As to your ability to conceal, I suspect you have already surpassed Stewart. You slip into the best role for any situation like a master of the masquerade."

"I'm not sure what you mean, Grace. It was you and Anne who pressed me to don the clothes of a gentleman."

"But it was you who made the Chelmsfords and Kendall believe they were in the company of a man born to privilege, not merely an imposter in a suit of clothes. Don't think I haven't noticed this uncanny ability before. With Duncan, you might have been the twin of Waddell, gentling a confession from a tormented man. I don't care to know how you convinced Fanny Snoot to tell you what she saw in the alley, given the intense distrust between prostitutes and the police, but it cannot be the same means by which you made Lynch believe the only threat you posed was naivety."

Charlie couldn't quite decide whether it was the best compliment he had ever had or an accusation of duplicity. He searched her expression for signs of teasing, but saw nothing but sincerity. "If what you say is true, it was unconsciously done. I hope you don't think I have deceived you, Grace. Or your great-aunt. You are one of the few people with whom I feel able to be truly myself."

Her hand reached out to clasp his arm with a firmness that left warm, finger-shaped dents. "I did not mean to suggest that there was any deception involved, Charlie. On the contrary, you have an instinct for understanding the nature of a person and thus how best to engage with them. I truly hope you may continue as a detective. It is what you were born for."

Her hand dropped away, but he could still feel the pressure of her touch. "Grace, when this investigation is over, I hope we might continue our friendship, without compromising your place in society."

"Of course! I cannot imagine how dull life would be without you, Charlie, whereas I care less for so-called proper society than for a boil in want of lancing."

Charlie spluttered with laughter. "I dare you to say that to Mr Edmund Chelmsford."

"There now. It is good to see you smiling again. You ought to do it more often. Promise me you will set aside the serious business of chasing criminals and enjoy yourself on the arm of a pretty girl at this evening's entertainments."

Charlie racked his brain to figure out what she was talking about.

"Charlie, please tell me you haven't forgotten that it is Thursday." Grace paused, waiting for him to recall whatever it was he was supposed to be doing. "You promised to take your young lass to the New Zealand and South Seas Exhibition this evening. I believe you were to pick her up at seven o'clock. For goodness' sake, don't let her down again or she may never forgive you."

Her sweet laugh followed him up to the door of the hotel, as he wondered if forgetfulness could possibly set in at so young an age.

"Molly and I plan to come to the Exhibition too," she called after him, "but I promise not to distract you from the lovely Miss Fraser." Grace walked away with hips swinging, half-turning at the corner to give a pert little wave over her shoulder, in perfect mimicry of the shopgirl.

All the fun of the fair

With the prospect of novel entertainments to look forward to, against the backdrop of a perfect summer evening, Grace gave herself over to frivolity. She abandoned her usual white and grey in favour of an emerald green silk shirtwaist with puffed sleeves and a dark skirt with an embroidered hem.

In a fit of joie de vivre, she added a flower-sprigged straw hat, which hadn't seen the light of day since the church's spring fete. As she grinned at her reflection in the looking glass, she concluded that Charlie Pyke wasn't the only one who needed to work less and enjoy life more.

Anne had engaged a cabriolet to take them to the Exhibition, picking up Molly Sugden along the way. Her mother came out of the house to see her off, adjusting Molly's straw hat and brushing a loose thread off her Sunday-best white muslin dress with motherly pride.

The city streets were awash with people, all heading down to the Jervois Street entrance for the evening opening of the New Zealand and South Seas Exhibition. The chatter of the crowd intensified as the cupola-topped turrets of the entrance came into view. An enormous dome rose over the entrance, its Moorish design magnificently out of kilter with the workaday brick buildings around it. Octagonal towers guarded each corner of the vast construction, adding to the impression that they were being drawn into the gates of a wonderland from the pages of *Arabian Nights*.

Molly peered out the window, her body quivering with excitement. "Oh my, that dome must be as tall as ten houses, don't you think? Have you ever seen so many people in one place? My friend Alice has visited three times already and still hasn't had her fill of it."

They stepped down from the carriage into a flood of eager visitors. Anne had the presence of mind to grab their arms as the crowd swept them past the decorative portico and through the turnstiles into the main hall, for the price of a shilling apiece. Inside, the dome rose high over a statue of Queen Victoria. Glorious friezes led to each of the main avenues. A multitude of lights and mirrors added to the air of enchantment, eliciting oohs and ahhs from silk-clad ladies and freshly scrubbed coal boys alike.

Anne steered them to a quieter eddy by the wall. "Which way first, girls?"

"Anywhere!" Grace replied, as Molly gasped, "Everywhere!"

They chose the path least travelled. Or, more precisely, the way with fractionally less of a crush than the rest.

For the next hour, they wandered amongst a fantastical juxtaposition of nature, science and art. A fernery and rock-pool behind a large plate-glass window, an aviary, art galleries and a concert hall, an oriental tearoom, and endless courts filled with the pride of New Zealand industry, as well as displays from Australia and around the world. Paintings, porcelain, woollens and linens, homewares, agricultural implements, transportation, mining – every conceivable variety of human endeavour was on display.

When they passed the tearoom for the second time, Anne declared herself in need of rest and refreshment. Grace and Molly dutifully accompanied her, but were delighted to find a cabal of Anne's elderly friends already resident, which meant that the two young women could continue their exploration.

Without hesitation, they both turned towards the outside area, which was rumoured to be as wondrous as the interior. Gardens, a band rotunda with continuous entertainment, and, at the far southern end, delighted and terrified shrieks coming from an amusement area.

Molly stopped to crane her neck as a line of open cars rattled up and down the switchback railway, around a scale model of the Eiffel Tower. "Dare we try it, do you think, Grace?"

Grace, who was not fond of heights, watched the precarious contraption with trepidation, but she couldn't deny the thrill to her friend. "I will, if you will". Another pass of screaming daredevils drowned out her words. "Perhaps we might start with the merry-go-round before we risk our necks on the rails?"

One good turn on the merry-go-round led to another. The joy of being whirled around in a little suspended boat, surrounded by barrel-organ music and lights, had both women in fits of giggles. As an antidote to the events of the past few days, it was unbeatable.

As they supported each other after the second ride, still hopelessly dizzy and weak from laughing, they stumbled into Charlie and his girl. Grace made the introductions, noting that Miss Fraser was clutching Charlie's arm like a life preserver.

"We're just about to go on the switchback railway," Molly said. "Would you two like to come with us?"

"If you're game, then I am too," Charlie replied.

By the time they reached the head of the queue, Miss Fraser was already looking green from watching the cars plunge over the last dip in the rail. "Can't we go on the merry-go-around instead, Charlie?"

Charlie glanced longingly at the switchback. "As you wish, Miss Fraser. Might we stay to watch the intrepid Miss Sugden and Miss Penrose take their lives in their hands?"

"I would be happy to stay with Miss Fraser, while you go," Grace offered. "It looks no safer than Kendall's loom, and I really don't care for the thought of my vertebral column being wrenched to kingdom come."

Charlie needed little encouragement. In a trice, he had helped Molly into a seat. Then they were off, racing up and down the undulations, accompanied by the screech of metal and the shrieks of the riders.

Grace was so intent on watching, she didn't see the man talking to Miss Fraser until the ride was almost over. When Grace caught his eye, he wandered away again. A rush of wind as cars flew past drew her attention back to the railway. The cars whizzed up the final hump, teetered at the top, then plunged down, leaving behind a trail of screams.

Charlie had to lift Molly from her seat, which she was clasping with white knuckles. After a little deep breathing, Molly returned to her normal good cheer, gushing with excitement as she described every rattle and lurch of the ride to Grace, who felt queasy merely hearing about it.

"You have the heart of a lion, Molly. What shall we do now?"

"I've had more than enough thrills for the moment. Might we head inside and look at more of the exhibits?"

Grace turned to invite Charlie and his girl to come with them, but they had disappeared. She linked arms with Molly and they set off for the section of the exhibition they had not yet seen.

They hadn't gone far when Molly spotted a group of friends. Grace wandered over to a nearby exhibit, leaving them to chat. She was admiring a display of exquisite embroidery when she heard a familiar voice call her name. Edmund Chelmsford.

"Mr Chelmsford, good evening." She strolled over to the Chelmsford Textiles exhibit, nodding to Mr McIntyre. "What a splendid array of goods you have on display."

"Miss Penrose, a delight to see you again. I expect every soul in Dunedin is proud of this magnificent exhibition. Wares from near and far, hundreds of thousands of visitors. I couldn't be happier that we have pride of place in this pavilion."

"My friend and I are certainly having a marvellous time."

Edmund stepped to her side and bent his head to her ear. "May I ask the name of the young woman who is accompanying you?"

Grace leaned away with him to touch a wonderfully soft scarf of the finest imaginable wool. "Miss Molly Sugden."

His intake of breath would have been audible across the room. "Not the union activist? That girl is a disgraceful troublemaker." His hand reached out to grip her arm. "My dear, I admire your charitable works, but I must caution you to be more circumspect about your social companions."

Grace shrugged his hand off as she fixed him with a steely glare. "I will certainly be very careful to whom I talk in the future." Perhaps the note of sarcasm was a little overdone, but honestly, the gall of him, questioning her choice of friends.

"Excellent. I knew I could rely on your discretion. Now that we are courting, my dear, it might be best if you ventured out into society only in my company."

She gaped at Edmund, entirely at a loss for words. When the appropriate words finally came to mind, she bit them back, in the interests of not causing a scene. Sterling Chelmsford's donation to Lavender House had better be prompt and exceedingly generous.

"I'm afraid I must go, my dearest, as duty calls," he went on, apparently unaware of her inner turmoil. "The Mayor is about to show several very important dignitaries around the exhibits and they have expressed an interest in the advanced techniques we pride ourselves on at Chelmsford Textiles."

He bowed and disappeared into the crowd around the Chelmsford stand, leaving her unsure whether to scream, laugh or cry. After only two meetings, neither of a social nature, how could he think they were courting? Had she been too forward with him, allowing herself to be flattered by his attentions? Grace felt woefully prepared to deal with his attentions.

She turned to find Charlie watching on with interest. "Why didn't you rescue me, you rat. A moment longer in his company and you might have had another murder on your hands."

"I was so shocked to see you speechless, I couldn't move." His grin disappeared. "It looked as if you and Edmund Chelmsford were sharing serious words."

"I have to concede that you were right and I was wrong regarding his intentions. I am going to have to send a carefully worded letter of rejection tomorrow and risk the ire of my great-aunt if his father stops funding her charity. Men, honestly – is it really so hard to tell when a woman is being polite and when she loves you?"

"The workings of the female heart are a complete and utter mystery to all men, I assure you, Miss Penrose. Come now, wipe that fierce look off your lovely face and come outside for a dance. Or we could go to the concert hall, if choral and orchestral music are more to your taste."

"But what about your pretty companion, Miss Fraser?"

"Gone." Charlie huffed. "Apparently, another constable saw her with me and took delight in telling her of my dismissal from the police force, before whisking her away right under my nose. It would seem that my feeble charms are not enough to overcome a deficit of stable income."

"I'm sorry. It would appear that I am not the only woman who has been an exceedingly poor judge of character. Cheer up, Charlie, if Miss Fraser is so easily fooled by another man, then she is not worthy of you."

"She would be a fool to choose any policeman," Charlie replied. "Long, irregular hours and miserly pay is not something that most young women would tolerate long."

"Come along then, let's forget the foibles of others and dance our cares away. Just give me a moment to see if Molly and her friends wish to join us." Grace dashed through the crowd to find her friend.

Molly had been keeping an eye on her, too. "That rather splendid young constable cannot keep his eyes off you, Grace. And no wonder, with you blushing so prettily."

"What rot, Molly. He is just being kind after I made a fool of myself. Would you and your friends like to come dancing with us?"

"I'll leave you in Constable Pyke's tender care a while longer, if that is acceptable to you. Let's meet in the tearoom in an hour."

Outside, the long summer evening was fading into night, rendered magical by twinkling lights. The brass bands had relinquished their hold on the small band rotunda, complete with a thatched roof, and a Scottish dancing band had taken their place. The crowd, buoyed by the excitement of the evening, had taken over the courtyard and gardens for an impromptu ceilidh.

Dozens of couples twirled in time to the frenetic sawing of bows over fiddle-strings, egged on by a clapping, stomping audience. Grace was scooped up by a man she didn't know from Adam. Her annoyance at Edmund Chelmsford vanished, as she was swung with joyful abandon from one partner to the next, Stripping the Willow.

Charlie managed to nab her for the next dance, a Dashing White Sergeant. They reeled, toe-stepped, and swung each other to an increasingly frenetic tempo, which outstripped even the merry-go-round for inducing dizziness. The fiddlers sweated their way to a soaring end, receiving a wild burst of applause and whoops from the dancers. The band took a bow and left the stage for a well-earner breather, while a light orchestra took over the entertainment.

As the strains of a waltz began, Charlie murmured, "May I?" and took her hand.

Grace set one hand lightly on his shoulder, as his other hand barely grazed the base of her scapula. Rather to her surprise, Charlie was an accomplished dancer, twirling and pivoting her expertly through the dense throng of couples and around the smaller of the two Eiffel Tower replicas. Her cares flew away as she lost herself in the music and the novel feeling of being completely in tune with a dance partner.

A fumbling couple of novice dancers almost knocked her off her feet at one point, but Charlie simply gathered her closer, until her head was resting in the soft dip under his clavicle, so close she could feel his breath ruffling her hair. His arm tightened around her and they danced on, feet flying, pulses racing.

When Charlie glided to a halt, she stayed within the warmth of his arms, wondering why he had stopped dancing. Suddenly, she realised the music had ended and several couples were looking at them with amusement.

A Missing Friend

Grace stepped back out of his arms, feeling like a fool. "Where did you learn to dance like that, Charlie?"

"My mother was of the opinion that every young man should be taught social graces, whether they wanted them or not." Charlie smiled down at her with his golden cat-eyes glowing. "But, in truth, I have never danced quite like *that* before."

"No, nor have I. Might we take a break while my pulse returns to normal?"

He linked her arm with his. "Would you like a refreshment? I have a piece of good news to share. Mostly good news might be more accurate."

They found an empty bench seat in the depths of the garden, away from the crush of the crowd, and sipped lemonade from glasses etched with the name of the Exhibition. The surreal atmosphere of the evening was palpable even in this quiet spot, heightening her acute awareness of his presence beside her.

She and Edmund might be fire and water, but with Charlie it was more like fire and kerosene. Powerful when harnessed, explosive when unleashed. Relishing the heat was all very well, but she didn't need reminding what happens to those who play with fire.

Grace eased along the bench, leaving a more respectable gap between them. "You have good news?"

"I have confirmation that the missing workers are all at the new Chelmsford factory near Mosgiel. The local constable added a note that he was impressed at the excellent conditions in the factory. His only concern was that they are rather trapped out there, unable to travel to see their families on account of the distance and isolation of the farm and mill. He also mentioned that some of the girls complained that the cost of their meals and lodgings was taken out of their wages, leaving them with little to spare."

"Well, that's one mystery solved," Grace said. "Thank heavens nothing untoward has happened to them, although it doesn't sound like the paradise of Chelmsford's vision."

"Enough about work. We promised ourselves a night of frivolity. What would you like to do now, Grace? Go up the Eiffel Tower? A hundred and thirty feet tall and a splendid view from the top, so they say."

In theory, she was happy to go anywhere with Charlie, but in practice, the thought of being wound up inside a wooden tower by a steam-powered motor to such a height was rather terrifying. Not wanting to be seen as a coward, she allowed herself to be guided into the eager crowd queuing by the tower.

Before she could change her mind, they were ascending with fourteen others inside an elevator cabin. They rode to the top, where they stepped out onto a deck lit by electricity and topped by a searchlight.

The startling brightness of the lights was like nothing Grace had experienced before. "Imagine if an entire city could be lit by electricity. One might read all night without straining the eyes. Or see an end to the filthy coal smoke that clings to the nostrils wherever one goes."

"Amazing, isn't it?" Charlie guided her straight to the edge of the platform. "What a view!" He must have noticed her reluctance, as his arm tightened on hers, clamping it to his side. "I won't let you fall, Grace."

Suddenly, his body stiffened. "Look, there's Nolan."

By the time the elevator reached the ground, Constable Nolan had disappeared into the dense crowd. They searched for a while, but saw no further sign of him.

Charlie stopped beside a row of sideshows and stalls. "We're wasting time looking for Nolan in this crowd. Let's allow ourselves this one night of amusement, without a care in the world. Toffee, milady?"

"Too sweet for me. I don't wish to ruin my reputation as a sour old sawbones. Would you mind if we went to the tearoom? I don't want Molly and Anne to think I have abandoned them entirely."

The tearooms were packed, with no sign of Molly, but Anne spotted them and waved them over. "Grace, what excellent timing. Mrs Boyle has offered me a lift home. You may come with us or stay a little longer, if Charlie will see you safely home."

"It would be my pleasure, Mrs Macmillan," Charlie replied. "May I ask if you have seen Molly?"

"Not since Grace and Molly left me in the tearooms. Is everything all right?"

"No cause for alarm, Mrs Macmillan. May I see you ladies to your carriage?"

"What a polite young man," Mrs Boyle replied. "I thank you, but Mr Boyle will escort us. I'm sure you young folk have better things to do."

"What now?" Charlie asked as he held the door open for Grace.

"I expect Molly is having such a grand time that she has lost track of the hour. Shall we make a quick circuit of the pavilions to see if we can spot her?"

Finding a single person amongst the throng was close to impossible. After twenty minutes of pushing through jostling bodies, Grace pulled Charlie aside. "Let's check the tearoom again. After that, I'm afraid we'll have to go back to the Chelmsford Textiles stand, as that is the last place I saw Molly. Can I count on you to rescue me if Edmund Chelmsford sees me?"

"Pistols at dawn if he dares lay a hand on you, I promise."

"Very gallant, assuming you know how to shoot a pistol."

"I can knock a tin can off a fence post at fifty feet. I have never shot at a man before, but the larger the target, the easier it ought to be."

"Let's just stick to words, not bullets, shall we?"

Her concerns were for naught, as neither of the Chelmsford men were there. The stand was manned by Mr McIntyre – a hard man to miss, given his six-foot stature and bushy red beard. Grace had no trouble imagining him clad in tartan, bellowing on a bagpipe or wielding a pike on the battlefield at Culloden.

"Mr McIntyre, have you seen a girl in a white muslin dress?" Charlie asked.

He waved a hand at the milling crowd. "Several thousand wee lassies in white dresses. Take yer pick."

"She was standing right here about an hour ago with Miss Penrose."

"Ah, Molly Sugden, was it? From the union? Had a fit of the vapours. No doubt the excitement of the Exhibition was too much for her, though I'd have taken her for a stouter lass than that."

"What happened?" Grace heard the panic in her own voice and forced herself to calm down. "Is she recovered?"

"Miss Sugden asked me if I'd seen Mr Finlay lately. I said I hadn't seen the poor man and wasn't it a tragedy. After I saw ye this morning, I looked in the newspaper and there it was. A terrible thing being brutally bashed by yer own brother. Poor lass let out a howl that would've wakened William Wallace himself. Then she fainted. She doesn't strike me as the delicate sort, so perhaps she knew him. I ought to have taken more care with my words."

"Poor Molly," Grace said. "I should have been here to help. Where is she now?"

"Mr Sterling Chelmsford helped me to take her out the back, where there's an area for exhibitors to take a break and store their wares. He's a rare decent man, especially considering she is a union lass. He stayed with her while I came back out to attend the stand. I didn't see Miss Sugden again, or Mr Chelmsford for that matter, so I presume she recovered and went home."

Charlie interrupted. "May we look out the back to be sure?"

"Not allowed, I'm afraid, exhibitors only." He paused as Charlie reached for his badge. "My apologies. I forgot you were a policeman. I'll show you through."

As McIntyre led them down a narrow corridor, Grace asked, "Are either of the Mr Chelmsfords still here?"

189

"Not now, lass. They've both gone. Only came to meet the Mayor and his dignitaries."

A few people were milling around the area behind the exhibits, packing or unpacking boxes, or resting with a cup of tea or a dram of whisky, but there was no sign of Molly Sugden or Sterling Chelmsford.

Charlie handed one of Stewart's cards to McIntyre. "Thanks for your help. Could you contact me if you hear anything?"

The Exhibition was about to close for the night. Attempting to move upstream against the flow of the crowd proved impossible, so they went to the exit and waited to see if they could spot Molly coming out. After a long wait, the last few reluctant visitors dribbled out, chattering and exclaiming at the sights they had seen.

"Couldn't we go back in and search for her?" Grace pleaded.

"I'm not sure there is much point. The most likely explanation is that she went home after hearing the news about Finlay, if she was upset."

"I can't believe she would go without telling me or Anne first."

A pair of uniformed staff members began to close the gates, supervised by a man in a top hat and natty suit. Charlie flashed his police badge. "There's a young woman missing. Similar build and age to this lady, but wearing a white dress. Could I ask you to inform the staff to keep a lookout for her while they are tidying up?"

"Very well, Constable. We have several dozen missing persons every night, what with the crowds, so I expect you'll find her soon enough, safe with friends or at home. But we'll keep our eyes open too."

Grace trudged away from the domed entrance, feeling the weight of exhaustion and disquiet dragging at her feet. "Might we visit the Sugden home on the way back? Molly must be there, but I would like to know for sure."

Charlie slipped his arm through hers, his strength providing much appreciated support. "Molly Sugden is a robust, sensible young woman. I find it hard to imagine her swooning over the news of Finlay's death." He paused, frowning, then slapped his free hand to his

190

forehead. "I'd forgotten that Jack Finlay had a girl who was about to become his fiancée. Could it have been Miss Sugden?"

Grace stopped abruptly, turning to stare at him. "Molly did have a young man she was in love with. A clever young man, who was too busy with work to take her to the Exhibition. Charlie, this is awful. To think we have known about his death for three days, while poor Molly was ignorant of the tragedy."

"The pamphlet from Temperance House. That would make sense if Finlay was going to hear Molly speak. He must have been proud of her." Charlie took a few more paces forward before stopping again. "Oh my lord, I'd quite forgotten that Jack Finlay and his cousin Bart Nolan had fallen out over a girl they were both in love with. If that girl was Molly and Nolan was at the Exhibition–"

"Hell and damnation." Grace felt her knees go weak at the thought that Nolan might have gotten to Molly after she left the care of Mr Chelmsford. "Perhaps he thought Molly might know something about Jack Finlay's death? I feel terrible we didn't put the pieces of the puzzle together sooner."

"Me too." Charlie put an arm around her waist, holding her steady until she stopped trembling. "We need to see Mrs Sugden, and hopefully Molly, to confirm their connection. Even if she went off with Nolan, surely he would not harm her."

They hurried to the Sugden's home, where a single candle burned in the porch window. Molly's mother answered their knock with startling promptness. Her worried expression told them all they needed to know. Molly was not yet home.

"May we come in, Mrs Sugden?" Grace asked. "This is a friend of mine, Constable Pyke."

"Of course, dear. Where are my manners?" Molly's mother led the way to the kitchen table and waved vaguely at the chairs. "She knows she must be home by ten o'clock and it's gone eleven. My Molly is never late – she knows how I worry about her."

"Molly and I got separated when she stopped to talk to some friends. I'm sorry to say that we could not find her again. Do you have any idea where she might be, Mrs Sugden?"

"My Molly has more friends than hot breakfasts. And her devoted young man, of course, although he could not go tonight."

Grace's gut contracted, but the question had to be asked. "I don't think she ever mentioned his name to me, Mrs Sugden."

"Jack Finlay. Such a gentle and clever young man with excellent prospects. He is going to make his fortune with their inventions. Just between you and me, my dear, I would bet a pound to a penny that Jack is about to ask Molly to marry him."

Grace braced herself to tell Molly's mother the tragic news, feeling sick to her stomach, but Mrs Sugden got in first.

"I can see what you're thinking, Miss Penrose, but my Molly would never elope or nothing silly like that. She's a good girl with a steady head on her shoulders."

"I believe she also knew Jack Finlay's distant cousin, Bart Nolan," Charlie said.

"Odd that you should mention him, Constable Pyke. I haven't seen him in an age, but I would swear I saw him standing outside the house the other day. But Molly hasn't said anything about seeing him, so perhaps I was mistaken. I believe he had an eye for her once, but he must have had the wrong end of the stick, because it was always Jack Finlay that my Molly was mad for."

Charlie looked at Grace and inclined his head towards the teapot. She nodded and went to fetch hot water.

"Mrs Sugden, I am very sorry indeed to be the bearer of bad news. Mr Finlay was found dead on Monday night. Molly only found out by chance tonight, which might explain why she has gone off with a friend."

Grace searched the kitchen shelf for sugar, adding a heaped spoonful to a dark brew of tea. She placed it by Mrs Sugden's hand. Molly's mother kept staring straight ahead, as if she hadn't heard a word. Grace put a hand on her arm, feeling the chill seep up into her palm. "Blanket, Charlie."

"Mrs Sugden, is there a friend or neighbour I could call on to stay with you?" Grace took the blanket from Charlie and wrapped it over the protruding bones of the mother's slumped shoulders. Molly must have been a twilight baby.

"I can't believe it." Molly's mother picked at the tassels on the edge of the blanket. "Jack's dead? Are you sure?"

"Absolutely sure, I'm sorry to say," Charlie replied gently.

Tears fell down her cheeks, silently. Not a woman to make a fuss, as Grace's mother would say.

"Poor Molly. Her dear, sweet Jack gone. They meant the world to each other." She accepted a handkerchief from Grace with shaking fingers. "What happened to him?"

Charlie searched Grace's face for permission. She blinked in response. The truth was always best.

"It appears that a thief entered Jack's office intending to take his designs and patent application. He killed Jack, making it look like an accident. I don't wish to alarm you any more than I already have, but we cannot rule out the possibility that the person who killed Jack is … wanting to speak to Molly too."

Instead of venting grief or rage or fear, Mrs Sugden seemed to shrink further into her shell of a body. "Mr Chelmsford visited tonight, wanting Molly's copy of the designs."

"Mr Chelmsford?" Charlie kept his calm admirably, despite a dozen emotions flitting across his face, from surprise to disbelief, before settling on shock.

"He saw Molly at the Exhibition and she had agreed to meet him here to give him the papers, which she was holding for Jack. It seems Mr Chelmsford had agreed to purchase the design for a large sum of money. Enough to set Jack and Molly up for life."

"Did you give the papers to him?"

Mrs Sugden lifted red-rimmed eyes. "I wasn't keen to hand them over, seeing as how valuable they were. My Molly was the one who had the idea for it, though of course Jack did all the drafting and business side of it. But Mr Chelmsford is a powerful man and I couldn't say no, what with him promising to pay for them. I would never have let them out of my sight if I'd known Jack was dead."

Grace hurried next door to see if someone could come to look after Mrs Sugden tonight. Luckily, the neighbour was an old friend, who immediately dusted off floury hands and led the way back, as Grace quickly outlined the situation.

"Flo dear, there now," the neighbour said as soon as she was through the door. "You drink your tea, love, and I'll pop a hot brick in your bed to warm it."

Flo Sugden sipped her tea automatically as the neighbour bustled around. Grace leaned over and whispered that she would be back tomorrow. As she stood up again, Flo's hand shot out and clasped her arm with shocking strength.

"You'll find my Molly, won't you, Miss Penrose? I know in my bones she's alive."

Too Many Suspects

Charlie woke before first light, feeling ravenous and on edge in equal measures. After a quick wash, he tiptoed down the stairs to the kitchen.

"Porridge?"

"Holy smoke, Grace, you scared me halfway to the moon. What are you doing up so early, slinking around in the dark?"

"Couldn't sleep for worry and guilt." She picked up the teapot and poured him a cup. "Who do you think is behind this, Charlie? I've spent the night twisting it into a tangle and I'm still none the wiser."

"I wish I knew." He glopped porridge into a bowl as he gathered his thoughts. "It worries me that Sterling Chelmsford was the last person known to have been with Molly and quick off the mark to secure the second copy of Finlay's designs. Or Molly's designs, if Mrs Sugden is correct."

"But Chelmsford had already agreed to pay a large sum for the design. Why would he kill a man, and risk his reputation and life, when he could afford to pay, especially when the new machines were already being tested in his factory? Besides, we know he was at the Grand Hotel for a reception on the Monday night until late, so he cannot be the murderer."

"Perhaps he decided it was more expedient to get the design for free and make a second fortune from selling the rights to use it," Charlie said. "I would imagine it's not so hard to find a hired killer in this town, if the price is right. Although I concede that the evidence doesn't fit with a hired thug. The gentleman's scarf, the fact that Finlay let the killer into his office and accepted a drink from him – it all points to somebody he knew."

"Nolan seems the most likely suspect to me. Disgruntled, jealous, greedy, and a known liar, not to mention hanging around Molly's house and being at the Exhibition."

Charlie swirled milk and sugar through the oaty glop, watching the disparate elements slowly combine. If only detecting was so straightforward. "Nolan is a corrupt bully. It would make my day to toss him into gaol and throw away the key. But we have no evidence against him for the murder, aside from his failure to report his cousin's death. And we still haven't ruled out Duncan and Kendall, let alone all the other potential employers and acquaintances of Jack Finlay who haven't been investigated yet."

"Charlie, we haven't time to investigate all of Finlay's contacts. Molly might be in grave danger."

Grace had her head in her hands, but her distress was evident in her voice. He desperately wanted to gather her into his arms and assure her that everything was going to be fine, but he wasn't about to lie.

"You're right, Grace. I have to solve this fast." Charlie banged his fist on the table in frustration, catching the edge of the spoon. The spoon catapulted a glob of porridge across the table, landing on Grace's hand and in her hair. "Oh no, I'm so sorry."

He watched her lift her head from her hands, expecting either anger or tears. Grace licked the porridge off her hand and wiped it out of her hair without saying a word. Then, with deliberate care and a grin that slowly spread to include mischievous eyes, she filled a spoon from her own plate and hovered it in the air. She wouldn't – would she?

Charlie cringed, waiting for the splatter, but Grace moved the spoon to her mouth and swallowed with a "mmm".

"About the only person I'm sure didn't kill Finlay is you," he grumbled.

"Is that a wise assumption, Detective Constable? As far as I recall, you have never asked my whereabouts on Monday night."

Charlie contemplated her for a moment. Of course, he knew Grace hadn't killed Finlay, but she had a point. Had he made unwarranted assumptions about other potential suspects? "Unless you wish to confess, my assumption stands. Lady V … Fanny said it was two men in the alley."

"Fair enough. Decent of you to put your trust in the honesty of a scarlet woman."

"And you have an alibi for last night." Charlie reached across the table and wiped a splodge of porridge off her cheek. "Was that why you danced with me, to divert suspicion from yourself?"

Grace gave him a long, hard stare, then pushed her porridge away half-eaten. "You know, if this was a medical problem, I would say we lack the information to make an informed diagnosis."

"Agreed. We need a plan to identify critical pieces of information …"

"…and an efficient means of collecting said information."

"I like your rational thought processes, Miss Bones. Not bad for a woman, not bad at all."

"Do you want to wear porridge to work, Detective Constable Pyke?"

"It might provide welcome sustenance for what I am sure will be another busy day, Miss Penrose."

It was all very well to ease the tension with a bit of light banter, but there was no getting away from the seriousness of the situation. Charlie had turned his brain inside out, trying to figure out a better way to get information quickly, without putting Grace or Johnny or their friends at risk. But he had little chance of securing help from the local police force and no one else he could trust. Grace and Johnny it would have to be, although only for low-risk tasks. The rest he would do himself, with Stewart working the upper levels of authority.

"Grace, do you think you could rally a contingent of women to check the union, hospitals, churches, and so forth for any sign of Molly?"

"Of course. I'll visit Mrs Sugden again too and get a list of Molly's friends. And you?"

"I need to see DI Stewart and Johnny Todd again. They might have more information on Nolan and our other suspects. And I'll file an official missing person report. Not that any action will be taken after so short a time, unless we uncover evidence of foul play."

"God forbid," Grace said. "Send word to Lavender House if you find Molly. Otherwise, shall I come to Wains Hotel around noon, so we can compare results?"

"Perfect. Talk to DI Stewart if I am not there. Tread carefully, Grace. I don't have to remind you that there is a killer on the loose, and he will be desperate if he thinks we are getting close. For heaven's sake, don't take any chances."

"You too, Charlie."

The first blush of dawn glowed as Charlie made his way into town. He had planned four stops on his roundabout route to Wains Hotel and two of them had to be early. The first was to the neighbourhood of Finlay's office, to see if he could find anyone who saw what happened on Monday night. He would have done it days ago, if it had been his case to investigate.

The first few premises he tried were locked up tight. Eventually, he noticed a bleary-eyed night watchman shuffling his way home. The man acknowledged his badge with a reluctant nod.

"Where exactly do you work?" Charlie asked.

"I work for a shipping company, down the road a way," the night watchman replied, gesturing at a warehouse. "Plenty of valuable imported goods stored there, so they pay me to keep a good lookout for trouble."

"Did you see any activity at Mr Finlay's offices on Monday night?"

"A dreich night like Monday, it was hard to see much of anything."

"Nothing untoward or nothing at all?"

"Well, the secretary left, as usual," the watchman recalled. "Always six o'clock on the dot, Miss Abercrombie, and a pleasant word to me as she passes. And Mr Finlay arrived around sundown. Don't know him well, but he works late at night oftentimes." The guard rubbed his chin, which was rough with whiskers after a long night on duty. "Not long after, there was a copper, in and out in a few minutes, as I recall, so he probably saw the lamp on and went in to see that all was well. I remember him passing by the warehouse on his way in, thinking it was good to see a copper on the beat, there being too many scoundrels about for my liking."

Charlie's pulse kicked up a notch. An observant witness was a rare treasure. "Can you describe the constable?"

"They all look the same on a drizzly night in their uniform."

Charlie pulled out his notebook and flipped to the sketch of Nolan. "Does he look familiar?"

"I reckon it might have been him. Broken nose rings a bell. Wouldn't swear to it, though."

"And this man?"

"Will Finlay. Cannae recall seeing him on Monday or any other night. He tends to stay within the walls of the foundry, not liking to show his face in public, I expect, poor man."

"What about any of these men?" Charlie flipped through his sketches slowly until the watchman jabbed a finger at the page.

"Reckon I saw him recently, though I couldn't say if it was Monday night or not. Only saw the outline of a man passing the gaslight as he came down the street from the other direction, but you don't see a figure as round as that every day. Come to think of it, I recall how odd he looked in the misty light, so perhaps it was Monday."

Mr Kendall. Miss Abercrombie said Kendall had visited Finlay's office on Monday, but Finlay was out. Kendall had told the secretary he would return. What if he had returned later that night, without his wife's knowledge? If Grace was right about Mrs Kendall using a sleeping draught herself, it would be easy enough to do.

Charlie crossed his fingers and asked the critical question. "If it was Monday night you saw this man, would it have been before or after the constable?"

"That I cannae say."

"One final question. Did you see two men leaving the office that night, or Mr Finlay alone."

The watchman shook his head. "Not that I recall. I'm not always at the front gate, though. Every half hour or so, I walk around the yard and warehouse, ensuring that everything is in order."

"Thank you, sir. You have been very helpful indeed."

Charlie continued on to his second task for the day, having a word with Johnny Todd before he headed to school for the morning. Charlie didn't want to stir up trouble for the lad by pulling him out of class, so it had to be early.

Johnny greeted Charlie with relief. He pulled out of his mother's clutches, as she attempted to hold him still and comb his hair flat with copious quantities of water.

"Gotta go, ma." Johnny barged past him and out the door, where he sank to the step and shook his head, sending the neatly flattened hair flying back into its usual rumpled spikes.

"I got some juicy titbits for you, Copper Charlie. Nipper, what works as a messenger boy, had a run to do at the Dunedin Club last week. He needed a piss, so he went around into the bushes at the side. Reckons he saw Fingerless Fergus – that's Mr Duncan – talking to a toff. Duncan came away with a mile-wide smirk on his face and a fat wad o' cash in his hand, according to Nipper, and he ain't no liar."

"Did Nipper recognise the man?" Charlie asked.

Johnny flipped through the sketches Charlie had given him. "That's the gent, he reckons. Real fancy cove – top hat, walking stick and all. He got into one of them covered buggies with a curly 'C' on the side, pulled by a pair of greys."

Sterling Chelmsford paying off Fergus Duncan, well, well. Charlie was having a successful morning, but the information gathered only seemed to add to the confusion of suspects swirling around the investigation. Too many motives, too many suspects, not enough hard evidence.

He slipped Johnny another two coins. "Terrific work, lad. Split that with Nipper."

A thought occurred to him, belatedly. "Nipper was sure it was this older gentleman, not the younger one? They look rather alike, being father and son, aside from the age difference."

"Aye. Nipper took a good look at the sketch of the young one, which he saw first, looking puzzled like. Soon as he saw the older one, he was dead sure. He's seen the young one around town too, always hanging around the kind of gambling halls where only the nobs visit."

Another black mark against Edmund Chelmsford. But gambling was only a vice for weak men, not a crime, unless he frequented illegal gambling dens. Charlie would warn Grace next time he saw her, but there was no need to be alarmed, especially as she had declared herself horrified by the thought of being courted by Edmund Chelmsford.

On the other hand, Sterling Chelmsford was another kettle of fish. Rotten fish, judging by his dealings with Duncan.

"Nothing else on any of the men in the sketches? Nobody seen in the alley the night of the murder?"

Johnny shrugged. "Monday wasn't the sort of night people hang around."

"Thanks, Johnny. Keep an eye out for Miss Bones for me. The Chelmsford father and son are keen to pursue their acquaintance with her. I'd not see her hurt for the world."

Charlie's next stop was the Grand Hotel. Sterling Chelmsford could not be the killer if he was at a reception there on Monday night. Which is not to say that he hadn't hired someone to do the job for him.

He talked to the doorman, who had been on duty on Monday night. The doorman recalled both Chelmsford men, but he had only seen them entering at the start of the evening and leaving amongst the last guests after midnight.

The clerk at reception confirmed this information and added that Sterling Chelmsford had given one of the many speeches that night. "The speeches went on for some time, Detective Constable." The clerk leaned across the desk and whispered discreetly, "I recall the hotel manager becoming a mite concerned that Mr Chelmsford would never stop, thereby upsetting the timing of the supper."

Charlie's next stop was the police station. Fortunately, Sergeant Lynch was not on duty. The desk officer confirmed that there were no reports of young women being found, dead or alive, in the vicinity of the Exhibition, or elsewhere. Charlie filed a missing person report, which was accepted with minimal interest.

He made it back to Wains Hotel on the dot of noon. Grace hadn't arrived yet, so he discussed progress with Stewart.

The Detective Inspector had been busy all morning in meetings regarding the forthcoming Sweating Commission, as well as liaising with the local detective branch. Unfortunately, Stewart had no information from them on the whereabouts of Bart Nolan or any further progress on Finlay's murder. The only positive news was that Stewart hinted he was actively pursuing his corruption investigation into the local force, although he was tight-lipped about the detail.

"The autopsy results arrived," Stewart added, pointing at the topmost file on Charlie's desk. "Suffocation by a woollen object given as the cause of death, after being knocked out with chloral hydrate, as you deduced. The fibres in the victim's nose matched those of the scarf you retrieved from the alley."

"And the head wound was post-mortem?"

"Just so. What have you found out, Pyke?"

"First up, I'm afraid I am the bearer of bad news, sir. A young woman went missing from the Exhibition last night. Miss Molly Sugden, the fiancée of the murder victim, Jack Finlay. Nolan was there, along with half of Dunedin. Nolan was also spotted outside the Sugden house and at Finlay's office on the night of his death."

"Hmm. I'll have a word to the station about redoubling efforts to bring him in."

"The last person to have seen Miss Sugden was Mr Sterling Chelmsford, who also visited the Sugden house shortly afterwards to uplift the only other known copy of Finlay's designs. In fact, the designs are a collaboration between Sugden and Finlay, which may have a bearing on her disappearance. Also, a witness saw Sterling

Chelmsford paying a large sum of money to Mr Duncan, the foreman at Kendall's factory."

Stewart drummed his fingers on the desk. "I can't say I'm happy to hear of so many possible links to Sterling Chelmsford. The Premier and Police Commissioner will not be pleased at all, Pyke. If Mr Kendall is considered beyond reach, Mr Chelmsford is ten times more so, as a man of great wealth and influence, almost certain to become a powerful politician in the near future."

"Are you ordering me to exclude Sterling Chelmsford from the investigation, sir?"

Stewart's shocked look was answer enough. "Good heavens, no. Justice must apply equally to all, whether high or low. But walk softly when you are gathering evidence and keep me briefed at all times. Make sure you do not put a foot out of line on this, Pyke. And definitely do not talk to Chelmsford again without me being present. Is that understood?"

"Yes, sir."

"Don't look so despondent, lad. You're making good progress in an exceedingly complex case."

"It feels more like I am taking two steps backward for every one forward, sir."

Stewart gave the slightest of shrugs. "That is the way of it, more often than not. I know you young coppers want to unravel every twist in the blink of an eye, but most cases are a long, slow slog, interviewing and re-interviewing, floundering around in the dark until a chink of light appears."

Or, in this case, too many chinks of light, throwing so many cross-beams that the truth was obscured. Charlie sighed and bent to the task of writing up his notes. The more evidence he gathered, the more it seemed as if every one of the suspects was guilty of something.

Most of all, he was worried about Sterling Chelmsford's potential involvement, given his obvious desire to become Grace's father-in-law, despite her protestations to the contrary. What if Grace had confided the details of their investigation to Edmund Chelmsford, and he had passed them to his father? The thought that Grace might be in danger turned his stomach upside-down and inside out.

He glanced at the clock. Almost one o'clock – where in the name of Chronos was she?

A Monstrous Injustice

Frustration and anxiety had burned Grace's nerves to a frazzle as the morning passed with no news of Molly. She and half a dozen other concerned women had worn their boot soles out on the streets of Dunedin, with nothing to show for it. No sightings and no sign of her at any hospital, church, union or friend's house.

There was only one other place she could think to ask, and Charlie Pyke was most definitely not going to like it.

Grace slunk across town, expecting to see him lurking at every corner. But his unerring ability to catch her during risky escapades appeared to have deserted him today. Soon, she was safely standing in front of a forbidding brick edifice. Although "safe" was perhaps not the best choice of words in the circumstances, as the building was the Dunedin goal.

The echoing clang of the bell drew curious stares from passers-by, but no sign of activity from within. On the second ring, she heard shuffling footsteps. A hatch opened with a thud in the thick oak door, just above her head, then the door swung open.

The guard scrutinised her card with less care and attention than she had received from the doorman of Wains Hotel. Perhaps it was only those attempting to leave the gaol who raised his interest. Or perhaps the guard was used to visits by well-meaning women carrying a member's card of the Ladies' Society for the Advancement of Prison Reform, which she had borrowed from her great-aunt this morning.

"I would like to visit Mr Will Finlay," she stated.

The guard deigned to raise an eyebrow at that. "He's a monster, that one, and a murderer to boot. Are you sure it's him you have to visit?"

"Yes."

Grace half-hoped he would deny her access, allowing her to escape back to fresh air and blue sky. However, he only shrugged and gestured for her to put her bag onto a small table in the lobby.

"I'll leave my medical bag out here, if I may, and take in this smaller bag."

The guard upended the small bag with casual disregard for the contents, scattering them across the table.

"What's this?" he queried, holding up a small jar of salve. He held it to his nose briefly, before jerking his hand away at the sharp smell of peppermint, menthol and arnica.

"Medicinal salve, for his face."

The guard considered it, then pushed it back across to her. The jar was so small, it wasn't as if she could be concealing a file or rope ladder in it, nor was it a drug anyone would want to ingest. Aside from the salve, she had brought only some bread, cheese, biscuits and fruit. The guard took his fee – a roll, a peach and three pieces of shortbread – then gestured for her to pack the bag again.

"We don't have a matron here, so I cannot search you." His gaze flicked up and down her body, as if wondering whether he might get away with it.

Grace gave him her best evil eye. "I should hope not. I am a personal friend of Detective Inspector Stewart, who is on special assignment to the Dunedin police force. Please show me to the prisoner."

The guard led the way down an exceedingly gloomy corridor, lined with cells and smelling worse than a pigsty. None of the prisoners could see them, as the peepholes were closed and latched, but evidently they could be heard. The crash of tin mugs against metal was decidedly unnerving. She dreaded to think how they would react if they could see the visitor was a young woman.

The guard stopped outside a cell and unlatched the peephole. "He's chained up, so you should be safe enough if you stay by the door. I'll search him when you leave, so don't be tempted to slip him anything other than what is in your bag."

"Thank you, you may leave me. I will call for you when I am finished."

"Your funeral, lass."

Grace stepped into the cell. The door slammed behind her with a heavy finality that sent a jolt of panic spiralling through her body. Her hand reached instinctively for the door. Only the thought of Molly – somewhere out there, in need of help – kept her hand from hammering on it to bring the guard back.

She turned to the man slumped in the corner, with his head between his knees and his arms wrapped around for extra protection. Had she made the right decision coming here? Charlie believed that the giant sitting a mere few feet from her was innocent and she trusted Charlie with her life. The man had not moved since she entered, but one eye looked sideways at her with disconcerting intensity.

No point in procrastinating. She stepped forward with an outstretched hand. "Will Finlay? My name is Grace Penrose. I have come to see you because my friend, Constable Pyke, believes you are innocent. We are working hard to clear your name and catch your brother's killer."

His head came up a little higher, but he made no response. Hardly surprising that he was no longer quick to trust a stranger.

"Please, Mr Finlay, come and sit with me. I am here to help you, truly." She reached for his enormous arm and tugged gently, as if her tiny hand could move him against his wishes.

He twitched at her touch, showing his face for the first time in his surprise.

"I'm also training to be a doctor. I have some salve that might ease your pain. And fresh food. I don't imagine the food in her is quite up to the standard of the Grand Hotel."

This feeble joke elicited a grunt. She tugged at his arm again, and he got up obediently. His muscular bulk towered over her, sparking another round of heart palpitations. A mental picture of him bending metal bars in the foundry left her in no doubt that he could pick her up in one hand and crush the life out of her in an instant.

Instead, he allowed her to lead him to the narrow bunk. They both ignored the chain clattering across the stone floor behind him.

Grace had discussed his condition with Anne and Lily this morning. After they got over their horror at her proposed visit to the gaol, they had made a few useful suggestions. The consensus was that there was nothing they could do for his twisted bones, but they might be able to relieve the pain from the inevitable muscle tensions his condition would cause. Lily had made up the salve to bring him relief, with the hopeful side effect of winning the man's trust.

"Please, take a seat," she said, as if she was hosting a tea party. "Would you care for a fresh bread roll stuffed with cheese and pickle?"

He looked at her as if she was quite mad, then let out a rumbling noise. After a moment, she realised he was laughing. "Yes plez, milady."

Grace tipped her bag out between them on the none-too-clean blanket. Just as well it was summer, if this thin, moth-eaten scrap of wool was all Will had to keep him warm. She passed over a roll. "I do apologise for forgetting the linen napkins."

He waved a dismissive hand. "Nex' time."

"I rather hope we will have you out of prison too quickly for me to visit again, Will. But I would be delighted to invite you for a proper luncheon when you are released."

While Will ate, Grace explained how he should rub the salve into the muscles of his face and neck, massaging any spots that were painful to ease the tension.

When he finished the roll, he pushed the rest of the food aside and took up the jar. He sniffed and shied back at the pungent smell, then took a tiny dollop and massaged it into the muscles running up his neck. With a sigh of relief, he dug out a larger dollop and set to work on the muscles around his enlarged jaw.

"Tha' helps, thank you." He put the lid of the jar back on with great care and slid it inside the straw mattress. "Wha' can I do to help you?"

"Do you know Molly Sugden, Will?"

Will gave her a twisted smile. "Jack loved 'er. Lovely lass. Kind t' me."

"I'm sorry to say that she has disappeared. We have checked with her mother and friends, at the Tailoresses' Union, church and hospital. Can you think of anywhere else she might go?"

He thought for a moment, then shook his head.

"We'll find her, Will, and bring her to visit you. She would have come earlier if she had known about Jack's death and your arrest." Grace patted his hand, which brought her another wry smile.

"Will, do you know anything about the design for machinery that Jack and Molly were working on? Jack had done the drawings and was preparing to file a patent, but the documents have disappeared. Jack's killer took the original file from his office safe and Mr Chelmsford took the copy Molly had at her house. I am told the patent could be worth a fortune, but I cannot fathom Chelmsford's involvement. He had Jack's new design at his factory already and claims to have agreed to buy the patent outright. Why would he need to take the papers?"

"No, not true." Will shook his head vigorously. He took a breath and continued with slow deliberation, carefully enunciating each word. "Jack and me made the Chelmsford machines las' year, before he met Molly. Spinning, carding, looms, all better, safer than other factories. But only a little better. The patent is for a new design – much safer and much, much more efficient. Revolutionary, Jack said, worth a fortune. Molly and Jack designed them together. Her da was an expert weaver, and she knows everything about sewing and weaving. Very clever, our Molly."

Will leaned back against the cold, unyielding wall of the cell, as if the effort of so long a speech had tired him. Grace considered his revelations and the implications, as Will selected a piece of shortbread and nibbled it with drawn-out pleasure.

"So, if Mr Chelmsford didn't pay a fortune to secure the patent for his sole use, he might have been driven out of business by whoever had the new design?"

"Jack only agreed to sell to Chelmsford cos he needed the money to get married and buy a house. And to pay for a surgeon for me." Will looked directly into her eyes for the first time. "He was a good brother, Jack. Always treated me like a real person."

"I know Molly thought the world of him. I am sorry for your loss." Grace patted his hand again. A trivial gesture, but it was all she could do. "Thank you, Will. You have been very helpful. I hope to see you again soon, under better circumstances."

Will touched one of his plate-sized hands to her arm. "Find Molly, Miss. Jack would want to see her safe."

She hammered on the door and called for the guard, setting up a clamouring and hooting along the corridor. When she turned to wave farewell to Will, he had his eyes closed as he bit into a juicy peach, wearing an expression of complete contentment. The outsized effect of even the tiniest act of kindness never ceased to amaze her, when the recipient was a person in a seemingly hopeless predicament.

Kendall's Lament

The morning had flown by. With time running out before her noon rendezvous at Wains Hotel, Grace hurried across town and up Walker Street, on route to Lavender House, where Anne was coordinating the search. With any luck, Anne might have good news about Molly to take to Charlie.

She heard the low rumble of angry voices before she saw the two men at the entrance to Kendall's factory. Grace crossed to the other side of the street, but couldn't resist a sidelong glance.

Mr Kendall was standing on the top step, his fists clenched, but down by his side rather than raised. His shrill voice carried across the road. "Keep away from here, you hear me. I won't take it anymore."

The other man had his back towards Grace. He leaped over the intervening two steps and grabbed Kendall by the lapels of his coat. His voice was a low hiss, so Grace could not make out the words, but his threat was clear by the way Kendall pulled back, his eyes bulging. Judging from his sweaty brow and beet-red face, Kendall was on the verge of an apoplectic fit.

The man released him suddenly, sending Kendall stumbling backwards into the door and sliding to the landing. He slumped there, bent over, with his hand on his chest, as the aggressor watched on.

Grace was caught between her desire to flee and her duty to help. Too late, the decision was taken out of her hands. The man turned and spotted her. He was across the street before she could escape, grabbing her by the wrist and thrusting his face to within inches of hers.

"You again. The nosy busybody always interfering in other people's business. Was it you or the old man who laid a complaint about me to the Inspector? Or did Pyke tell tales about me behind my back?"

"Constable Nolan." Grace flicked a glance up and down the plain clothes he was wearing. "Or is it former-constable Nolan now? You want to be careful who you threaten. You never know who might be watching. Threatening a fellow constable in front of a senior officer is foolish enough, but it's downright suicidal when that old man is also in charge of an investigation into police corruption."

His grip tightened on her wrist. "What the hell do you mean?"

"Didn't you recognise the old man who intervened between you and Pyke? Detective Inspector Stewart. Surely you must know of him – famous detective, decorated hero, crusader against corruption. Not a man to give in to a bully like you, Nolan. Now, kindly remove your hand from my wrist."

Nolan let out a string of oaths. But instead of letting her go, he seized the other wrist too and twisted it hard. "What does Stewart know? Tell me, or I'll break your arms."

An icy twinge of fear crept through her veins, as Grace realised she had been a fool to provoke this beast. He might look like an overgrown choirboy on the outside, but inside he was pure venom. "I have no idea what Stewart knows. Not much, I imagine, as he has only been in Dunedin for a couple of days. Please, let me go."

"So you can go crying to Stewart, telling him what you just witnessed? I don't think so. Tell me, Miss Penrose, do you have family or friends who you care about? People you would not want to see hurt?" He twisted harder, until the pain became excruciating.

"Help!" she screamed. "Somebody, please help!"

He smirked and twisted harder. "You're in the wrong part of town, you stupid cow. Nobody around here cares two hoots about some self-righteous little whiner, unless you're willing to flash your fanny."

A deep male voice growled from behind her. "You will let Miss Bones go immediately, or you'll have me to answer to."

She twisted around, seeing an unfamiliar man of intimidating bulk. He let out a piercing whistle. Three more men appeared from the carriage-works a few yards up the street. Big, grease-stained, working men, who looked as if they could toss a caber half way across town without breaking a sweat.

Nolan dropped her arms and backed away. "Just a misunderstanding, gentlemen."

Her saviour pinned Nolan against the brick wall, none too gently. "Put a hand on our Miss Bones again and you'll be singing soprano for the rest of your natural." He turned to her. "Did he hurt you, Miss Bones?"

Grace held up her arms, showing the angry red welts. When she saw the tightening of her saviour's jaw and the bunching of biceps as he pulled back his arm, she thrust her hand out to stop the blow. "Wait. I don't want you getting into any trouble. This man is a policeman. Rotten to the core, but a copper nevertheless."

The man narrowed his eyes and kept Nolan pressed against the wall for a few more seconds, before releasing him so suddenly that Nolan collapsed to the pavement. "Now, scram, before I change my mind and feed you to the fishes. And don't show your ugly face around here again."

Nolan crawled clear of the looming bulk, pushed himself unsteadily to his feet, and scrammed.

Grace sagged against the wall, massaging her burning wrists. "A close call. How can I thank you gentlemen, for coming to my rescue?"

Her rescuer doffed his cap. "No need for thanks, Miss Bones, the honour was all mine. You and Mrs Macmillan saved the life of my wife and son two days back."

She registered the shock of red hair. "You must be Mr Campbell. A tricky breech birth, but nothing to worry about. How are they both doing?"

"Just grand, thanks to you. The bairn is a strapping wee lad, the light of my life. Angus, here," he continued, pointing to another of the men, "near lost his missus to fever a few weeks back, before you and Mrs Macmillan came by with your medicine. We look after our own around here, Miss."

"Are you all right, Miss Bones?" Angus asked. "Cuppa tea? Take you to Lavender House?"

Grace realised she was shaking. With every ounce of willpower that she could muster, she pulled herself together and attempted a weak smile. "No need to keep you from your work. Thank you again for saving me from that brute. I must see to Mr Kendall." She picked up her dropped medical bag, nodded farewell, and crossed the road.

Kendall was still slumped in the doorway, his face ashen. Grace wondered why none of his workers had come to his aid. But, as she walked up the steps, she realised the factory was silent. The place felt eerily lifeless without the thump of the steam engine and the clatter of machinery.

She put Kendall into a more comfortable position and loosened his cravat and collar. He was conscious, but his breathing was shallow and laboured. A whiff of smelling salts pulled him back from the edge. Gradually, he regained his normal colour and breathing.

She helped him into his office with difficulty, given his bulk, and heaved him unceremoniously into a low armchair.

"Thank you, young lady. Miss Penrose, isn't it? Aren't you the one who got Duncan's hand out of that cursed loom?"

"That's right, Mr Kendall." She took his pulse and deemed him sufficiently recovered to answer a few pertinent questions, realising that there might never be a better opportunity to get to the truth. "The same loom that killed Alfie Watts."

The colour drained from his face again, but he took a deep breath and shook his head. To her surprise, a teardrop sparkled in the corner of his eye. Far from the arrogant, heartless factory owner she had taken him for, instead he seemed contrite – a beaten man in need of a confessor.

"A terrible tragedy. It keeps me awake at night, to think of that poor lad. I had the tarnation loom fixed only the week before. The engineer gave me his word that it was in perfect working order, but it broke down again the next day."

"Was the engineer Mr Finlay?" Grace asked.

"Yes. I blamed him at first. Yelled at him and threatened him, if I'm honest. Told him I wouldn't pay."

"And he threatened to sue you in return?"

Kendall looked up sharply. "How did you know that?"

"Then what happened?" she countered.

Kendall sank back into the armchair, his fleshy chin falling to his chest as he unburdened his conscience. "Finlay agreed to come and fix the loom again on Saturday morning. Told me it seemed to him as if someone had deliberately damaged it, so it would fail to operate properly. I dismissed that as bluster, but sure enough, the darn thing wouldn't work on Monday morning again. When I examined the loom, I saw someone had tampered with it. I got Duncan, my foreman, to fix it and went down to Finlay's office to apologise. Or, to be honest, to seek his advice on how we could make it unbreakable."

"Did Finlay accept your apology?"

"He wasn't there on Monday morning. However, when I went back in the evening, he accepted my apology like a true gentleman. We shook hands on it. He was to come to my factory again this week, but he never showed up. Most unlike him. He is a hard worker, that lad. I'm sorry I blamed him."

"You didn't know that Finlay died on Monday night?"

His head jerked up again. "What! No! That's dreadful. Such a clever, pleasant man. That would explain why I never heard from him. What with the boy's death and my life descending into the pits of hell, I never gave him another thought. Accident, was it?"

"Murder, Mr Kendall. You didn't see anyone loitering around his office when you left?"

Kendall gasped, then began trembling as the implications hit home. "No, no one. Finlay was alive and well when I left. I swear it. It was getting late by then, but he wanted to keep on working. How awful. Shocking news, indeed." He shook his head, as if unable to take it in.

"Mr Kendall, you must think me impertinent to be asking these questions, but I have been helping the police with their inquiries. It would be helpful if you could explain what was behind your argument with Constable Nolan."

"That blackguard. I am ashamed to admit it, Miss Penrose, but I see now that the truth must come out. Nolan has been bleeding me dry for months. It started with requests for small amounts of money to ignore a few minor complaints from my workers. I had a couple of malcontents back then, trying to stir trouble for no reason."

"And then?"

"Nolan threatened to fabricate more complaints against me if I didn't keep paying him." Kendall hunched in the chair like a chastened child. "I should have stood up to him right from the start, but my situation was desperate and he had me bailed up in a corner. I couldn't afford any more problems, any more than I could afford his increasingly extortionate demands. On Tuesday morning, I told him I would no longer pay. If I'm going to have the ignominy of bankruptcy, at least I want to go down without the shame of paying any more to an extortionist."

Grace dropped a hand to his shoulder, feeling it shaking under her fingers. She went to the sideboard and poured him a stiff brandy. "Was it Nolan who pushed you to bankruptcy, Mr Kendall, or were there other problems?"

"Nolan was just the last blow in a long battle. Cheap imports and local sweated labour have been undercutting profits. And Chelmsford has been ruthless, swinging his influence and money about like a scythe, cutting out the smaller operators like us."

His gush of anger dribbled away into misery. "I've been in business over thirty years. I was a respected man once, Miss Penrose. Now, I cannot bear to look in the mirror. The contract to make tartan was my last hope. A golden goose in this city, as you can imagine, with all the pipe bands. I suspect Finlay was right. Someone deliberately damaged the loom in order to drive me out of business." He waved a hand towards the silent factory floor. "As you can see, they have succeeded. I am ruined."

"Who do you think damaged the loom?"

"I hate to say it, but I have concluded that my foreman, Mr Duncan, must be the traitor, though it pains me to accuse an employee of such long service. He was the only one with the access and the knowledge."

Although Grace could not acquit Kendall of putting his workers at risk in terrible working conditions, she felt an unexpected pang of pity for him, knowing the extent of his financial troubles. "Is there no hope, sir?"

"None at all. The trial order of tartan was due today. Given that I failed to meet the deadline, the contract is now worthless. I hear Chelmsford has been sniffing around, waiting to jump in and seize the contract off me, merciless dastard that he is. He won't stop until he controls every woollen mill and clothing factory in the land, by fair means or foul."

"You've had a successful business all those years, Mr Kendall. Can you not find another way to make it profitable? Clean this factory up, make it a safe and healthy place to work, pay better rates to get the best out of your skilled workers. I may not know much about hosiery and shirts, but even I can tell that your workers do fine work here under dreadful conditions. Think how much more productive your workers might be under good conditions."

"Fine words, Miss Penrose, but what am I to use as capital? Nolan has drained my purse to the last penny."

"I rather think Nolan is heading for a nasty downfall, Mr Kendall. Perhaps we can recover some of your money. I will put in a word for you with Detective Inspector Stewart. I cannot promise anything, mind, but it's worth a try."

Kendall raised his head, looking at her as if she was an inmate of Bedlam. "Why are you helping me, Miss Penrose? After all the terrible things I've done? All these years, I've thought no more of the girls than the machines they work, seeking only to make every last shilling out of them."

"I am doing this for your workers, Mr Kendall, who need their jobs. And because every repentant sinner deserves a second chance."

Grace left him sitting in the chair, his head between his hands, sobbing, aware that she was running hopelessly late for her meeting with Charlie.

A Reckoning

Charlie watched the hands of the clock tick around to one o'clock. Had Grace forgotten their plan to meet at noon? Or had something happened? Either way, the waiting made him sick to the stomach.

He jumped a foot off the chair when the door opened at last. Grace rushed in, her hair falling loose from its pins and her face flushed. "I apologise for being so late, Charlie. What a morning! Still no sign of Molly."

She flung her hat onto a side table and flopped down into an armchair, with her arms sprawled over the armrests. Below her shirt cuffs, angry red marks blazed on her wrists.

Charlie was on his knees beside her in an instant, reaching for her hands. "Grace, what happened to your wrists?"

"Nolan and I had words, but never mind that now."

He pushed her sleeves up as gently as he could manage, but still she winced. The sight of the painful welts triggering a wave of fury. "Nolan did this to you? He's going to regret it for the rest of his wretched life."

"Mr Campbell has already seen to that." Grace pushed her sleeves down and clasped his hands in her own. "Please, don't do anything reckless, Charlie. Nolan must suffer the rest of his punishment at the hands of the law, not at the end of your fist."

"Only if the law gets to him first," Charlie muttered.

"Please, promise me. You cannot lose everything you have worked for over that lowlife."

"I haven't much left to lose, Grace."

"You have everything to lose." The words snapped out with an intensity that startled them both. "I promised Lily I wouldn't get your hopes up, but she says that Stewart is highly impressed with your work. As he should be."

219

"DI Stewart has spoken to my aunt about me?"

"He's been going to Lily for treatment. He certainly looks a great deal happier now that he can walk without pain. I don't want to speak out of turn, but it would seem they enjoy each other's company as well. Don't tell me you haven't noticed?"

"I've noticed, but while Stewart is my superior officer, I choose to avert my gaze so he doesn't feel awkward with me." He couldn't resist lifting the edge of her cuff with one finger to see if the red welts were still there. "I'll take Nolan down and bring him in for justice to take its course, I promise." But woe betide Nolan if he tried to put up a fight.

"Charlie, I need to share some information with you. Only, you must promise not to get cross with me."

He closed his eyes and counted to ten. Dear Lord, what had she got herself into now? "Continue."

She sat back in the chair, shaking her head. "We had it the wrong way around. It wasn't Kendall who was offering to pay to make the complaints against his factory disappear. It was Nolan who was demanding money, making up allegations, and threatening Kendall if he didn't pay. Kendall thinks Duncan might have been damaging the loom on purpose, so that the factory would be driven out of business."

"That makes sense. A witness saw Duncan taking money from Sterling Chelmsford. Maybe Chelmsford was paying Duncan to disrupt the business."

"Kendall said it was Chelmsford who stood to gain from his loss of a lucrative contract. Called him a ruthless dastard. The thing is, I have been sceptical of Chelmsford's involvement with Finlay's death because he already had the new design of machinery on his factory floor. But I was wrong. Finlay had sold him an early design, which was only a little better than standard machinery. The designs Finlay was intending to patent were a great deal more efficient – revolutionary, in fact."

Charlie rose from his knees and paced the room, allowing the new information to tick over in his brain. "You went to see Will Finlay, didn't you? He's an accused murderer, for heaven's sake. How did you even get in to see him?"

"You know he's innocent and I know you could not see him, given that you are not officially on the case, so I had no choice. With what we have found out, especially if we can get Duncan to admit being paid by Sterling Chelmsford–"

His exasperation boiled over. "Grace, I have the deepest of admiration for you, but this has become far too dangerous. I won't have you within a mile of any of them." He crouched down beside her again to soften the harsh words. "I'm going to take you home, where you will lock the doors and not let anyone in. Tiny Tim can stand guard while I hunt down Duncan and Nolan."

She cupped his face in her hands. "Charlie, there's no need to–"

He closed his eyes, relishing her soft touch, but he was determined not to be swayed. "It would destroy me to see you hurt again, Grace. Please, just this once, I am begging you to do as I ask."

Charlie waited for her to refuse. If she did, he would have no hesitation in forcing her into safety, even if he had to tie her up and lock her in her room for her own protection. Perhaps she heard that resolve in his voice.

"I agree. To be honest, I feel exhausted and far more shaken by Nolan's attack than I care to admit to anyone but you, Charlie."

He gently pulled her up and brushed the loose hair off her face. "If I'd looked after you properly, Nolan would never have got to you. Come on, let's get you home. A bite to eat and a decent rest will have you back to your old self."

On the way out, he sent a messenger boy to Lavender House with a note asking for Tiny Tim to be sent to the Macmillan house as soon as possible.

Less than an hour later, he had Grace settled on a chaise longue in the drawing room with a pile of cushions, a soft wrap, a soothing salve for her wrists and a pot of tea. Johnny stood guard until Tiny Tim returned from an errand. It would have to do. Nolan was unlikely to come to the house anyway – he'd be lying low somewhere.

Charlie gave strict instructions to Johnny to let no one enter the house, then went back inside to say goodbye to Grace. Her eyelids were already fluttering closed, so he tucked the blanket around her and left.

He was halfway down the street, feeling wrung out with the shock of Nolan's attack on Grace, when he realised he had forgotten to mention Edmund Chelmsford's dubious character and gambling debts. No need to wake Grace. That unwelcome news could wait until she was feeling stronger.

Duncan proved elusive. Kendall's factory was shuttered and silent, not even a wisp of smoke coming from the brick chimney. Nor was he at home, although Mrs Duncan found time to suggest that he try St Andrew's church, in between tending a bubbling pot, a grazed knee, a dripping nose and a screaming baby.

A melodious burst of choral voices washed over Charlie as he entered the church, taking him back to his childhood Sundays. He stopped for a moment and let the joyous harmonies lift his sorely tested spirits.

A soft voice behind him caught him unawares. "A fine sight to see a policeman caught up in rapture, rather than flailing a truncheon."

"Joy is a rare commodity on the beat, Reverend Waddell. I was hoping to find Mr Duncan here."

Waddell waved a hand towards the south. "I believe he has gone to the cemetery to visit with the son he lost a year ago and the lad who was killed at the factory. Duncan paid for Alfie's burial, as Mrs Watts could not."

"That was a kind gesture." Kindness perhaps, guilt certainly, but no need to tell that to his minister, before all the evidence had been gathered. "You haven't seen a young woman by the name of Molly Sugden, have you?"

"Mrs Macmillan sent a woman to inquire after her this morning. I last saw Molly two days ago, when she and Miss Penrose came to ask after the women who were to testify at the Sweating Commission."

Waddell's frown deepened. "I am deeply concerned that so many women have gone going missing, and now Miss Sugden as well. As one of the Royal Commissioners, I can tell you that their evidence is vital if we are to achieve significant reform of labour conditions."

"I have good news on that score, at least," Charlie said. "The missing women have been located, having taken positions at the new Chelmsford woollen mill out near Mosgiel."

"I am delighted to hear it. That might explain why Mr Chelmsford asked for a morning to be put aside for him and his workers to give evidence to the commission. We granted his request, naturally, but I wondered what purpose he had in mind, other than to highlight the superior conditions in his own factories. Now I see that he may have intended his workers to give evidence of their past situations. We are lucky to have such an enlightened Christian as a business leader."

Charlie refrained from adding that Chelmsford was less likely to be doing it from Christian charity than for the cold, hard profit to be gained by undermining his rivals. Instead, he thanked the Reverend Waddell and went in search of Duncan.

He found the foreman kneeling beside the freshly tamped earth of a new grave, marked by a simple wooden cross. Duncan swung around at the approaching footsteps, a flicker of fear sparking as he saw Charlie.

"Mr Duncan, good of you to pay for Alfie's burial."

"He deserved better, Constable Pyke."

"He did indeed. You must feel a terrible guilt, Mr Duncan, as you are directly to blame for the lad's gruesome death."

Duncan scrambled to his feet. "I … I don't know what you mean. It was an accident."

"You took money from Sterling Chelmsford to interfere with the loom, so Kendall would lose the contract to make tartan."

Tears forced their way out from under Duncan's tightly battened eyelids. "I never meant for anyone to be hurt. I … I was desperate for the money to feed my family and Kendall refused to raise my lousy wage."

Charlie closed the gap between them, looming over Duncan with all the authority he could muster. "Did Chelmsford pay you to murder Jack Finlay as well?"

"What? No! I had nothing to do with his death. I swear on the boy's grave." Duncan dropped to the ground and placed his hand on the cross.

"Chelmsford would have paid you well, I expect, to do such a terrible deed. But the patents you stole were worth a fortune. You, as a factory foreman, must have known that."

Duncan clutched the cross so hard his knuckles turned white. "I had nothing to do with that. I swear it, before God. I am not a killer or a thief. May He smite me down if it's not the truth."

Charlie contemplated the wreck of a man hunched in front of him. Duncan's obvious contrition was all for the dead boy, and he had freely admitted to taking money from Chelmsford to damage the loom. His denial of the murder felt genuine. But if not Duncan, then who? Nolan? A hired killer known to Finlay?

"Mr Duncan, I suggest you pray for your soul and that of the boy. Don't leave town until I say so, or I promise I will hunt you down and haul you back to the gallows myself." Charlie spun around and left the man to his guilt.

Retribution

Charlie stopped off at Lavender House on the way back into town to check for any news of Molly.

Anne enveloped him in a hug as soon as he came through the door. "Charlie, we've been looking everywhere for you. Some boys playing hooky from school found Molly in a grove of trees near the Exhibition. Fortunately, they had the good sense to come here. Lily and Tiny Tim took the rickshaw down to pick her up about an hour ago."

Charlie pushed down his unease that Tiny Tim hadn't got the message to guard Grace. Rescuing Molly was the more urgent priority. "Are they not back yet?"

"I told them to take Molly straight to the hospital. The boy who came to us said she was unconscious and stone cold. The other lad stayed with Molly and wrapped her in his coat, bless him."

"If Tiny Tim comes back, send him to your house. Chelmsford's up to his neck in this wickedness and I wouldn't trust Nolan as far as I could throw him."

"Sterling Chelmsford? Surely not?"

"He paid Duncan to disable the loom that killed Alfie Watts. He was the last person known to have been with Molly and wasted no time in taking her copy of Finlay's valuable designs."

Anne's walking stick fell with a clatter to the floor as she clutched her hand to her heart. "What about Edmund? How could I have been so stupid as to force Grace to consort with him for the sake of a donation? Where is Grace? Is she safe?"

Charlie took Anne's elbow and saw her to a chair. "Don't you worry about Grace, Mrs Macmillan. You wouldn't want Edmund Chelmsford as your nephew-in-law – he's a weak man and in debt to a very unpleasant gambling boss – but I have no evidence he is involved with either the boy's death or Finlay's murder. I've got Johnny guarding your house, while Grace catches up on sleep, although I'd be happier if Tiny Tim could lend his muscle to the job. Just out of caution, not that there is any genuine concern. Grace had a painful encounter with Nolan earlier, so better safe than sorry."

Miss Newland appeared with a cup of tea and a sweet biscuit. "There now, Mrs Macmillan, no need to worry, I'm sure."

Anne took a sip and put the cup down. "I have two patients I must see to, then I will go home and stay with Grace. And you, Charlie?"

"I need to find out who attacked Molly. Without her evidence, I cannot be sure who is behind this tangle of evil. Honestly, I don't believe Grace is in any real danger, otherwise I would be with her myself."

Anne planted a kiss on his cheek. "I know you would, dear boy. We're lucky to have you around, Charlie, and your lovely aunt. Off you go to the hospital now. The sooner you sort out these vermin, the better for all of us."

The warm feeling of being included within a loving family almost overwhelmed him for a moment, reminding him how much he missed seeing his own parents. He returned the kiss and left her startled but smiling.

Quarter of an hour later, Charlie ran up the stairs into the hospital, where he found Lily talking to a nurse. "How is Molly, Aunt Lily?"

"Alive, thanks to those boys finding her. Molly was lying in her own vomit, so perhaps that cleared out her stomach and saved her from worse. Even so, she was still heavily sedated when we got to her. Now that we have her tucked up in a warm bed, her colour is improving and her pulse is regular. She will recover. I've sent Tiny Tim to get DI Stewart."

"Won't they let you sit with her?"

"I saw her settled in, then I left her to talk to the doctor who examined her. Can't find him anywhere. I was just about to ask the nurse."

"You'd have more chance of finding a needle in a haystack, ma'am, than a doctor in a hospital," the nurse said, as he laid out a tray of metal objects, which looked like implements of torture.

"May I see Miss Sugden now?" Lily asked.

"Only one visitor at a time," the nurse replied. "Her gentleman friend arrived a few minutes ago."

Charlie showed the nurse his badge. "What does this man look like?"

"Young man, blond, crooked nose."

"Nolan!" Rage and fear flared with equal intensity, followed by an iron-hard determination to stop this brute in his tracks, once and for all. "Stay out here and see if they have a security guard on duty at the hospital."

"Ward Six," Lily shouted after him. "Second door on the right."

Charlie skidded around the corner on the newly waxed floor. Nolan was bent over Molly's bed, his hand on her lifeless face. "Get your hands off her, Nolan."

Nolan glared back. "What's it to you, Pyke? You ain't even a copper anymore."

"That's Detective Constable Pyke to you. On secondment to Detective Inspector Stewart, who has issued a warrant for your arrest."

"On what charge?" Nolan sneered.

"Corruption, extortion with menaces, assault, covering up a murder. That'll do for a start. When they interrogate you, I'm sure there will be further questions about your cousin's death. Last man to see him alive, first to see him dead – it's not looking good for you, Nolan."

Nolan had slowly risen from the chair, puffing out his chest like a cockerel strutting in front of his rivals. "Bollocks. How dare you threaten me, you lily-livered cretin?"

"I'm not threatening you. I'm arresting you. Move away from the bed, Nolan."

The other man sank back into the chair and took Molly's hand. "Why should I? Molly Sugden is a dear friend in need of help."

"How did you know she was here?"

"I happened to see two disreputable characters carrying her body on a wheeled contraption, so I followed them to the hospital." Nolan feigned a look of injured innocence. "Look, Pyke, I know you are eager to prove yourself, but I don't know what happened to Jack Finlay. His death was nothing to do with me."

"Then why were you at Finlay's office on Monday night?"

Nolan blinked. "If you must know, I heard my cousin was about to come into some serious money, so I touched him for a loan. Rotten swine threw a shilling at my feet and told me never to come back."

"That must have made you furious."

Nolan stared straight at Charlie, with his pretty blue eyes narrowed to slits, then slowly got to his feet. "What makes me furious is listening to your muck-raking. I never touched Jack Finlay, never mind that he deserved a good thrashing for his arrogance. Now get out before I kick you out."

Charlie took a long, slow breath and kept his fists under control. Grace had been right – it would do him no good to lose his job over this lowlife. But neither did he give a single inch as Nolan came towards him. If he so much as swung a fist, all bets would be off. After what Nolan did to Grace, he would welcome the chance to take him down.

"Get out of my way, Pyke."

"No chance, Nolan. You're coming down to the station with me. There's a warrant for your arrest, remember?"

Nolan swung his fist with shocking speed, catching Charlie on the ear as he ducked. His arm went around Charlie's throat, tightening until breathing was impossible. Charlie stamped back with his heavy boots on Nolan's shins, but the arm only cut deeper into his throat. Dots swam in front of his eyes as he punched backwards with his elbow, but Nolan twisted to avoid the blow.

An almighty screech reverberated around the ward. Nolan's grip loosened enough for Charlie to twist around. Lily was clinging to

Nolan's back, like a butterfly on a bull, boxing his ears and clawing at his eyes.

Nolan grabbed for her hands, but Charlie was not about to allow him to hurt another loved one. He slammed his knee upwards into Nolan's thigh to off-balance him, while whisking Lily off his back. Nolan howled and collapsed to the floor, clutching his nether regions.

Stewart skidded to a stop in front of Nolan's writhing body. "Ouch. Remind me not to make you angry, DC Pyke."

"Sorry, sir, I was aiming to take out his leg, but the idiot twisted at the last moment." Charlie set Lily down and watched Stewart clip a pair of cuffs on Nolan, while Tiny Tim held him down. Every eardrum in the hospital would be bursting with the screams and curses emanating from the former constable, even those in a coma or lying on a cold marble slab.

"Quiet down or I'll gag you, you pathetic excuse for a man," Stewart commanded. "Don't worry, Pyke, I saw and heard enough to know it was self-defence." He gestured at the bruising around his constable's neck. "Are you all right?"

Charlie nodded, fearing his voice would give away his still-smouldering rage.

Stewart slapped Tiny Tim on the back. "Fancy a job as a copper, lad?"

Tiny Tim's eyes widened at this ludicrous thought. He shook his head firmly. "I'll help you take him to the nick, but that's as close as I'd want to be to a police station."

"Fair enough. Hold him here for me, will you, while I have a word with Pyke." Stewart turned to Charlie. "Did Nolan hurt Miss Sugden?"

Molly! He had forgotten about her in the heat of the moment.

Fortunately, Lily was already at her side. "Miss Sugden is fine, Detective Inspector Stewart."

The hard lines around Stewart's mouth softened as he smiled at Lily. "You were very brave to take on Nolan, Mrs Wu."

She flicked a hand dismissively. "Not brave. Just darned mad to see that fiend hurting my nephew."

Stewart led Charlie down the corridor to a dead end, where they were out of earshot. "Good work, Pyke. You'll be pleased to hear that I have detained Sergeant Lynch for questioning too. The local inspector had his eye on Lynch and Nolan, even before I came to investigate corruption. Between the three of us, we have a watertight case against both of them. I'm sorry that I couldn't take you into my confidence earlier."

"I understand, sir. You were right to keep me out of it, seeing as I had my own axe to grind with both of them. Thank you for telling me now."

"There's more, Pyke. The inspector was making regular checks on Nolan, in light of rumours that he was shirking his duties. The constable who checked up on him on Monday night reported that he found Nolan collapsed in a grog shop, dead drunk, at the time of the murder. I'm sorry that I didn't think to find out about this earlier, but events have been moving at rather more than an ordinary pace these last few days."

"You mean–"

"There is no way that Nolan could have murdered Jack Finlay."

An Odd Proposal

Grace woke up slowly, feeling groggy with that horrible afternoon-nap wooziness. Headache, irregular pulse, fatigue. Her condition wasn't hard to diagnose – shock, dehydration, lack of food, too many sleepless nights.

She had not intended to fall asleep. How could she, with Molly still missing? Her plan had been to wait for Charlie to leave, then return to Lavender House to help with the search. Allowing him to ply her with comfort and warmth had been a mistake. Time was wasting.

To her surprise, the tea was not yet completely cold. She guzzled two cups of the tepid brew and forced a biscuit down, hoping Molly was out there somewhere, sitting down to a nice cup of tea with a friend.

The alternative made her sick to the stomach. If only she had stayed by Molly's side at the Exhibition last night, instead of getting distracted. The thought of the loathsome Nolan forcing her friend to go with him, while she was dancing outside without a thought in her brain, other than the delicious sensation of a man's arms around her … she would never forgive herself if Nolan had harmed Molly.

Not that she knew for certain it was Nolan. After all, no one had seen Molly after Sterling Chelmsford took her away. Chelmsford had bribed Duncan to destroy Kendall's business. Would he stoop to murder and abduction too? He was rich and influential already, but she was not naïve enough to believe he didn't crave more money – especially the kind of wealth that sole possession of a valuable invention might bring. With Finlay out of the way and Molly's copy of the patent in his hands, wouldn't he have to silence Molly as well?

She shivered, feeling grateful for the locked doors and Johnny watching for trouble outside. Tempting as it was to wrap herself in the soft blanket and sink back into temporary oblivion, she forced herself to her feet.

The front door opened and voices drifted over the sound of a scuffle in the hallway. Johnny's boyish voice protesting, a man's voice reassuring, the maid giving Johnny a piece of her mind for being cheeky. Grace twisted her loose hair in a coil, pinning it with haste as footsteps approached the drawing room. She heard whispered words outside the door and the maid giggling, as she straightened her wrinkled clothes. The door opened.

"Miss Penrose, please forgive me for calling unannounced."

Her hammering heart eased back to a fast thump, as she realised it was only Edmund Chelmsford, not his father. "Come in, Mr Chelmsford."

The maid giggled again and picked up the tea tray.

"Sadie, would you stay here please," Grace ordered.

The maid looked from Grace to Chelmsford, receiving a sharp nod from the latter. "I'm sure you'd rather be alone, Miss Penrose."

Grace watched her retreating with an equal measure of annoyance and foreboding. "Mr Chelmsford, I very much regret that I cannot possibly see you now. I have pressing matters to attend to."

"Please, my dear, call me Edmund. We haven't known each other long, but I like to think of myself as a man who can spot a gem and act promptly to secure it." He went down on one knee and pulled out a ring box.

Grace wasn't sure what she had been expecting from him, but it certainly wasn't this. They had only seen each other three times, and not one of those times had been more than a business meeting or a chance encounter. How could this be happening when she counted him as no more than a casual acquaintance? Was Charlie right, that she unwittingly given the wrong signals to a man who was clearly desperate for admiration and attention?

"Mr Chelmsford – Edmund – you flatter me, but please believe me that now is not the time." To her dismay, the last words came out as a sob.

"My dear, whatever is the matter?" The ring box disappeared into a pocket as Edmund took her arm and pushed her gently down onto the chaise longue. He sat with his knees touching hers, looking at her with sincere concern.

"I am afraid I am in a state of upset. A friend of mine went missing at the Exhibition last night and nobody has seen her since."

"I'm mortified to hear it. How may I be of assistance? Whatever it takes to make you happy again, my dear, it shall be done."

"Thank you, Edmund, you are very kind." Grace extracted her fingers from his grip and clasped her hands in her lap. "Perhaps you could ask your father where she went. She took a turn at the Exhibition and your father took her behind the stands to recover."

"Father said nothing of the matter to me, but naturally I will ask him for you. Can you describe your friend?"

"I believe you saw her with me. Miss Molly Sugden." The woman Edmund had dismissed as nothing but a union troublemaker.

"I recall seeing her with you, my dear, but not after that. Are you sure she hasn't gone off with some fancy man or other?"

"Mr Chelmsford, I resent the implication that she was that sort of girl. She was the devoted fiancé of a Mr Jack Finlay, who was murdered on Monday night. We think she was unaware of his death, which is why she collapsed at your exhibition stand, after hearing of his murder. Finlay worked with your father."

Edmund didn't bother hiding his disbelief. "Finlay murdered? Surely not! You are overwrought, my dear."

"Did you not see it in the newspaper? The police have arrested Finlay's brother, but Detective Constable Pyke and I do not believe he was the killer."

"Darling Grace, you must not allow yourself to be dragged into anything so abominably sordid. Finlay's death cannot be anything to you, surely. A good man and a great loss, notwithstanding."

Grace couldn't be bother explaining the complex tangle of events. "It is Molly I am most worried about at present."

233

"My dear, you look awfully pale. Allow me to get you a glass of brandy."

"No, really, Edmund, it is not necessary." Alcohol was the very last thing she needed, but he had already moved to the decanter to pour out a slug of liquor.

"Just a nip, to calm your nerves," he said, thrusting the half-full glass into her hand.

She figured she would get rid of him quicker if she didn't make a fuss, although she never drank brandy. She knocked it back, gagging at the unfamiliar taste.

He fussed around, putting cushions behind her, stroking her wild hair back from her face. "Are you feeling better now, my darling?"

She wanted to tell him to stop using such endearments, but he was being so kind and, truth be told, she was feeling slightly calmer. She allowed him to whitter on about what he would do to help in the search for Molly, as her own thoughts drifted with a lamentable lack of focus.

With a start, he let out an "oh!"

"What is it, Edmund?"

"I believe I recall seeing her again, after all. She came out from behind the stand and asked me to thank Father for his help. She met a young man as she walked away from our stand. I remember feeling pleased she had his arm to lean on."

Grace dragged herself upright from the comfortable nest of cushions. "A young man?" Nolan's face jumped into her mind. "Tall, blond, muscled, freckles, broken nose?"

The tension seemed to drain out of Edmund's body. "That's the man. Looked like a prize-fighter. Or perhaps more like the man beaten by the prize-fighter. I'm so glad that I could help locate your friend."

Grace sank back into the cushions. Edmund seemed so delighted to have helped that she didn't have the heart to tell him that his news only made the situation worse. If Molly had fallen into Nolan's clutches, then the need to find her had become even more desperate.

But Charlie had been right. She absolutely must have some rest if she was to be of any use. She felt as if she could sleep for a week.

Meanwhile, Edmund was droning on about how successful the Exhibition had been.

"Edmund, you have been very considerate, but I'm afraid I must ask you to leave. I barely slept last night, and I feel terribly tired."

Tired was an understatement for the wave of exhaustion swallowing her. Drinking brandy on an empty stomach had been a mistake. She tried to get to her feet, but Edmund gently pushed her down on the chaise longue with the sweetest of smiles.

She sighed, the will to get up oozing away, as he lifted the soft woollen blanket towards her drooping head. The blanket was so soft. As soft as a finely woven scarf.

In a Lather

Charlie stared at Stewart in shocked silence.

Detective Inspector Stewart asked the inevitable question. "So, if Nolan didn't kill Jack Finlay, who did?"

"I'm not sure you'll want to hear it, sir, but I have uncovered additional evidence pointing to Sterling Chelmsford's involvement."

Lily ran out of the ward, waving to catch their attention, and cutting off Stewart's reply.

They raced down the corridor. In the ward, Molly's eyelids were fluttering. Lily propped her up with pillows and gave her a few sips of water. Molly's eyes roved unsteadily around the group before focusing on Charlie.

"Charlie from the switchback railway?" she queried, in a voice as wobbly as a drunk's.

"Acting Detective Constable Charlie Pyke, at your service. And this is Detective Inspector Stewart and my aunt, Mrs Lily Wu. You remember going on the switchback railway with me last night?"

"Vaguely. I remember a man saying Jack is dead. Or was that a nightmare too?"

"I'm very sorry to say that it's true, Miss Sugden. My sincere condolences."

Molly squeezed her eyes closed, but the tears refused to be held back. "I loved him."

Charlie took her trembling hands between his. "He loved you too, Molly. When you feel better, Miss Abercrombie has a beautiful ring that he intended to give you. He was a fine man, by all accounts."

Molly nodded, clearly unable to speak. Finally, she let out a long sob. "Thank you, Charlie."

"I'm deeply sorry, but I need to ask you about last night. I wouldn't bother you if it wasn't urgent. What can you recall, Molly?"

"I must have fainted after I heard…" Molly took a series of gasping intakes of breath. With an obvious effort of willpower, she continued. "When I recovered from the faint, Mr Chelmsford was looking after me, giving me a glass of brandy. Next thing I know, I woke up here." She looked around. "Where am I?"

"Dunedin hospital." Charlie squeezed her hands, wishing he could take some of the pain away, or at least not inflict any more. But they needed to know. "Mr Chelmsford gave you the brandy?"

"Yes. His father had brought me tea, but Mr Chelmsford said brandy was a much better restorative than tea. I don't drink alcohol at all, but he insisted. I suppose I must have been overwhelmed by the brandy and wandered off, although I don't remember leaving the Exhibition. I remember being violently ill and that's it."

"Being sick probably saved your life, Molly." Her exact words finally hit Charlie square in the gut. "Wait. Did you say the father gave you tea, but the younger Mr Chelmsford gave you the brandy – Mr *Edmund* Chelmsford?"

"Yes. Ever so kind he was. He said he and Grace Penrose were to be engaged and that it was his duty to take good care of her friends."

"And you only drank the brandy, not the tea?"

"Yes."

"Molly, Edmund Chelmsford drugged you. Grace may be in trouble." He was on his feet, pulling on his cap. "My Aunt Lily will stay here to watch over you. You can trust her completely."

"Charlie, wait," Lily said, catching his arm. "I haven't had a chance to tell you what I found out this morning. I asked a few questions at the Grand Hotel. The cook there is a friend. He said that several of the young gentlemen sneaked out of the reception on Monday night, so they could drink and smoke out the back during the speeches. I showed a copy of your sketches to the staff and the kitchen hand recognised Edmund Chelmsford as one of the men."

"Edmund Chelmsford left the reception on Monday night? So, it is possible that he could have walked the short distance to Finlay's office, killed and dumped him, then gone back to the reception without anyone realising?"

Charlie dashed his hand to his forehead. "I've been an idiot. I didn't ask Mrs Sugden to specify which of the Chelmsford men had taken the patent application, assuming it was the father." Another memory surfaced, causing him still greater anguish. Grace, at the Exhibition, stroking a scarf of the finest wool, as Edmund leaned over her possessively.

Stewart took charge. "Pyke, see to Miss Penrose. Lily, stay here with Miss Sugden. I'll alert the hospital's security guard. I have to get Nolan to a jail cell, then I'll round up a few constables to detain both Sterling and Edmund Chelmsford. Report any developments to the police station."

Charlie didn't wait to hear any more. He sprinted out the door, skidding on the wax and cursing like a docker, running as if the hounds of hell were nipping at his heels. The bruising on his neck made breathing painful, but the throbbing only drove him faster.

He didn't stop running until he pulled up outside the Macmillan house, lungs straining like bellows, dripping with sweat. To his horror, there was no sign of Johnny guarding the house.

Charlie barged into the hall, yelling before he had stepped across the threshold. "Grace! Grace! Where are you?"

The maid came out of the kitchen. "Whatever is this fuss about, Mr Pyke? Miss Penrose has gone out with Mr Chelmsford."

Charlie wanted to shake the stupid girl, but he forced himself to be calm. "*Edmund* Chelmsford?"

"Of course, sir. He arrived not long after you left. Dead romantic, it was. He asked me to leave them so he could propose. She must have said yes, because they went off together. Ain't that just lovely? Well, naturally she said yes to such a handsome and wealthy man. Lucky her, I say."

He resisted the urge to slap her, allowing the sting of his words to convey the urgency. "Do you know where and when they went?"

The maid took a step back, clearly shocked by the panic in his voice. "Mr Chelmsford couldn't have been here too much longer than a half hour. I expect they must have gone to see Mrs Macmillan to ask her permission, though I could not say for sure."

Charlie glanced at the mantelpiece clock. He had brought Grace home over three hours ago, so they were long gone. Damnation, why hadn't he stayed to look after her. "Were they in the drawing room?"

At her frightened nod, he pushed past her and strode into the drawing room. The shape of Grace's head was still visible in the cushions, but there was no trace of warmth. Only the faint scent of Grace's perfume, teasing his senses and mocking his stupidity. He pulled himself away from the cushion and scanned the room.

His heart skipped a beat when he saw the brandy bottle and glass on the sideboard, concealing a small bottle of chloral hydrate, tipped on its side, empty.

Where would they have gone? Surely, Chelmsford House was the most likely place. But what if Edmund was taking her somewhere to dump, as he did to Molly and Finlay? Safer to take the time to send messages to all the search teams, rather than take the chance of being wrong.

Charlie slammed the front door and leaped over the porch steps, almost knocking Johnny Todd over as he ran through the gate. The lad was a lather of sweat and anguish.

"I'm sorry, Mr Pyke. Tiny Tim hadn't arrived yet and Chelmsford was stronger than he looks. The maid told me off and said he could come into the house. I couldn't stop him."

"Never mind that now, Johnny. Do you know where he took Miss Penrose?"

"She came out of the house in his arms, looking up at him all dreamy-like, and the maid was congratulating them on being engaged. But he had to lift her into his buggy, which didn't seem right to me."

"He drugged her. Did you see which way they went?"

"I jumped on the back of the buggy and hung on as far as the corner of Anderson's Bay Road, where I couldn't hang on no longer. Chelmsford was driving the horse hard."

Charlie flung an arm around the startled lad and hugged him. "Great work, Johnny. At least we know they are heading out of town. But where?"

Mrs Macmillan's voice startled him from his frantic thoughts.

"Charlie, what is happening?"

"Edmund Chelmsford has taken Grace, Mrs Macmillan. Johnny says they were heading out on Anderson's Bay Road."

"Chelmsford has a house out on the peninsula." Anne frowned. "Is there something amiss, beyond my niece going for a seaside jaunt with a gentleman without my permission?"

"This is no jaunt. He drugged and kidnapped Grace. Edmund Chelmsford is the man behind Molly's disappearance and Finlay's murder."

Anne clutched at the gatepost for support. "What are we to do?"

"I will follow them as fast as I can. Mrs Macmillan, you stay here in case they come back. Johnny, you must run as fast as you can to the police station to tell Detective Inspector Stewart about the peninsula house. Have him gather a few stout men and meet me there."

Anne nodded, her expression terrifying in rage and anguish. She threw her purse at Charlie. "Use this to hire the fastest horse in the stable. The house sits on a promontory, about half a mile this side of Glenfalloch House. Bring my girl back safely!"

A Room with a View

Grace floated back to consciousness on a wave of nausea, feeling as if her head was stuffed with barbed wire and wool. The pillow beneath her head was soft and scented with lavender, the sheets starched white, and her wrists hurt like the blazes.

Was she dreaming? The last thing she remembered was Edmund's face above hers, but that was at her great-aunt's house, not this unfamiliar place.

She pushed herself upright, fighting against the urge to lie back and let oblivion claim her. When the room stopped whirling, she took stock of her surroundings.

A trickle of sunlight filtered around the heavy velvet curtains, lightening the gloom enough to see that the bedroom was hung with tapestries and filled with furniture of baroque taste, but undeniable quality. The canopied bed dominated the space, surrounded by gilded chairs upholstered in pale silk, with matching tables bearing antique vases and dried flower arrangements. A lady's boudoir.

Two doors, presumably one to the corridor and one to a connecting room. A garment caught her eye, laid out across a large travelling trunk. The cream silk gown had a ridiculous number of ruffles and flounces. A special occasion dress, suitable for a woman of florid tastes.

Her throat felt parched. A carafe and glass stood on one table. Could she trust the water in it? Grace slid out of the bed, making her way around the room, using the wall for support. A sniff and a sip suggested the water was untainted, so she gave in to thirst.

Feeling marginally revived, Grace wobbled her way across to the nearest door. Locked. The second door was too. With a flicker of hope, she pulled the curtains back from the window, revealing, to her astonishment, a stunning seascape. Ink blue sea, sapphire blue sky and a distant horizon of verdant hills, curving around to the north end of Dunedin city.

Edmund had taken her to the Otago Peninsula while she slept, where nobody would think to look for her.

The faint sound of waves lapping on a rocky shore taunted her. Inevitably, the window was locked too. The air seeping through the cracks around the window carried the tang of salt with a whiff of pungent animal. Anne had taken her on a sightseeing jaunt to Otago Peninsula when she had first arrived. A truly marvellous place, where malodorous fur seals basked on a rocky coast and giant albatrosses took flight out to the ocean.

More to the point, the magnificent view was made possible only by the location of the window, high on the third storey of a house. With no convenient trees or ladders to scramble down, she was trapped, like Rapunzel in her tower.

The voice of Mrs Watts came back to haunt her. *A princess in a castle, set on a rock above the sea, where giant birds circle and mermaids sing.*

Grace flopped back onto the bed and allowed herself a minute to assess her options for escape. A few seconds would have been enough. The door was the only way out.

She rattled the door handle again. A tiny clink on the other side had her crouching down, peering through the keyhole, which was blocked by a key. It would be easy enough to push it out with a hairpin, but how could she then retrieve it?

A hasty rummage through the draws rewarded her with a piece of stiff card, which she slipped under the door to catch the key as it fell. Pulling it back under the door was trickier, the chunky old key catching once, twice, before she managed to wiggle it to the wider gap at one side of the door. Seeing it sliding into her hand was a minor triumph, but not one she lingered over.

Grace stood by the door, ears on the alert. The house was quiet, aside from the gentle wash of waves and the sigh of wind through the trees. Her first instinct was to run. She would have, but for the possibility that Molly might be here too. Instead, she would allow herself ten minutes to search for Molly and for evidence of what Edmund was up to, then she would flee.

With infinite care, she unlocked and eased open the door, pulse pounding as the hinges squeaked against the silence. She tested the door opposite, which was locked, and hissed Molly's name as loudly as she dared. Silence. Two other rooms on that side of the corridor were also empty.

The only other door on this floor of the house was the one beside the room she had woken up in, which yielded to her touch. The coat and gloves thrown on the bed told her the bedroom belonged to Edmund. Thankfully, the room was empty.

A quick reconnoitre revealed a separate dressing room and an adjoining study, with a connecting door to her room. The suites of the master and mistress of the house.

Grace started her search in the most obvious place – the desk. Edmund had virtually no documents relating to the woollen mill and clothing business, although he had a pile of papers pertaining to racehorse breeding, a disturbing number of annotated race cards, and a veritable avalanche of terse notes requesting repayment of alarmingly large debts.

Ten minutes had long since passed when she slipped into his dressing room, but her perseverance was rewarded. A travelling trunk sat in a corner. With a little gentle persuasion from a paper knife, its inadequate lock yielded.

Underneath Edmund's clothes and sundries, she found a small box of white powder. Grace thought back to the morning of their visit to the factory, when Edmund's eyes had sparkled with uncharacteristic fervour, which had ebbed away to dullness as the hours passed. How could she have been so blind?

At the bottom of the trunk, wrapped in an overcoat, she found a leather satchel. Amongst the documents it contained were two copies of the patent application, complete with technical drawings. One copy had an attached letter purporting to be from Jack Finlay, assigning all rights to the patent to Edmund. He must have forced Finlay to sign the letter, under duress, that night in Finlay's office before he killed him.

What a fool she was to have felt anything but revulsion for this murderer, who had every advantage in life, yet still fell prey to addiction and greed. To think she had felt sorry for Edmund Chelmsford's weaknesses. If only she had listened to Charlie.

The sound of floorboards squeaking jolted her back to the present. The door to the adjoining bedroom, where she had woken up, opened with a creak, followed by the sound of an oath and a frantic search of the room.

With heart thudding, Grace packed the satchel away in the trunk and looked around frantically for a hiding place for the documents she had removed. A hat box sitting on top of a wardrobe caught her eye.

She was still balanced on a narrow chair, with the hat box in her hands, when she heard footsteps in the corridor and the rattle of door handles from the rooms opposite. Grace flung the hat box back where she found it and dashed back into the bedroom.

Too late. Footsteps stopped outside the door. She raced to the window, but it was an impossible drop – three storeys onto a steep slope, falling away to the edge of a cliff.

"I wouldn't jump from there, my dear. My father insisted on finding the most dramatic spot for his grand pretension. When William Larnach and George Russell built their mansions on the peninsula, my father was not to be outdone."

Grace spun around, her heart plummeting into her boots at the sight of Edmund Chelmsford in the doorway, holding a long, needle-sharp dagger in his hand with casual menace.

"My mother died after leaping from that very window. She was quite mad by the end. My father drove her to it." He paused, bringing his palm to the point of the dagger, leaving a pin-prick of blood. "I know how she felt. Father dearest made me move into this room after her death to spare himself the daily reminder of his sin. He cared nothing for the effect it would have on me, naturally."

Grace eased away from the window, edging her way inch by inch across the room to the connecting door. "You don't have to be like your mother, Edmund."

Edmund stepped into the room, closing and locking the door behind him. "I do not intend to be, my dear Grace."

Another slow step. "Is Molly here too?"

He darted between her and the connecting door. "Alas, the meddlesome Miss Sugden is dead. I gave her a much bigger dose than I gave you."

Grace stifled a sob and forced herself to focus. Somehow, she had to beat this insane killer before she became his next victim. She dropped her voice to a soft purr. "Edmund, you must stop this. If you leave now, you can escape the noose."

"I would never have faced the noose if that damned policeman friend of yours hadn't stuck his nose in."

"Do you mean to kill me too, Edmund? Pyke will hunt you down to the ends of the earth."

"Kill you? Only as a last resort. I have become fond of you, my dear, despite your insatiable curiosity and unladylike pursuits. The problem is, you appear to know too much." Edmund gave her a sweet smile, which curdled her insides. "However, there is a convenient solution to my dilemma. Did you know a wife cannot give evidence against her husband?"

"You cannot think I would marry you, after all you have done?" Grace stepped back towards the window, her only option for escape. She would sooner risk a three-storey drop than marriage to this lunatic.

"What have I done? A couple of unimportant people disposed of, and a fortune is mine. Ours. We could have a wonderful life, my dear, away from my oppressive father and his sordid factories. I rather fancy a trip to the Continent. Paris, Nice, Monte Carlo. A marvellous spot for a honeymoon, don't you think? We would settle in England, of course. A grand home and racing stables, near Ascot or Newmarket."

He made it all sound so delightfully normal, as if he was mad enough to believe such a fanciful life was possible. Grace pushed down her panic. "And how do you mean to escape justice here?"

"Simple. I have two tickets booked already. Our ship sails on the next tide."

Grace was absorbing the enormity of his words when he moved beside her.

"I must thank you, my dear. You showed me what it was like to feel loved. You encouraged me to break free of my father and follow my passions."

She clamped her dropped jaw shut. Arguing with a madman would serve no purpose. "Did you arrange for the factory girls to go missing too?"

"That was my father's idea. He even managed to make a profitable deal out of it, as usual. The other owners wanted to be rid of them so they couldn't bring their fanciful tales of exploitation before the Royal Commission. They paid him a tidy sum to take the worst of the unionists off their hands. The amusing irony was that my father was double-crossing the other owners, taking their unwanted militants away, but planning to get them to testify on his behalf."

"He traded their lives for money?"

"Hardly, my dear. He offered them an exceptional opportunity. The new factory is a working-class utopia. Fresh country air, miles from the ills of the city, with everything they need provided. We house them, feed them and work them. A grand new way of creating a healthy and efficient workforce."

Penned and used like a herd of dairy cows. "And they may leave at any time?"

"They have all signed a two-year contract," Edmund said. "And why would they want to leave? Their homes in Dunedin were appalling hovels."

"They would want to see their loved ones."

"Oh, you may rest assured that no one loves them. They are not proper women, you see, just worker drones with a bee in their bonnet about their so-called rights, and no desire for home nor hearth."

Edmund Chelmsford opened the connecting door to her room and gestured with the dagger for her to go through. Her skin raised goosebumps as she passed within touching distance.

"You may put on your wedding dress. The minister will be here soon. It took me a while to find one on short notice who would ignore the trifles like reading the banns, but money always works wonders in the end."

"Why on earth would you want to marry me? Most men would run a mile from my beliefs and sharp tongue. I want to be a doctor, not a wife."

Edmund chuckled, as if she had made a joke. "Oh, I think you will find that being my wife has far more attractions than slaving for a living amongst the sick and destitute. As my father rightly pointed out, a robust, intelligent woman with five brothers is a sound proposition for a man who wishes many healthy sons to carry on the family name. The simpering daughters of the in-bred elite are no match for your robust bloodlines."

"And if I don't agree to be your breeding sow?"

"If I cannot silence you by marriage, the alternative option is still open. That would be a terrible waste, my dear Grace. So young and lively. A very great shame indeed."

"May I have time to reflect?"

"Of course, my dear. A marriage proposal is such an exciting time for a young lady, naturally you wish to savour the moment before agreeing." The twist of his lips confirmed he hadn't become so divorced from sanity that he meant these outrageous words.

Edmund locked the connecting door, taking the key, and moved to the main door to the bedroom, pausing at the threshold. "Perhaps I ought to mention that the lives of several other people hang in the balance? Refuse me and I assure you that the odious Charles Pyke will be the first to meet a painful demise, followed by Mrs Macmillan, and any others dear to you. After taking the life of one man, you see, there is no further penalty for killing again."

Grace didn't doubt for a second that he meant it. No wonder his mother took her own life, with Sterling Chelmsford as a husband and this lunatic as a son. But Grace knew she couldn't be responsible for Charlie and Anne suffering. And the marriage would be a short one, with any luck. She had never been a supporter of capital punishment, but right now the hangman's noose seemed like a beacon of hope, although the prospect of the intervening long voyage as his wife didn't bear thinking about.

With a roiling stomach, she spat out the words he wanted to hear. "I accept your proposal." If nothing else, her acceptance would buy her time to think of a better plan.

"Excellent. Please put the gown on."

He watched on with a proprietorial smirk as she stripped to her undergarments and slipped on the silky gown, which smelled of lavender and disuse. The gown had been made for a woman of more generous proportions than her own, which sent a shiver down her spine. Dear Lord, was she not the first to be held in this room and given the devil's choice?

With a wriggle to settle the ruffles and flounces into place, the bride was as ready to meet her fate as a condemned man awaiting the gallows.

Until Death Do Us Part

Edmund led Grace down the stairs, through a reception hall with stunning views across the harbour, and into a room large enough to hold a ball ... or a wake.

The design brief must have specified "ancient baronial style", alongside admonitions to spare no expense and to the devil with good taste. Wood-panelled walls, lined with the stuffed heads of game animals that had never set foot in New Zealand, and a floor of polished hardwood bedecked with four-legged hairy rugs, crowned by an oppressive ceiling, intricately carved from the cornices to the chandeliers. An enormous fireplace – wide enough to roast a boar – dominated the near wall, with a heraldic shield above it.

A thoroughly pretentious folly, given the Chelmsford family's less than noble origins.

To top off the decorative excesses, a cluster of scientific display cases lined the side wall, featuring iridescent tropical butterflies, a long-necked skeleton of a moa and unidentifiable fleshy specimens floating in large glass jars. Pride of place went to a domed glass case filled with enough stuffed finches to make Charles Darwin salivate. On a normal day, this eclectic display of the world's fauna might have intrigued Grace, but today it twisted her stomach in knots.

The sound of a carriage on the gravel driveway brought hope and dread in equal measures. Was that Charlie's heavy tread on the steps? Or the renegade minister, come to seal her fate? The odds were not good. The minister was definitely coming, while Charlie had no earthly idea where she was or even that she was missing.

As the heavy oak door opened, Edmund tightened his grip on her arm with one hand and pushed the tip of the dagger into her back with the other, sending a prickle of pain through her nervous system. "Not a word, Grace."

"Edmund, I didn't expect to see you here." Sterling Chelmsford closed the door behind him. "And Miss Penrose, looking most charming." His mouth puckered as his eyes took in her dress. "Forgive me for staring, but your gown reminds me of my first wife's wedding dress."

With a slight shake of his head, he forced a smile. "I do apologise for disturbing you two love-birds, but my son did not inform me of his visit." Sterling glanced around. "You have a chaperone or maid, I trust?"

Edmund pushed the knife into her back and answered for her. "I have sent the servants out for an hour or two, Father, while I show my fiancée around the estate."

"You're engaged? Well, well, that is splendid news. I look forward to many clever and lively grandsons to carry on the family empire."

Edmund whispered in her ear. "Try smiling, my dear. Think of what a horse crop would do to Pyke's dreary face."

Grace's attempt at a smile would fool no one with an ounce of compassion, but Edmund seemed satisfied. Her last chance was to appeal to Sterling Chelmsford and hope that he had played no part in his son's crimes. Better to risk the knife in her back than to give in to despair.

"Your son murdered Finlay and stole his designs," she blurted out, before the butt of the dagger jabbed into her lower back, sending a spurt of pain up her spine.

"Say a word more and you will die," Edmund whispered, twisting her wrist painfully in the exact spot Nolan had twisted.

Sterling Chelmsford moved from the door into the room, jabbing his silver-topped walking cane in her direction as he digested her words. "What are you talking about, girl? What's this about Finlay? He has already agreed to sell me the design for an extortionate sum."

His frown deepened as he processed the rest of her accusation. "And murder? What rot. Edmund is too spineless to hurt a flea."

Grace felt the tension rising in Edmund's grip on her as his father's callous jibe hit home. Did she dare say more?

"My darling Grace is rather light-headed after taking a sleeping tonic, Father. I fear she must be confusing reality with a nightmare."

Sterling came to a halt a few feet from them, tapping his boot with the cane, a frown furrowing his brow. "Why would she agree to marry you if she doubted you?"

Grace didn't dare say a word, but she was able to angle her face away from her captor and send a silent plea to his father.

The elder Chelmsford appeared uncertain. No doubt an unusual feeling for so powerful a man.

"You do not wish to marry Edmund?" At her minute shake of her head, he directed his puzzled frown back to his son. "Let her arm go, Edmund. Can't you see you are hurting her?"

Edmund stepped away, hooking her ankle and jerking her arm up as he did so, tipping her to the floor. Grace felt a sharp pain as her ankle twisted.

Her abductor ignored her cry of pain and pointed the dagger towards his father. "I've listened to your demeaning insults for twenty-five years, Father. No longer. I will soon have the money to live my life away from your suffocating shadow."

His father eyed the knife with commendable sangfroid. Or perhaps merely a foolish disregard for his son's true nature.

"Money?" Sterling sneered. "How would you make money, Edmund, when you're high on cocaine by dinner, drunk on gin-slings by supper, and drugged with sleeping draughts all night? You care about nothing but yourself, your damned racehorses, and squandering your allowance on gambling and vice."

Grace melted into the floor, as still as a snake in the grass, hoping she would be go unnoticed. Was she hallucinating, or was that the sound of hoofbeats on the road below? She prayed the renegade minister would put his greed aside and try to stop Edmund from murdering them all.

With glacial movements, she tested her ankle. Agonising, but hopefully not bad enough to stop her putting her weight on it, if she absolutely had to. She started sliding across the floor, towards the door, as Edmund fixed his father with a poisonous glare.

"You won't be so high and mighty when I sell Finlay's design to the highest bidder. Every woollen mill and clothing factory in the Empire will have efficient, safe machinery, and all your devious tricks to claw your way to the top of the pile will be for naught."

"Edmund, don't be a jackass fool. With Finlay's invention, we can both be rich." Sterling Chelmsford stared at his son, perhaps seeing him clearly for the first time. "Or is it me who has been the fool, not seeing that you are as insane as your mother?"

"Don't you dare insult my mother." Edmund's screech echoed off the ceiling. "A sweet, loving angel, destroyed by your contempt. Did you think I wouldn't remember how you turned your back on her?"

Anger flashed across his father's chiselled profile. "Your mother failed at the one thing required of her – producing a half-decent heir. Her only progeny, you, turned out to be as pathetic as she was. You will do as I say, Edmund, or I will cut you from my will entirely."

"Enough!" Edmund yelled. "You will do as I say, for once in your damned life. Tell me this – did my mother jump or was she pushed?"

Sterling whipped his walking cane into the air with a furious up-swing. It hung in the air over Edmund's head, until, with equal abruptness, his father dropped his arm. "How dare you ask such a thing? Your mother was not in her right mind. I had every reason to be angry with her. She was the one who shunned me, then she sent away the one woman who brought joy into my life."

"Hannah Watts." As soon as the words burst out of Grace's mouth, she realised she was an idiot for calling attention to herself. Her insatiable curiosity would get her killed this time.

Sterling whirled around. "How did you–?"

The truth was, she hadn't been sure until he confirmed it with his reaction, although she should have recognised the resemblance between Alfie Watts and Sterling Chelmsford earlier. Hannah must have left this house not long before Mrs Chelmsford's death, presumably sent away when her mistress found out she was with child.

252

No wonder Edmund hated his father, if he believed Sterling had driven his mother to her death in revenge.

With both men staring at her, all she could do was stoke the fire of their animosity. "Did you know that Hannah Watts bore you a fine son, though she died doing it?"

For the first time in their acquaintance, Sterling Chelmsford showed signs of genuine emotion for another human being. "My poor, sweet girl. I never knew what happened to her." He raised his head and looked at her with a flicker of hope. "You say she bore me a son? Did he live?"

"A clever, lively lad called Alfie Watts, with the look of his mother, but your nose and chin. A son to be proud of."

"Where can I find him?" Sterling asked, his voice cracking with longing.

Grace was long past any trace of empathy for either of the Chelmsford men. "Alfie is newly laid to rest in a pauper's grave. He lived a hard life and died in a factory accident that should never have happened." She spat out her next words with all the vitriol he deserved. "You paid Fergus Duncan to disable the loom that killed him. How does it feel to know that your son lived and died in agony because of your own despicable actions?"

The cane clattered to the floor. Sterling sank to his knees, whimpering like a wild animal in distress.

"Now who's the cry baby?" Edmund snarled. "You bed a lowly maid, young enough to be your daughter, right under my mother's nose, yet you weep for her and her bastard, but not for your wife. Have you no shame?"

"Get the hell out of my sight, Edmund. I cannot bear to look at you. If only I had known I had another son."

Edmund let out a demented shriek and lunged forward, holding the dagger like a rapier.

Sterling Chelmsford scrambled for his walking cane, striking the tip of the dagger away as it descended to his chest. The length of the cane gave him the advantage, but only in defence. In attack, it would be no

253

match for the sharp blade of the dagger and his son's mad fury. Grace took the chance to slide closer to the door.

Edmund dodged and feinted, slashing like a maniac, until a desperate upward sweep of the cane flipped the dagger out of his hand. The knife skittered away across the wooden floorboards, coming to rest under the display cases.

Both men lunged for it, but Sterling was quicker off the mark. He grabbed the hilt of the dagger, turning the point on his son. Edmund stared at the blade, his face rigid with hate, as his father slowly withdrew his arm and turned the dagger away.

"If only I had understood how much you were suffering, Edmund. I am truly sorry that I allowed my work to take precedence. I promise I will arrange the best of care for you. Seacliff has an excellent reputation for–"

"You would send me to a lunatic asylum?" Edmund's voice rose in shrill incredulity. "I'd sooner jump from the window." With whip-fast speed, he seized the case of stuffed birds, using it as a shield as he advanced on his father.

Sterling stumbled backwards, waving the dagger in front of his body. "Put that down, Edmund. It cost me an absolute fortune to get those specimens of Darwin's finches."

"Survival of the fittest, Father dearest," Edmund snarled as he brought the display case down on his father's head.

Sterling lurched sideways, but the case still caught him with a shuddering blow. The glass shattered and cascaded over him, as he slumped to the floor with a guttural moan amidst a shower of feathered bodies.

Grace froze for an instant, fighting the reflex urge to help him. Self-preservation prevailed. She forced herself to her feet and ran for the door, ignoring the pain shooting through her ankle. The over-long dress and the thick rug in front of the hearth were her undoing. In a panic at the sound of his footsteps behind her, she tripped and fell. When she looked up again, Edmund was between her and the door, with the dagger back in his hand.

"Edmund, enough," she cried. "For heaven's sake, leave the country as you planned, but don't add any more murders to your overburdened soul."

"I didn't want to kill anyone, but he left me with no choice." His simpering smile looked as out of place as rouge on an undertaker.

"Please, Edmund, go now, while you can, I implore you. The ship will be sailing soon."

The smile wavered as he considered her plea. "You'll come with me? We'll be rich. We can go wherever you want."

Grace closed her eyes and fought to remain calm in the face of his delusions. "No, Edmund. You will go alone and make your own way in the world."

Edmund's eyes narrowed to slits, as her refusal finally lodged in his brain. "You lured me with your sweetness and kind words, but you're no better than the rest of them." He twirled the dagger in his hand. "Give me one good reason why I shouldn't kill you too, you deceitful harpy."

As the dagger flicked closer to her face, Grace curled into a ball with her arms over her head, praying for a miracle.

The door exploded open and a booming, inhuman roar rent the air. Grace heard Edmund's scream and the sound of two bodies smashing together. A sickening crack reverberated through the floorboards. Then silence.

She pushed herself to her knees. Edmund lay stock-still, with his head seeping blood into the bear-skin rug in front of the stone hearth. A second body lay close by, creating its own pool of rapidly spreading blood.

"Charlie!"

Last rites

Charlie's face was as pale as the hospital sheet that covered him. Grace swallowed her fear and cradled his hand. Her voice rasped from begging him to live, by way of alternating whispers of devotion and threats to chase him to the pearly gates if he dared give up on her.

Bandages swathed his upper arm, concealing a long, shallow slash wound. Although he had lost an alarming quantity of blood, his pulse was now stable.

Lily had spent hours sharing the vigil at her nephew's bedside, between shifts attending to the needy at Lavender House. Anne came and went with harried regularity, bearing tins of cake and words of heartfelt apology for her role in throwing her beloved great-niece into the path of Edmund Chelmsford.

Molly Sugden visited too, looking drawn and red-eyed, but wearing the garnet ring Miss Abercrombie had delivered to her bedside. Molly hugged Grace fiercely, like a long-lost sister. "Dearest Grace, how glad I am that you survived. Mrs Macmillan has told me what happened, although I suspect she spared me the worst of it. How is Charlie?"

"As well as can be expected. Unless the wound becomes infected, he should make a full recovery, although he'll have a nasty scar. And you, Molly?"

"I'm relieved to hear you found the missing women. Harriet Morison says some are content where they are, whereas others have come back to town. A couple have even returned to Kendall's factory. I would never have believed it in a thousand years, but Harriet says that Mr Kendall has repented his sins and promised to improve conditions in his factory with the profits from the tartan contract."

"So, you'll have your prize witnesses to testify before the Sweating Commission?"

Molly smiled for the first time. "The truth will out."

Grace clutched her friend's hand. "And how are you, Molly – honestly?"

"Feeling like the devil has ripped my heart out. Will and I will try to keep Jack's business going, though how that's to be done without the patent, I cannot say."

"Molly, what an idiot I am. With all that's happened, I completely forgot. Ask Detective Inspector Stewart to have the hat box retrieved from the top of the wardrobe in Edmund Chelmsford's dressing room. I hid the patent application and design documents in it."

Molly stared at her with tears in her eyes, before clasping her in another rib-crushing hug. "Grace Penrose, you are a life saver. It would mean everything to me to see our inventions making their mark on the world. Safer, more efficient factories. What better memorial for my darling Jack?"

"Go. We can talk later."

Grace settled back in her chair. The patent would set Molly and Will up for life and the world would be a better place. A silver lining on a thunderously dark cloud.

Detective Inspector Stewart arrived soon after, his face grim at the sight of Charlie's closed eyes and pallid face.

"What news of the other patients, Detective Inspector?" Grace asked.

"Sterling Chelmsford has been discharged from hospital with no more than severe bruising and glass cuts to his face."

"For all his sins, he did save my life by turning up when he did. If it hadn't been for the swift actions of his coachman and footman in getting us all back to town, Charlie might not have survived. What of Edmund?"

"He died early this morning. They think he was haemorrhaging around the brain. I suppose it makes my life easier, although I would have preferred to see the villain stand trial for the murder of Jack Finlay and the attempted murder of Molly Sugden, his father and you. Now that he's dead, I'd not be surprised if the whole thing is hushed up. Sterling Chelmsford is a powerful man."

Grace felt a prickle of relief that the set of three deaths was now complete. She might not believe in superstitions, but right now, she was willing to grasp hold of anything that favoured Charlie's recovery.

Stewart was regarding her silence with sympathy, so she diverted the conversation. "I trust the Premier and Police Commissioner are pleased with your success?"

"They are satisfied that the police force can no longer be accused of corruption and failing to act on complaints."

"And what of the boy's death?" Grace asked. "Will there be justice for Alfie Watts?"

Stewart shrugged. "That will be for the court to decide. Fergus Duncan and Sterling Chelmsford are both refusing to say a word. But Duncan's prior confession to Pyke and the witness account of him accepting a payment from Chelmsford are in our favour, along with the other evidence you and Pyke uncovered."

Grace was about to add a few pithy comments on the fickleness of justice when she noticed a twinkle in Stewart's eye.

"There was an incident this morning, when Chelmsford was heading to prayer at the First Church. A group of street urchins ambushed him and pelted him with pig dung and rotten eggs. They accused him of Alfie's murder in front of an appalled congregation of the city's most eminent citizens. I think it is fair to say that Sterling Chelmsford will struggle to regain his standing in society. Unfortunately, the urchins escaped."

Grace returned his smile. "Shocking. I fear the slums of Dunedin are a breeding ground for persons of the lowest moral character. A veritable Devil's Half Acre."

"Indeed, Miss Penrose. Thank goodness we have the upper classes to set a better example."

Her hoot of laughter surprised them both. "I'd almost forgotten what it's like to laugh. Good to see your leg is better, by the way."

"Mrs Wu is a miracle worker. And a charming lady as well." Detective Inspector Stewart left her with a cheery wave and strolled off down the corridor, whistling a lively tune.

As the sun went down on the second day of her vigil, Grace was finding it increasingly hard to keep her eyes from flickering shut.

A gentle hand on her shoulder shook her awake. She lifted her head from the crook of Charlie's uninjured arm and saw that the sky was now inky black.

"Grace, you must rest. You'll be no use to Charlie when he wakes up if you're exhausted." Lily applied gentle pressure under her elbow. "Up you get, my dear. The nurse says there is a spare bed in the women's ward. I'll stay with him for a few hours."

Grace allowed herself to be guided to a hospital bed with corners so tight she struggled to get in. Lily pulled the sheets back for her and removed her single boot, the other foot being wrapped in a bandage. She sank into the crisp cocoon, her eyes closing almost as soon as her head hit the pillow.

Sunlight was pouring into the ward when Grace woke up. She hobbled down the corridor, fearful that Charlie might have taken a turn for the worse in her absence. Instead, she found Anne holding a cup of water to his lips. Her great-aunt's beaming smile told her all she needed to know.

"It seems St Peter is not yet ready to welcome Detective Constable Pyke through the pearly gates." Anne rose from the bedside chair and gave Grace's arm a pat. "Go easy on the poor man, Grace. He has lost a great deal of blood on your behalf."

Grace took the vacant chair and reached out for his hand, feeling the warmth of his fingers as he clasped her hand to his chest. "Charlie. I'm so sorry I wasn't here when you woke up."

His smile was weak, but a smile nevertheless. "The nurse told me you had been here for forty hours straight until Lily dragged you away."

"It was the least I could do after your heroic rescue." She reached over to straighten the pillow under his head, resisting the urge to run her fingers through his silky black hair. "Although, next time you save my life, do you think you could do it a little earlier, before the villain tries to stick me with a dagger?"

"I thought it might be more dramatic if I waited until the last moment." His fingers tightened around hers. "Can't make it look too easy."

"Oh, Charlie. I can't tell you how good it is to hear you tease me. Now I know you are on the mend."

"They say you saved my life, Grace, with your quick thinking and medical skills."

Anne came back with a fresh jug of water. "A shame you had to rip up your lovely wedding dress to make a tourniquet. But then, with your charming fiancé gone to sup with Satan, perhaps it was not such a great loss." Anne put the jug down on the side table and kissed them both. "I'll see you two later."

The smile dropped from Charlie's lips as Anne left. "Far too close a call on all accounts. I blame myself for letting you get involved in the investigation. I hope your enthusiasm for detection has run its course, Miss Bones?"

"As it happens, I have received a letter from Professor Scott, inviting me to be a student at the medical school this year." Grace was expecting effusive congratulations, but all she saw was hesitancy. "Charlie, are you not happy for me?"

"Of course, I'm delighted for you. An extraordinary achievement, to be the first female medical student in the country." He raised her hand to his lips and brushed a light-as-air kiss onto her knuckles. "I have received an offer too. Detective Inspector Stewart came in first thing this morning, while you were asleep. He wants to take me on as his permanent Detective Constable."

"Charlie, that's marvellous." Again, the look of pain on his face. "Isn't it?"

"He is based in Wellington, Grace. Perhaps it was a foolish dream, but I had wondered – hoped – that if you didn't get accepted to medical school in Dunedin…"

"That I might be going home to Wellington too?"

Charlie nodded, releasing his hold on her fingers and letting his hand drop to the starched white of the hospital bed. Grace took his hand again, holding it in both of her own, the silence stretching, as neither found the right words to say.

Eventually Grace formed the words she knew must be said. "Charlie, you must follow your dream, just as I must follow mine, even though I will miss you terribly. It need not be forever." A tear forced its way through her closed lids, betraying the light tenor of her words. "Promise you will write to me? Please."

"I promise. I suppose you'll want to hear all about my investigations of suspicious deaths, so you can give your expert medical opinion." The softness in his voice, and the way his fingers entwined with hers, spoke louder than the words.

"Naturally, what other reason could I possibly have for asking you to write to me?" She bent down to whisper in his ear. "And don't hold back on the gruesome details."

Read on

In Book 2, *Murder Most Melancholy*, Penrose & Pyke are driven to desperate measures to solve an old family mystery.

When a dying woman whispers her final words, they appear to be the ravings of a madwoman. But what if there is truth behind her shocking claims? The answers lie behind the locked doors of a sanitorium for wealthy women with delicate constitutions, where high walls and dark corridors conceal more than one dreadful secret.

Thank You

Thank you for reading this story. If you enjoyed it, I would be very grateful if you would leave a rating or review to help other readers discover it.

Find out about other books and sign up for new release notifications at https://RosePascoe.com

Also available: the **French Legacy trilogy**, featuring a young Anne Godwin Macmillan

Set during the French Revolutions of 1789 and 1830, as well as London, New Zealand and present-day France, the French Legacy trilogy follows several generations of courageous women, who become the protectors of a priceless family heirloom.

Historical Notes and References

Although this story is a work of fiction, elements of the story were inspired by the real events, characters, and conditions of Dunedin in 1890.

The three historical characters who play a part in this novel each blazed a path towards a better society with their hard work and sacrifices. Their roles in the story are entirely fictionalised.

Harriet Morison was one of New Zealand's pioneering feminists, campaigning for the rights of working women as Vice-President of the Dunedin Tailoresses' Union from its inception in 1889. She also played an important role in the campaign for women's suffrage and the temperance movement.

Professor John Scott was the driving force behind the development of the Otago Medical School, the first in New Zealand, from 1877 to 1914.

The Reverend Rutherford Waddell had an outsized impact on a wide range of issues – women's suffrage, education, temperance, penal reform and even conservation. But he is best known for his sermons, lectures and writings on the "Sin of Cheapness". The combination of an economic depression in New Zealand and mechanisation during the Industrial Revolution left many skilled tradespeople and crafters in desperate circumstances, having to accept appalling conditions and pitiful pay – the alternative being starvation.

Waddell was the minister of the St Andrew's parish, in an area so notorious for drinking and debauchery that it became known as the Devil's Half Acre. It was so bad that Walker Street, which is the epicentre of events in this story, was later renamed Carroll Street in an attempt to blot out the taint. The elements of the story relating to the conditions endured by the area's inhabitants are drawn from first-hand accounts where possible, although the fictional Kendall factory gathers all the most extreme elements under one roof.

Waddell's sermons raised awareness of the dire conditions in factories, especially after the publication of an investigation by the *Otago Daily Times*. The government responded by setting up the Sweating Commission of 1890, which first convened in Dunedin on the tenth of February, with Waddell as one of the commissioners. In some cases, workers risked losing their jobs if they gave evidence.

The report concluded that sweating did not exist, in the sense of the accepted definition, albeit with three dissenting commissioners, including Waddell. However, the evidence of long hours, poor conditions and inadequate pay was undeniable. The Liberal government subsequently made significant changes to labour laws, including the Factories Acts of 1891 and 1894. The full report can be read at:

https://paperspast.natlib.govt.nz/parliamentary/AJHR1890-I.2.3.2.5

At the same time, Dunedin was hosting a major spectacle, the New Zealand and South Seas Exhibition, which was open from 26 November 1889 to 26 April 1890. It was so popular that more visitors were said to have gone through its gates than the entire population of New Zealand. For a superb summary of this extraordinary event (and yes, there really was a scaled-down Eiffel Tower with an elevator), visit my website or this wonderful blog about New Zealand history:

https://the-lothians.blogspot.com/2016/06/the-new-zealand-and-south-seas.html.

The first female medical student in New Zealand, Emily Seideberg, began her studies at Otago Medical School in 1891, but is by no means the model for the feisty heroine of this novel. Emily quietly went about the vocation of becoming a doctor and gave exceptional service to her community over her lifetime. So too did the second female student, Margaret Cruickshank, who was so revered that the Waimate community erected a statue in her honour.

Emily Seideberg is commemorated by a plaque in her home town of Clyde, in Central Otago, right outside the schist cottage where I was staying (and where my grandparents used to live). So, in a twist of fate, Grace Penrose was born.

Many Chinese immigrants arrived in New Zealand during the Gold Rush and settled in the poorer areas of Dunedin afterwards. Sad to say, they were not treated with the dignity and equality they deserved, as reflected in a small measure by the challenges faced by the two part-Chinese characters in the story.

The New Zealand Police Force had been established in 1886, just a few years before this story is set, and went through more than a decade of challenging adjustment, moving from its military-style predecessor, the Armed Constabulary, towards a more modern form of preventative policing. Poor pay and lack of opportunities for advancement provided fertile grounds for lax enforcement and kickbacks amongst a minority of officers, especially with regard to enforcing liquor laws.

I am grateful to the Toitū Otago Settlers Museum for their wonderful displays of the early history of Dunedin and to the Hocken Library and National Library for their collections of historical photographs. Information on the history of various buildings was sourced from a variety of sites, but particularly Heritage New Zealand (https://heritage.co.nz) and https://builtindunedin.com.

A number of published books provided useful historical background, including:

Carmalt Jones, D.W. (1945) *Annals of the University of Otago Medical School, 1875-1939*. A.H. and A.W. Reed, Wellington, New Zealand.

Dougherty, I. (2009) *As Others See Us: Historic Dunedin Through Visitor's Eyes*. Saddle Hill Press, Dunedin, New Zealand.

Dougherty, I. (2018) *Pulpit Radical: The Story of New Zealand Social Campaigner, Rutherford Waddell*. Saddle Hill Press, Dunedin, New Zealand.

Grimshaw, P. (1987) *Women's Suffrage in New Zealand*. Auckland University Press, Auckland, New Zealand.

Hercus, Sir Charles and Bell, Sir Gordon (1964) *The Otago Medical School Under The First Three Deans.* E. and S. Livingston Ltd, Edinburgh and London.

Hill, R.S. (1995) *The Iron Hand in the Velvet Glove: The Modernisation of Policing in New Zealand, 1886-1917.* Dunmore Press, Palmerston North, New Zealand.

Johnson, D. (1993) *Dunedin: A Pictorial History.* Canterbury University Press, Christchurch, New Zealand.

Maxwell, M.D. (1990) *Women Doctors in New Zealand: An Historical Perspective, 1921-1986.* IMS (NZ) Ltd, Auckland, New Zealand.

McLean, G.J. (1981) *Spinning Yarns: A Centennial History of Alliance Textiles Ltd and its Predecessors, 1881-1981.* Alliance Textiles Ltd, Dunedin, New Zealand.

Page, D. (2008) *Anatomy of a Medical School: a History of Medicine at the University of Otago, 1875-2000.* University of Otago Press, Dunedin, New Zealand.

About the author

Rose Pascoe writes historical mysteries with a dash of romance, when she isn't plotting real-life adventures. She lives in beautiful New Zealand, land of beaches and mountains, where long walks provide the perfect conditions for dreaming up plots and fickle weather provides the incentive to sit down and actually write the darn things.

After a career in health, justice and social research, her passion is for stories set against a backdrop of social revolution. Her heroines are ordinary women, who meet the challenges thrown at them with determination, ingenuity, courage, and humour.

Visit her at: https://RosePascoe.com